I0556492

Crossroads Serenade

A novel by
Laurie Adair Grove

Laurie Adair Grove

Published by:
MacFadden-Grove Publishing
Copyright © 2012
All rights reserved.

Dedication

This book is dedicated to my father, David Charles MacFadden, for making my youthful summers extraordinary. Also, thanks go to my daughter Melanie for her many hours of editing and thoughtful input, and my brother Gary for actually making this book a reality.

Contents

Chapter 1

I will never forget his last words to me, in a letter I received when I was living far from home. "I know you are quite familiar with the workings of The Serenade, dear Meredith, but I trust you to follow my business plan until you are strongly on your feet." The handwriting was strange to me—pained and spidery. "Sam at the bank will be your financial advisor—check in with him often. Charlie and Mona will share my estate equally with you, although you are receiving The Serenade and some bare land, and they are receiving all bare land…"

"Mom?" Grant, my five-year-old son, asks from the back seat, jolting me back to the present. "Is this the place Uncle Duck left you?"

"Yes! This is it!" I say, reaching across the seat behind me to tousle his black hair. I rummage through my purse for the keys Sam Overgaard had sent me.

"Why is it so dark in there, Mom?"

I look back at him, noting worry in his blue eyes, even in the dimness of the car's dome light. "It's dark because it's been closed since Uncle Duck died. Nobody's in there. But we're going to change that! I love this place, Grant. I hope

you will too." I open my car door and take a deep breath of
the fresh northern Montana air. "Smell the air, Grant—it's the
best in the world!"

"It's too cold!" he says as he opens his window. Before
he closes it he takes a loud, deep breath that I'm sure to hear.
"Yep! That's good air, Mom!" The darkness of this late May
night can't hide the surrounding beauty from me. I know in
the light of day I'll see a wide expanse of prairie, dotted with
craggy outcroppings and stubborn patches of deep snow, the
magnificent glacier-laced Rockies on the horizon beyond.
Close by, red paintbrush, purple bitterroot and yellow sage-
brush buttercup will just be beginning to bloom, and ponderosa and quaking aspen around the property will provide shade
on the warm summer days to come.

"Well, it's late, so let's go take a quick look around inside, and then we'll carry some things in so we can get settled
for the night. There will be time for exploring tomorrow," I
say as I take Grant's hand to climb the fifteen flat log steps
to the hotel entrance. "Now let's hope Mr. Overgaard had the
electricity and phone service turned on for us, like he said he
would."

I separate the hotel lobby key from the others on the ring
Mr. Overgaard had sent and unlock the massive double pine
doors. Something skitters across the floor in the beam of my
flashlight, making us both jump. "Probably just a mouse," I
say, trying to sound confident.

I find the switch by the door. "Much better," I say, silently
adding a 'thank you' to Mr. Overgaard. I lead Grant down
six steps into the main body of the lobby, and my heart leaps
with pleasure that everything seems to be exactly as it was the
last time I saw the place. Three enormous unlit chandeliers,
fashioned from wagon wheel rims and wreaths of antlers
hang suspended over the lobby by sturdy black chains, the
air around them bisected by huge round yellow pine beams.
A polished river rock fireplace and chimney dominate the left

side of the lobby. Groupings of comfy overstuffed chairs and sofas fill the remainder of the room, more worn but still the same pieces I remember. The jewel of this room, though, is the magnificent hand-hewn knotty pine staircase to the second floor, which houses the hotel rooms.

"I'm scared, Mom," Grant says, squeezing his arms around my waist.

"Hey, honey, there's nothing to be scared of," I say. "When business really gets going and this place is full of customers, it's a lot of fun. You'll see. Do you want to see the building tonight?" I ask.

"Will it be dark?"

"I don't think so, but we don't have to go anywhere that the lights don't work."

"Well, okay, then, but only in the light places."

A few hours later, after a tour of the restaurant, kitchen and hotel, I tuck Grant into his sleeping bag on one of the sofas in the lobby. The odor of mice had permeated the entire place in the year it stood vacant. I imagine a lot of mice families have taken up residence. I'm grateful that rodents and some cracked ground floor windows are the only problems I am aware of as I sink wearily into an armchair next to Grant. I can almost hear Uncle Duck's jolly, booming voice resonating throughout the establishment, greeting customers and friends. He wasn't actually my uncle at all, just a dear friend who left me the gift of his beloved Serenade! And now I've come back to reopen it! And to try to do it justice after the years of tender care that Uncle Duck put into it. I guess he saw some strength in me that I hadn't seen in myself.

Of course Pete comes into my mind, as he does every day, unbidden or not. I remember his angular jaw and handsome nose. The cowboy hat he loved to wear which hid his sandy brown hair, and the musky scent of leather and hay that seemed a part of him. His hands were roughened by the nature of his work, but his caresses were tender, and his breath was warm and sweet when he leaned down to kiss me. As I do on so many lonely nights, I imagine his arms around me again, and remember the time we made love.

Crossroads, Montana, is the town I call home. Many of the twelve hundred inhabitants are descendants of the Swedish immigrants who founded it in the eighteen-eighties. It is surrounded by a sea of prairie, which is then embraced by jagged mountains. The highways from Crossroads lead north to Browning and Glacier Park, south to Choteau and Great Falls, west to the Hungry Horse area, and east to Conrad.

Our first morning in town, there is a sharp rapping at the hotel doors, and I jolt awake, reminded suddenly that Crossroads is like any other small town, where news and gossip travel at the speed of light.

"Who do you think it is, Mom?" Grant asks, his voice hoarse with sleep.

"I don't know, but I will in a minute," I say. I've slept all night in the chair, and I need to stretch out and have more sleep, not visitors, after our long drive. I hoist my sleeping bag up and wrap myself in it, then trudge barefoot, freezing my feet, across the lobby to one of the many-paned windows. Drawing back a gingham curtain, I peek out at the parking lot. "It's Dave!" I run to the doors and yank one open. "Oh my goodness! It's so good to see you!" I shout, joyfully throwing my arms around him.

"Hey, Meredith, great to see you!" Dave Bunsen, Crossroad's police chief, is a large man in his mid-thirties. He hugs me back in a great big bear hug. I pull back from him and see him surveying the lobby behind me until he sees Grant, a lumpy cocoon on a sofa.

"That's Grant," I say. "I imagine you've heard I have a son now?"

"Yes, I did!" he says.

"Grant, can you wake up enough to come meet my friend Dave? He's a policeman here," I add.

"I…I guess so," Grant stammers, unzipping the sleeping bag. In a few moments he's standing next to me, his toes curling up off the cold floor, while he looks up at Dave curiously.

"I'm happy to know you, Grant," Dave says good naturedly. He sticks his hand out to Grant, who answers with a small handshake.

"Do you want to go warm up?" I ask Grant, to which he nods and runs back to his sleeping bag.

"We got in late last night and it took a while to get situated, so we were sleeping in," I say, knowing that I must look pretty messy. "I slept in a chair all night—just fell asleep there!"

"I'm sorry I disturbed you," Dave says. "Sam Overgaard told me you'd be coming in, and I wanted to be the first to greet you."

"I'm glad you disturbed us," I said. "I wouldn't have it any other way. I've really missed you and Roma," I say, referring to his wife who was one of my high school friends. "How is she? Is she still teaching kindergarten here in town?"

"She's doing well, thanks, and yes, she's still teaching," he says. "I'm guessing Grant is about kindergarten age?"

"Yes, he is. So Roma will be my son's teacher!" I grin. I love it that one of my old friends will be teaching my son.

"Sam said he told you about those real estate developers who were here last year, after Duck got sick? That was really something. Duck sure got tired of their pestering! He told them he already knew who he was leaving the place to. So of course everyone was speculating about who it would be," he explains. "I thought it would be Mona or Charlie," he adds.

"Well, Uncle Duck was always surprising people, wasn't he?" I say, not wanting to discuss the terms of the will.

"Yes, he marched to his own drummer, and he didn't care what other people thought. I sure do miss him," he says.

"Me too," I say.

"I'm glad you decided to move back," Dave says, "but

I'm sure it was difficult to pull up stakes out there in Oregon to come on home." There's an awkward pause while he waits for me to say something, but I don't. I'm happy to see him, but I feel cotton headed from fatigue, and I'm not ready for a lot of talk. "Anyway," he continues, "people will be glad to get their old jobs back if you'll have them. Some of them are driving to other towns for work now."

"Uncle Duck did suggest it as an option in the business plan he left for me. I want to have this place open by the Fourth of July at the latest. That's what I'm aiming for, anyway."

"It'll be great to have The Serenade open!" he exclaims, then grasps me by the shoulders and holds me at arms' length, looking me over. "You look good, Meredith. Healthy. I guess being away hasn't hurt you, but I hope things'll work out for you so you'll want to stay home."

"I hope so too," I say. I want to find out if he knows anything about Pete, but I don't want to bring that up in front of Grant.

"Well, I have to get on back to the office now. It's great to see you," he says again.

"You too! Don't be a stranger, now," I say, hugging him again before he walks out the door.

I turn to see Grant snoring peacefully, so I burrow my way down into the seat sprung chair and doze off too, awakening later to a beautiful blue skied Sunday morning.

When Grant wakes up we munch on some cold cereal, then go outside. I show him the bark of the ponderosa trees which comes off in chunks resembling jigsaw puzzle pieces. Then I point out the quaking aspen trees, and a grove of scrubby, pungent junipers behind The Serenade.

"This will be a great place for you to play when the weather is good," I tell him, imagining him making roads and little towns between and under them, pushing his toy trucks and equipment to imaginary destinations. We walk around outside the building, and I point out the nearest part of the acreage Uncle Duck left me, which begins at the edge of the junipers. "Look at the mountains!" I exclaim, pointing to the snow covered range in the distance. "Those are the Rockies! Isn't that the most beautiful thing you've ever seen, Grant?"

"It just looks cold to me, Mom," he says.

"I don't suppose I thought much of the view when I was five, either," I say. "I guess you have to be older to appreciate it."

"I'll 'preciate it when I'm older, too, okay?" Grant says, looking up at me.

"Okay," I say. I survey the land around us, pointing out and naming some of the spring wildflowers.

"They're nice. I 'preciate those already!" he says, making me chuckle.

"I guess we better go inside," I say. "We have a lot of things to do to get this place ready. I lead him inside the hotel lobby and upstairs to the two adjoining suites that will be our home. Each suite has a small bedroom, sitting room, and bathroom—plenty of space for the two of us. I help Grant get started unpacking his things.

When he is happily sorting through his box of toys I go down to the hotel and start looking over the list of names of employees Uncle Duck left for me. There are twenty-eight, including waitresses, hostesses, cashiers, busboys, cooks, bartenders, desk clerks, hotel maids, laundry workers, and a handyman. The hotel is only busy during the tourist season, primarily inhabited by vacationers on their way to or from Glacier National Park. Most of the hotel employees I hire will only stay on for the season, except for a few, who will be offered jobs in the restaurant, because it operates more to capacity year-round. With the exception of bookkeeping and the handyman's job, (although I can turn a wrench and drive a nail), I've worked in every position at The Serenade, so I'll be able to jump in anywhere that I'm needed.

Uncle Duck built a successful enterprise, and I know he wants me to be successful too, so I read and re-read the detailed business plan he left for me. It's overwhelming. I wonder what on earth Uncle Duck was thinking when he decided to leave The Serenade to me. He didn't have children to leave it to, but I wonder why he thought I was a good choice. I'm honored, and I'll do my best not to let him down, but I'm scared to death. I can't wait to talk to Charlie and Mona, who were both with Uncle Duck from the beginning of this enterprise thirty years ago. Charlie was the first cook Uncle Duck hired, and Mona the first waitress. I doubt that either of them wants to work anymore, but I feel comfortable asking for their help, even if they turn me down.

I hadn't been back for several years, and being a single working parent, I had only had time for the rare phone call to old friends. I guess I never even imagined something happening to Uncle Duck—that he could get sick and die.

"Duck didn't want to disrupt your life," Mr. Overgaard had told me on the phone. "He didn't want you to see him sick and weak. He was so proud of the way you turned out— smart, considerate and loving. He always said if he had had a child of his own, he would have wanted one just like you. That's why you have been left this inheritance," he explained while I wiped away tears with my sleeve and tried to choke back sobs. "He trusts you to carry on with The Serenade. It will provide a good living for you, if you want to put the effort into it."

I told Mr. Overgaard I didn't know what to do. I didn't know how to manage a business, but he assured me that he would advise me, just like Uncle Duck had said in his letter. Uncle Duck had left money earmarked just for operating expenses, and if I didn't want the challenge, I had the option of selling out or hiring someone else to run it.

"It's a tough decision, Mr. Overgaard," I had said. "I have to think of how this is going to affect us. I mean, I have a job here and Grant loves his babysitter…"

"Take your time, Meredith," he'd said kindly. "This isn't a decision to be hasty about. Why don't you think it over for a few weeks, and get back to me."

The next two weeks I mentally sorted out whatever reasons there were for either moving back to Montana, or staying put. I wasn't sure at all that I could do Uncle Duck proud, but I thought from the beginning that I should try. I was also hopeful that Pete might come back into my life, even though that was a long shot. Grant and I would be giving up some good things we had gotten used to in Oregon, too: the mild winters, day trips to the beach, and some good friends we had made. But the biggest reason to stay away from Montana was that my stepfather, Raymond, still lived there. And if I never saw him again, it would be too soon.

"Meredith! Are you really back?" Mona exclaims when I call her. "I thought for the longest time that you had dropped off the face of the earth, then outta the blue I hear from Sam that you're splitting Ducks's estate with Charlie and me!"

"I know, I can't believe it myself," I say, not sure how to talk about it.

"I bet you 'bout fell over when you heard," she says.

"Yeah. But we lost Duck, and that's what I can't believe the most."

"I know," Mona agrees.

"I wanted so badly for him to meet Grant," I say, "and now it will never happen."

"Is Grant your husband? You actually gave up on Pete?"

"No, no. Grant is my son," I say. "He's five. Nobody told you?"

"Your son? I doubt many people know about him, if I don't," she says, and I'm sure she's right. "Well, congratulations! I would have said it sooner if I'd known," she says, and just by the way she clips her voice at the end of the sentence, I know her feelings are cut to the core.

"I'm sorry, Mona. Someday I'll explain it all to you— why you and nearly everyone else didn't know about Grant. But anyway, I haven't given up on Pete," I say, hoping to change the subject. "In fact, I'm hoping I'll see him. Maybe at our grand reopening, even."

"Wait a minute, back the truck up. Why can't you tell me about Grant now?"

"It's a long story," I explain. "I'd rather tell you in person."

"Dang! Way to leave me hanging," she says. "Well, I guess I have to wait." She coughs and says, "Okay, so what's the date you're hoping to open up?"

"Toward the end of June—or the Fourth of July at the latest! So, I'm begging here, Mona, will you come back to work?" I ask sweetly.

"I'll come back to help you start up, hon," Mona says. "But don't be expecting me to want to work forever! After all, I'm over fifty now, though you wouldn't know it to look at me!" she laughs, which triggers another cough.

"I'm sure you look as young as always," I say, glad that Mona's still struttin' her stuff. I thank her several more times for agreeing to come back. "Hey Mona, where is the land Uncle Duck left you, anyway? Is it just out of town here?"

"It's about sixty miles south of town! In fact, it's just next to the southern part of Pete's parents' ranch."

"Oh! So are you going to move out there?" I ask casually, hoping Mona didn't realize how the mention of Pete's parents, whom I adored, thrills me.

"I think I'll just hang on to it for now. We were already having a new house built right next to our trailer, since we love the property we're on and don't want to leave it. I wouldn't want to live clear out there anyway. Too far away from everything. I mean, you think I'm uncultured now?" she says with a laugh, setting off another round of coughing. "Hang on a sec, Meredith," she says. Through a muffled receiver I hear her shout, "Evan, bring my smokes, will you hon?"

"Mona, you quit smoking! I remember! I was a junior in high school, and I was working here part-time. What happened?" I ask, remembering the terrible nicotine fits she had suffered through.

"I dunno, hon. Things set me off and I start up. I should try again. Evan sure has been on my case about it. Don't worry, I still never smoke inside. Anyway, getting back to the subject—maybe I'll sell some of the property just so we'll have the money to go visit Jody and Frank in Arizona now and then. I miss them and my grandkids so much, but they're so busy all the time. I only get to see them a few times a year."

Before we hang up, Mona says she'll be happy to help me get started again. "It'll be kind of like my tribute to Duck. I think he'd appreciate it," she says, to which I truly agree.

Charlie, true to form, grumbles his way though the conversation when I call. Finally he agrees to come back to work.

"Sam told me you would probably call," he says, "and I already decided to help out, so don't think you're talking me into something," he says. Just like Charlie, I think, always wanting the last word. I don't expect him to bring up any particulars, like the inheritance, and I'm right.

I'm grateful that I'll have Mona and Charlie's experience and friendship on this journey. Energized by their promises, I spend the remainder of the afternoon calling the other former employees, explaining the tentative plans. I told everyone that Grant and I will be living upstairs in the hotel, so everyone will know to expect a child around much of the time. I also explain that he comes with a set of rules intended to keep him safe and out from underfoot.

By mid-June I've gotten all of Uncle Duck's former employees to agree to come back, with the exception of two; a hotel desk clerk, and Tom, the handyman. Danielle, a barmaid, had asked if there was an opening for a friend of hers, so I'll tell her about the desk clerk job—see if her friend fits the bill. Tom says he's just too old to come back full-time, but says he could help out until I find someone. I accept the offer, thank him, and make a note to talk to Mona about placing an ad in the paper.

If we stay on track, we'll be opening in two weeks. Mona and Danielle have been helping me get the place cleaned and organized, and Tom has been helping, but he reminds me every day that he's retired.

I grab a cup of coffee one afternoon and sit down with Mona at the break table in the kitchen. "We're one person short of a full staff now," I say.

"When you say it that way, it sounds like we're running a nut house," Mona says, and we both laugh.

"No, I mean we still need a handyman, but I just hired Cathy Olson as the other desk clerk," I say. "That was the friend Danielle wanted me to hire. I knew her from high school. Back then she was not a pleasant person, but hopefully she's over it."

"Oh, the Olsons. Yeah, I remember reading about her mom in the paper a few years ago," Mona says. "She was in a horrible car accident that left her paralyzed."

"That's right, that's what she told me," I say.

"I heard that when she was well enough to leave the hospital, Mrs. Olson insisted on having Cathy come home from college to take care of her. She absolutely refused to have anyone else. She just died last spring," she adds.

"That's really sad," I say. "I doubt Cathy really wants or needs to work here, but maybe she's just bored, waiting to go back to college in the fall?" I suggest.

"Why do you say that?" Mona asks.

"Well, she's an Olson, you know? Her great grandfather was a founding father of Crossroads, her father's at the bank with Mr. Overgaard..."

"Oh yeah, I forgot about that," Mona says. "So maybe she is just bored, after all. So all we're looking for is a handyman?"

"Yes, I hope we can find someone just by putting an ad in the Bugle," I say, referring to our local twice weekly paper. "I've never written a newspaper ad. What do I need to say?"

Mona takes a cigarette out of a white leather case on the counter. She holds it between two fingers but doesn't light up. She walks slowly around the table, her hands on her shapely jeans-covered hips. She bites her lip while she thinks. "Hmm…how about this: 'wanted: able bodied hunk of a man, tall and dark, or tall and blonde, with broad shoulders, rippling muscles, who can fix anything he lays a hand on?'"

"Uh, Mona, are you and Evan still happily married?" I ask with a laugh.

"Yeah, but I'm not dead!" she says, grinning. Mona has spunk that belies her age. When I started here at the age of sixteen, there were six waitresses, but it was Mona who took me under her wing. It wasn't long before she had me jotting down orders in waitress shorthand, asking customers 'what can I get for you, hon?' and balancing plates up to the crook of my arm. The tight pink uniform dresses that Duck had ordered were perfect for her curvaceous build, but even now, looking down at my less than full bust, there's no getting around the fact that all girls are not created equal.

"I think we better stick to business, Mona," I say now. "But I agree—a hunk of handyman would be okay."

"Hey, Meredith, I want to talk to you about something else," Mona suddenly says in a serious tone. "Grant won't hear us if we keep our voices down."

I stand and look over the waist-high wall of the play area Tom built for Grant in a corner of the huge kitchen, and see that he is happily playing with his toys.

"Okay, what is it?" I ask, figuring that not being in on my private life is really eating away at her.

"I know it's none of my business, but as an old friend I'm going to risk you being mad at me and go ahead and ask." She looks me in the eye and says, "What happened with you and Pete? Duck never mentioned it, even when I asked if he knew anything. And Pete certainly never said anything after you two split up. I only saw him a time or two after you left. And what about Grant? You told me you wanted to tell me in person, so here we are."

"Like I said, it's a long story," I say with a sigh.

"I'm listening," she replies, sitting back down at the table.

I refill our coffee cups, then sit down across the table from her and tell the story of what I was going through when Grant came along, and why Pete and I broke up—what only a few other people already knew. The telling of it exhausts and saddens me, as it does whenever I find myself reliving the details. When I'm finished, I just hold my head in my hands, staring into my cup.

Mona comes around to my side of the table, leans down and hugs me. "Thanks for telling me," she says. Then she adds, "I'm here for you," like she always used to say when I was struggling, whether it was from something that happened on the job, or something harder, like dealing with Raymond.

"Thanks, Mona. Just seeing you every day is a real help." I sit up straight and push my hair back from my face. "I have a question for you, now. Do you know anything about Pete these days?"

She doesn't speak for a long moment, then says quietly, "he was married for a while."

"Oh?" I ask, as my stomach sinks to my feet and a lump rises in my throat. "Who to?"

"A girl he met at college, after you two split up. But it didn't last. I think they were married less than two years. I don't know where he's living now, but his folks are still out on the ranch," she adds. "Why don't you call them and ask where he is?"

"I don't know. That just seems so forward," I say. "His folks and I really got along well, but after this long they really might not want me back in the picture."

"But what if they do?" she asks. "What if they miss you?"

"I don't know," I say. "I need to see Pete first."

"Okay, have it your way. I'm just trying to help," Mona says with a sigh.

"And I appreciate it, I really do," I say, patting her arm. "But I have to go with my instinct on this."

Chapter 2

Pete McBride was a new student in our high school the first day of winter term our junior year. Mr. Buxton, our homeroom teacher, had assigned him the only empty seat in the room, which happened to be next to me. Pete had sat down at the desk the teacher indicated, then looked across the aisle and exchanged smiles with me. He smelled wonderfully of leather and hay, and he wore his blue jeans just tight enough to create an effect I really appreciated.

In the afternoon of that first day I saw him staring out the classroom window across the snow covered prairie toward the jagged mountain range in the distance. Suddenly he glanced my way and caught me watching him.

"Daydreaming?" I whispered.

"Yeah. Something I do when I'm trapped," he whispered back. I felt an immediate connection with him. Another person, looking for a way out. Just like me.

A few days later, as the homeroom students noisily entered the classroom, I saw Pete at Mr. Buxton's desk. Mr. Buxton, who was from a ranching family, was talking about cattle, one of his favorite topics. I heard Pete reply that his dad had just bought his uncle's ranch ten miles out of town, and that he was learning the ropes so he could be a partner with his father some day.

"But I'm going to college too," he had added, "to get a degree in animal science. My dad and I think that would give me the best background for the business."

I sat at my desk listening to Pete's quiet, unhurried voice. I noticed when Mr. Buxton spoke, Pete sort of cocked his head, as though he didn't want to miss a single word the teacher said. Mr. Buxton must have said something funny next, because Pete's face broke into a wide smile, and he laughed a long, deep laugh. I was determined to get to know this guy.

In the following weeks it seemed that he was beginning to feel the same about me. If there was time before class we would talk a little, and if not, we'd just exchange a smile or two, but sitting next to each other was good just by itself. I had had other boyfriends, but none that made me so eager to get to school, and certainly none that I daydreamed about or thought about before I went to sleep at night.

About a month into the term, it was announced that the school talent show would be held in a few weeks. Though my performing experience was limited to singing in front of my best friend, MaryAnn, and her mom, DeeDee, I loved singing, and signed up to sing in the show. On the occasions that I had tried to sing for my mom, she said she didn't have time to listen, and Raymond, my stepfather, just told me to shut up.

"I'm really excited about the contest, but I don't have anything to wear!" I said one afternoon at MaryAnn's house not long before the show.

"I think I have just the thing," DeeDee had said. She went in her room and came out with a beautiful long cream-colored dress with a panel of forest green velvet down the front. She held it up on the hanger in front of me, and she and Mary-Ann said that it made my eyes look greener and my long hair

blonder. "This is a pre-twin dress," DeeDee had said, referring to the pregnancy that had produced MaryAnn's baby
sisters. "I doubt I'll ever be that thin again, and MaryAnn
doesn't like to wear that style, so if it fits you, you're welcome to it," she added.

"It's beautiful! Thank you, DeeDee!" I exclaimed. I tried
it on and we all agreed it was a good look on me.

"Mom, I think since you gave Meredith your dress, she
should sing for us," Mary Ann said with a grin.

"I think MaryAnn's right, Meredith. We'll sit on the
couch and be your audience," DeeDee said with a laugh.

I was happy to oblige them, and sang an upbeat song that
had been popular on the country charts a few years before.
When I was finished singing, MaryAnn and DeeDee clapped
and cheered.

"You're good enough to be on the radio!" MaryAnn said,
putting her arm around me.

I went home with a hopeful heart, the dress in a plastic
garment bag.

But DeeDee and MaryAnn had both been wrong. The
evening of the contest, I was in my room doing my hair when
I saw Raymond's reflection in my mirror as he leaned drunk-
enly in the doorway of my room. A wave of nausea engulfed
me when I saw the familiar look in his eye that meant he was
up to no good.

"Why are you getting gussied up?" he asked in a nasty
tone.

"I'm singing in the talent show at the school tonight," I
said.

"No, you ain't," he said.

"Mom said I could!"

I could smell the stink of alcohol on him before he even
grabbed my arm. "Did I say it was okay?" he asked, his
breath adding to my nausea.

"You were out of town when I had to sign up!" I reasoned.

"You ain't going nowhere, so just take that stupid dress off and wash that crap off your face," he said, grabbing a handful of tissues off my vanity and smearing the makeup across my face.

"Mom!" I yelled as I got up and tried to get past him. "Mom! Raymond won't let me go!" I yelled again as he smacked me in the eye.

"She ain't the one who tells you what you can do. I am. I pay your way, kid. I make the decisions. Why do you think a bunch of people want to hear you sing? I heard you sing once, and you ain't no star!" he sneered.

"You never give me a chance! You always tell me to shut up!" I scream at him.

"You are such an ungrateful brat!" he yelled back at me, hitting me again, this time across my mouth. I knew the evening was ruined for me, by the pain where he had struck me. And I knew I would look too hideous to perform even if I could somehow get there. I sat back down at my vanity and saw my eye and lip in the mirror, already swelling, then put my head down and cried.

I was so miserable. It was to have been a very special night. Not only was I going to sing, but Pete and I had planned to go on our first date right after the show. Now, Pete would think I had stood him up.

The next day I felt as horrible as I had the night before, but I didn't want to be in the house with Raymond. It was noon and he and mom were still sleeping, and I was sitting outside on the front porch in the cold, despising Raymond and grieving over the fact that I had lost my chance with Pete. I was pouring my guts out into my song notebook, writing a song of lost love, when I looked up and saw Pete in front of me. I could tell he was as shocked at my face as I was to see him.

"Pete, I'm so sorry I couldn't meet you last night," I started to explain, but my words sounded strange through my swollen lip.

"Never mind that. Who hit you?" he asked in an angry voice I hadn't imagined him using.

"My stepfather, Raymond. It's nothing new, don't worry about it," I said.

"It *is* something to worry about—a man hitting a woman," he said disdainfully. "I want to see him."

"It may not be such a good idea to ask him to come out," I warned, scared of what might happen, but also pleased that he had referred to me as a woman.

Pete insisted that I get Raymond. When Raymond finally lumbered out on the porch, still stinking, Pete went up the three stairs and asked him to his face if he had hit me.

"What if I did?" Raymond snarled, and Pete punched him hard, right in the face, and knocked him out cold.

Mom, hearing the commotion, had run out on the porch.

"What happened?" she shrieked. I told her, while Pete stood to one side with narrowed eyes. "I'm having you arrested!" mom screamed at Pete. Then she called the police, which made me angry, since she never called them when Raymond was knocking either of us around.

I was glad that when Raymond came to, Dave Bunsen had hauled him off to jail for a few days. He told Pete it would be best if he avoided Raymond after this, and that's what he did. We met other places, at MaryAnn's house, school and the park, completely avoiding my house from then on.

When summer rolled around, I got another chance to perform in the beautiful dress DeeDee had given me.

The Fourth of July brings out a level of excitement in our town rivaled only by the winter holidays. On our first Fourth of July together, Pete was entered in the bronc busting and calf roping in the local rodeo. I knew he had competed in rodeos since he was in grade school, so I was excited for him, knowing that he would get some good scores. He also signed up to ride his beloved palomino mare, Nadia, in the parade.

I was signed up myself, to sing in the talent show at the fair. "There's no way Raymond is keeping me from performing this time," I had told Pete, Duck, and Mona one afternoon when Pete had come to pick me up from my part-time job at The Serenade.

"Bring everything you need for the performance to work on the night of the third, and leave it in my office. Then you can change for the performance right after you work the next morning," Uncle Duck had suggested. "That way you won't have to see Raymond before the show."

"If he starts anything with you, I'm going to finish it," Pete told me seriously.

"Well I'm not giving him the chance," I said quickly. I was glad that Pete had defended me, but the idea of him ever punching Raymond again terrified me.

"You better watch yourself around him, Pete," Uncle Duck had said. "There's no telling what he might pull on you, especially now that you have one on him."

"He's never going to get away with hitting Meredith again," Pete said to Uncle Duck, then turned to me. "I love you, Meredith," he had said, embracing me. "I couldn't stand to see you get hurt again." It was the first time he told me he loved me. My friendships with Mona and Uncle Duck were very important to me, but this was different. It gave me a wonderful new feeling.

As I was hugging Pete, Mona caught my eye and smiled warmly. She had told me she thought Pete was a nice guy, and I could see that she was happy for me.

On the morning of the Fourth I set my alarm so I'd be sure to be out of the house before Mom and Raymond woke up. I was content to walk to work in the early blue dawn, breathing in the faint vanilla fragrance of the ponderosa pines that were scattered through town. It was hard to concentrate on my customers that morning, though. I was on pins and needles due to both my excitement and nervousness about performing, but I was also worried that Raymond would still manage to spoil everything again. Finally at noon my shift ended, and I went to Uncle Duck's office to get my gear.

"Don't slip out before I get a chance to say goodbye to you," Uncle Duck had said. "I wish I could be at the show, but I have some business that won't wait."

"I know, it's okay," I said, pleased that he was thinking about it.

"Before you go get ready, I just want to say that I've gotten good reports about you from Mona and Charlie. They both say you're doing a great job," he said. "Do you like working here?"

"I love it!" I answered truthfully, beaming with pride over the compliments.

"Well, we love having you here," he said. "I just wanted to tell you. Okay, you better go get ready. The show must go on!"

I was beside myself with joy as I got my things from Uncle Duck's coat closet and went to get ready in the employee restroom. I put on the dress, then curled my long blonde hair and put a green satin ribbon in it to match the velvet panel on the dress.

"You look beautiful!" Mona exclaimed as I walked proudly through The Serenade's kitchen on my way to say goodbye to Uncle Duck.

I appeared in his open doorway just as he looked up from some paperwork. "My gosh!" he exclaimed, "You look like an angel!"

"Thank you, Duck," I said, embarrassed and pleased at the same time.

"Meredith, will you sing a bit for us?" he had asked. "Some of the song you're singing in the show?"

"I guess so," I said. "If you really want to hear me."

"I really do, and I know Mona and Charlie would, too, if they can get away for a few minutes. I followed him to the kitchen, where he told Mona and Charlie what we were going to do, and invited them along.

"I'm not going," Charlie grumbled, but Mona told him there weren't any new customers in the restaurant right then and they could go for a few minutes. She winked at me, a sign I had learned meant that Charlie was just grumbling for the sake of grumbling, not that he was upset with me.

I walked up the steps to the little stage, then belted out the first verse of the song I had chosen. Mona and Duck applauded, whistled, and shouted for more, and I noticed that Charlie's brow wasn't quite as furrowed as it had been a few minutes ago. Happy to oblige, I sang the rest of the song.

"You sounded so good, if I wasn't your Uncle Duck I'd kiss you," Duck said. That was the first time he referred to himself as my uncle, but I wasn't sure if it was okay. I looked at Mona, who nodded her approval. That's when I began to call him Uncle Duck, which he loved.

The experience of singing to a football field full of people that afternoon was the most thrilling event of my life up to that point. I felt pretty in the dress, the sound system worked perfectly, and my voice cooperated, even though I trembled a little at first. By the cheers and whistles of the crowd, I believed I had done a good job, but the most important compliment of all came to me when I met Pete behind the stage a few minutes later. He had wrapped his arms tightly around me, leaned down to kiss me, and told me he loved my singing.

"You have the most beautiful voice I ever heard, Meredith," he said as we walked away from the backstage area. "And the rest of you is just as beautiful. I'm the luckiest guy on earth." We hugged again, right there on the fairgrounds in front of everybody. Pete stood with his arm around me as we watched the other performers. Between acts people kept coming up to congratulate me on a terrific job, and Pete agreed with every one of them while I thanked them for their compliments.

Unfortunately, Pete did not place at all in his events at the evening rodeo. The bronc threw him in a few seconds, and the roping calf did not cooperate. I felt a little guilty over my well-received performance earlier in the day.

The day had soured for Pete not only at the rodeo, but also at the parade that afternoon. A little white poodle had gotten loose from its owner and spooked Nadia, causing her to rear up and throw him off before he even got to the judging stand halfway through the route. I happened to be on the sidewalk close enough to where he landed that I could have reached out and touched him. Thankfully, his pride was injured more than anything else. He had glanced up at me, red-faced, then jumped up and ran after Nadia, swiftly catching her by the reins.

"I ran into my folks a little while ago," Pete said as we were walking to his truck after the rodeo.

"I saw you talking to them, when I was coming out of the exhibition hall," I told him. "Did they see your performances today?"

"Yes. We talked about it."

"I'm sorry about what happened, Pete."

We walked along silently for a few moments, as I imagined what his dad might have said about such a disappointing showing. Probably something upbeat, something positive. Occasionally, when I had been at the McBride's ranch, I had overheard Matthew giving Pete little pep talks when he was down about something. Pete knew his parents loved him, and I was glad that he had caring parents who took the time to give their son thoughtful advice. Now Pete put one arm around my shoulder and gave me a little squeeze, which I thought came indirectly from his chat with his parents. I happily squeezed him back with the arm I had around his waist.

"Want to go to the carnival?" Pete asked me.

"I was afraid you wouldn't ask!" I answered, and we spent the rest of the evening going on rides and walking down the little midway, our arms locked together much of the time. At the shooting gallery Pete had pointed at the ceiling and asked, "See that huge green stuffed dog? The biggest one up there?"

"Yes," I said.

"I'm going to win it for you," he said.

"I don't need the biggest one," I said laughing, "Any one will do."

"Well, that's the one you're getting!" he said. Apparently his luck had changed, and he shot like an expert. We walked away, Pete carrying the huge green dog over his left shoulder. I couldn't wait to see Mary Ann, to tell her everything about the day.

Chapter 3
ॐ

I have five applicants for the handyman position, all local men. I particularly like one of them. His name is Jacob, and I've seen him around Crossroads all my life, but I don't know him. I see on his application that he graduated five years before I did, so I wouldn't have known him in school, but I remember watching him drive at the stock car races during the summers. Raymond, a big racing fan, loved going to the circle track out of town, and sometimes mom and I went with him. I wasn't really into watching cars chase each other in an endless circle, but I did like watching the guys.

Jacob, who has been working as a mechanic at the local garage for several years, says that he and the owner have never seen eye to eye and that he just needs a change. He's medium height, has a muscular build, blond hair and brown eyes. He is qualified for the job I offer him, but it doesn't hurt that he's easy on the eyes, too. Mona is completely thrilled with the results of her ad when she comes in to work the day after I hire him. The first thing she sees of him is his lower torso and Levi covered legs sticking out from beneath the plugged up sink he's fixing in the kitchen.

"Yum! What have we here?" she asks me as she nods toward Jacob's legs.

"It's our new handyman. I'll introduce you when he's finished," I say.

"Okay, I guess I'll just enjoy the show for now," Mona says, and we both start giggling like schoolgirls. Charlie gives us a pained look.

"Charlie, your old face is going to freeze that way if you don't cut it out," Mona tells him loudly. She and Charlie worked together for so long that she knows how much she can dish out and when he's really had it.

Jacob finishes up and belly crawls backwards out from under the sink just as Mona and I finish our morning coffee. "Jacob," I say, "please come over here a minute. I imagine you've seen Mona before. She was the head waitress here as long as Duck was here. And Charlie, over here, was the head cook just as long. This is Jacob Carlson. You may have seen him at the auto garage, where he worked for the last few years."

"Welcome aboard, Jacob," Mona says in her flirty voice.

"When it's a half hour before your lunch hour, just write me your order on that pad and sign it. If you get it in late or don't sign it, you won't be eating on time, or maybe not at all," Charlie states gruffly.

"Yessir," Jacob says.

"And I'm Grant!" Grant yells, which makes us all laugh.

"Yes, that's my son Grant," I say. "Sorry Grant, I was going to introduce you in a minute but you beat me to it." I turn to Mona and ask her to show Jacob a few things that need his attention.

"No problem," Mona replies, giving me a sly look.

I shake my head slightly, and try not to laugh. "Well, I'd love to stay and chat, but I have to go take care of some paperwork," I say. I walk over to Grant's corner, where he's building a tower of brightly painted blocks that Mona's husband, Evan, made for him out of two-by-four scraps. The day Evan brought them in, Grant stacked them as high as he could and knocked them down on the linoleum, making an impressive crashing noise while Evan looked on, obviously pleased that Grant was enthused about the blocks. The next day, however, Evan brought in a thick piece of dark blue carpet to muffle the sound. Now Grant carefully balances a few tiny plastic people on top of the tower.

"I have to go to my office for a while, Grant," I say. "If you decide to go outside, you need to come tell me, okay? Otherwise, you have to stay in your corner so you don't get in anyone's way."

"Okay, I will, but wait, Mom," he says excitedly. "Watch how far my mens fly when I knock the tower down!"

"Okay, I'm watching!" I say, smiling at his word for his little toy people.

"One, two, three " he counts and rams a tractor into the bottom of the tower, causing the people to go flying.

"See that?" He asks, pleased with himself. "My mens went pretty far! Want to watch again?"

"Honey, I have to go to my office to take care of some paperwork," I say apologetically. "But I would like to watch another time."

Grant turns away from his toys and looks at me. "You never play with me," he says accusingly. "You say you will, but you don't. You used to lots of times at our old house," he adds, his voice sorrowful.

"I'm sorry, I just can't play right now. I promise I will as soon as I can." Mona gives me a sympathetic look, and even Jacob's face looks touched.

Grant gives me no reply. Guilt-ridden, I head down the hallway to my office. I'm torn by Grant's accurate account of the situation, and in a split second I decide to take the day off tomorrow to be with him. I think I'll show him Lower St. Mary's Lake, which has always been my favorite place in the area. Right now, though, I need to get some work done.

I sit down in front of the beautiful old oak desk, and suddenly an image comes to me of Uncle Duck's gentle hand as he cleaned the cuts on my face the first day I met him. Grant would have loved Uncle Duck, I think sadly. I imagine him sitting here, in this very chair, when he had first opened the place, doing paperwork, figuring the best way to run The Serenade. Only it wasn't called The Serenade at first, I recall Uncle Duck telling me.

He had built the place about thirty-six years ago, just after he came back from military service during World War Two. He first named it The Sentinel, a solid log sentry at the gateway to the mountains. But after a few years, he decided the name was too harsh, more war-like than peaceful, and didn't lend itself to the kind of good memories he hoped people would have of his place.

But the locals were already used to it being called The Sentinel, and he wanted them to feel like they were part of any change. With that in mind, he invited his customers and employees to take part in a contest to create and name a new drink, and if it was a good match, the name of the drink would become the name of the establishment.

Over a few weeks, Uncle Duck tried every one of the hundred-plus entries, and finally chose "The Serenade," a concoction submitted by good natured Tippy Svenson. Tippy, then middle aged, owned a little market, and had earned his nickname by way of his frequent visits to the bar. The explanation of the name of the entry said, "When I was away in the First World War, I missed my wife terribly. One of the things that kept me going was thinking of how we used to serenade each other with love songs." Tippy's recipe was printed on one side of the little advertisements Duck placed on every table in the bar and restaurant, and on the other side was printed in bright lettering: 'Sing to your Sweetie, have a Serenade!' accompanied by a drawing of a drink in a nice glass with an umbrella.

I met Tippy much later, and never shared a drink stronger than hot chocolate with him, but I will always consider him a true friend. We still serve the winning recipe. Sometimes people will have a few and start serenading their sweetie, or in some cases, anyone who will listen. Not many of them can actually carry a tune, but usually everyone has fun.

True to his word, Uncle Duck changed the name of his establishment from The Sentinel to The Serenade, and also decided that Saturday nights from late spring through early fall would be Serenade Night. On these nights there would be live music, food and drink specials, and in between sets, the singers in the band would walk around the tables and dance floor and sing to the customers. Also, the customers could sing, during specified intervals. Serenade Night was intended to be simply a fun evening for the hardworking citizens of the area, because goodness knew they needed it.

In a few hours I'm finished with my paperwork and go into the kitchen. Quietly I tell Mona and Charlie that I plan to spend the next day with Grant, and if the weather cooperates that I will take him to the lake. I remember countless plans over the years that had to be changed due to unexpected storms on the mountain front.

"Good plan," Mona says. "You haven't had a day off since you got here."

"And I owe Grant a little time," I add.

"It's not like the old days, is it," she says, "when we used to have so much fun around here. But I think we'll get back to that eventually."

"Oh, spare me," Charlie says sarcastically. "You two were a pair of nincompoops. I'm glad you finally grew up."

"What are you talking about, Charlie?" Mona says. "We were two perfectly behaved ladies and you know it!" she nudges me and we both laugh. "And we still are!"

"Oh yeah, you two could barely stop giggling to wait on the customers half the time," he replies. "At least now there's a glimmer of hope for you both. Remember that time, right after Meredith started working here, when she got the bean soup mixed up with the dishwater?"

"I had forgotten about that!" Mona says. "Remember, Meredith? You had a fifty gallon pot of that brown bean soup on the burner, and whoever was washing dishes for some reason put a fifty gallon pot of water on another burner to soak silverware in."

"Wait a minute, the dishwater was so murky that the two pots looked pretty much the same!" I defend myself.

"Why didn't you ask which one was which if you didn't know?" Charlie asks, just like he had on the day in question.

"Because she was just a kid, and she was scared to death of you," Mona says for me.

"It's true," I say, smiling at him. "But I'm not scared of you now!"

"You were right to be scared of me. Nobody ordered my bean soup for months afterward, and that really made me mad. It's a wonder we didn't get closed down!"

"Oh, we just gave everyone who ate it a free washing out," Mona says. "Most of them probably needed it anyway," she says, even getting a laugh out of Charlie.

"Then there was the time you poured bleach on the kitchen aprons and ruined a dozen of them," Charlie says, pleased with his litany of my mistakes. "Holes the size of my head in every one of them," he says, shaking his head.

"I'd never used bleach before," I said. Nobody told me how to do it, you just said 'Do it!'"

"Again, why didn't you ask?" Charlie says.

"Because you were such a grouch, and you still are!" I smile at him. "But I love ya, Charlie," I say, putting my arm around him. He mutters something unintelligible, but doesn't attempt to remove my arm.

"I remember the time I tried to teach you how to make an omelet," Charlie says to me. "I went through it step-by-step, maybe six times that morning, and you never turned out one that was edible. You any better at it yet?"

"I don't know!" I say with a laugh. "I've never tried it again! Want me to, right now?"

"Like we have time for experiments? How about buffalo burger, and steak? Did your cooking improve at all, is what I'm asking?"

"Well, let's see. .I haven't had a steak or a buffalo burger since I've been gone, so I don't know," I say. This is fun, so I don't tell him that I learned a lot just watching him dice, slice, sauté, and bake his way through the day, over and over.

"There's no hope for you," Charlie says in mock disgust. "But you're not the only hopeless one. I remember Mona was always trying to teach you to swing your behind like she still does."

"I quote from Waitressing 101," Mona says with a grin, "A female waiting tables who swings her hips gracefully in view of male customers will likely be rewarded with generous tips. It's always worked for me, anyway," she adds.

"Just like I told you back then, Mona, I wasn't blessed with a hip swinging figure like you were." I say. "I'm not curvy on the bottom and I wasn't blessed with much on top either."

"Well you know what they say," Mona says laughing, "more than a mouthful's a waste!"

"That's bad, Mona!" I say, pretending to be upset. "I never did get good at it anyway."

I hadn't realized that Grant is listening to everything we say. "What didn't you get good at, Mom?" he asks.

Knowing that I'm going to be taking tomorrow off gives me a little spring in my step. "I never got good at walking like Mona does, see?" I walk past Grant, swinging my derriere in an exaggerated movement, just as Jacob walks in the kitchen. Mona joins me, and Grant laughs uproariously as he tries to mimic us.

"This is interesting," Jacob says with a laugh.

"You ain't seen nothin' yet," Charlie says. "Wait until you've been here a little while. These two nincompoops are full of shenanigans."

Jacob just grins and looks at me and then Mona. He has a terrific smile, which I can't help but return.

"Well, this nincompoop has to fix her little nincompoop's peanut butter and jelly sandwich," I say. "That's something I've perfected, Charlie!"

"Let's add it to the menu," he says dryly.

"Hey, not a bad idea! Thanks!" I say as I set the peanut butter and jelly out on the counter. "Hey Grant! I'm spending the day with you tomorrow!" I tell him.

"Really? You don't have to work tomorrow?" he squeals happily.

"Nope! It's just you and me," I say. "We're taking a day just for us!"

"This is going to be fun!" he shouts. It's fun already, I think, just watching him.

At eight the next morning I look out the window. The sky is blue, dotted with fluffy white cumulous clouds. I turn on the radio and wait for a weather forecast, and am happy that no inclement weather is expected today.

"Time to get up, sleepyhead. Remember, I'm taking the day off? How would you like to go adventuring?"

"I'm too sleepy to get up," he says.

"I don't think so, mister," I say, laughing and shaking him playfully to get him moving.

In an hour Grant and I stop at the gas station to fill the tank of Uncle Duck's fifty-five Ford pickup before we leave town. He loved driving it, and I love it because it reminds me of him. It's probably just my imagination, but I think the inside of the truck still smells like him.

The drive toward Glacier Park is as beautiful as I remember it. I imagine that someone first named this the Big Sky Country on a day like this, when the sun was shining and the blue sky went on forever. Grant and I sing and play twenty questions along the way. After a while he needs a pit stop, so we stop at a tiny market where I have stopped before. While Grant is in the restroom I buy bread, cheese, lunchmeat, chips and root beer for a picnic when we get to the lake.

"Meredith?"

I turn around and see Pete's best friend, Jim Stewart, just coming in the store.

"Jim!" I say, happy to see him.

"What are you doing here?" he asks, his face lighting up.

"I'm living in Crossroads now," I tell him. "I've been back for a few weeks. Going up to the lake for the day."

"It's great to see you! I'm working on a ranch not too far from here," he says. "See that turn off out there?" he points to a secondary road that cuts off from the highway. It's about five miles out that way. Pete works there too."

"No kidding!" I say, my heart skipping a beat. "I thought he was going to go into business with his dad after he got his degree."

"Well, I should let him be the one to tell you about that," he says.

"Okay," I say, supposing Jim is referring to Pete's marriage. "How long have you guys been working there?"

"Oh, I've been there about eight months I guess. Pete started a few months before I did. I was lucky to get on at all—the drought is making it pretty tough all over. "

"That's what I've been hearing. I'm glad you were able to get on there; I'm sure it's good for you two to work together. Oh, here's my son," I say as Grant joins me at the register. "Jim, I'd like you to meet Grant. Grant, I went to school with Jim," I explain.

"Hi Grant!" Jim says. "You like it over there in Crossroads?" he asks, not giving Grant time to answer. "You better say yes! That's where your mom and I grew up, you know!"

"Yes!" Grant says, grinning.

"Okay, good!" he says to Grant. Then to me he says, "You should bring him out to the ranch. I bet he'd love it."

"Can we go, Mom?" Grant asks.

"Not today, hon. I'm sorry, Jim," I say, thinking that Pete probably wouldn't want us showing up unexpectedly at his work place. "But please tell Pete 'hi' for me. And would you please tell him if he wants to see me, he can find me at The Serenade?"

"Sure, I'll tell him. I'm really glad I ran into you guys. Hey Grant, take it easy, ok?"

"Okay, I will," Grant says, sticking his thumbs in his pockets like Jim does. "You take it easy too, okay?"

"You got it," Jim says, and we both laugh. Jim gives me a quick hug goodbye before we leave the store. As we pull back out onto the road I can't help but wonder if I did the right thing by declining Jim's invitation to the ranch. Pete has been married and divorced, so I know things can never be exactly the same between us again. But even with that knowledge, I still love him. I want to find out if it can work for us, but I'm not going to throw myself at him like I'm desperate. Like I always tell Grant—if something's meant to be, it will happen. I just hope it's meant to be.

I marvel at the lake's beauty, as I do every time I see it, before spreading a blanket on the shore and pulling the sandwich fixings, chips, and root beer out of the market bag. There is nobody else around. The sun is warm on our backs as we munch contentedly.

"You can wade in the water just a little ways, if you want," I tell Grant after we eat.

"I want to swim!" he says.

"There's no way I'm swimming in this freezing water. Let's stick to wading."

"Okay, chicken," he says, laughing at me.

"Fine, I'm a chicken. Cluck cluck. I don't care what you say, little man! This water is too cold!" I tickle him and we both giggle. He takes off his shoes and socks, and I roll up his pant legs a little. He walks the few feet to the water and sticks a foot in.

"Mom! It's freezing!" he shouts.

"Cluck, cluck," I tease playfully. He wades for just another minute, then comes to the blanket to warm his feet in the sunshine.

I think back to the last time I was here. It was graduation day. Pete asked me to come up here on an overnight trip. It was no problem for him, he said. He had been on overnight camping trips with his friends before, and his parents most likely felt he could take care of himself. I doubt that his parents knew I was with him. If they had had an inkling of it I think Matthew would have had quite a lot of wisdom to deliver to his son. At first I didn't even want to go, because I didn't think I was ready to spend a night with him.

"We'll just cook dinner over a campfire. I'll bring real warm sleeping bags to use in the back of the pickup. Nothing has to happen between us," Pete assured me. "I'll be happy just having you with me." I trusted him to let me take things at my own speed, so I decided to go. I asked my mom if I could spend the night after graduation with MaryAnn and come home late the next afternoon.

"What if they come looking for you?" MaryAnn had asked me.

"It's risky, I know," I had said. "If they do, just say you thought I was going camping at the lake with some friends. That way they'll at least know where I am," I told her.

"Meredith, you better be careful—I mean, you're going to spend the night with him?"

"I already told Pete not to expect anything," I told her.

"I know Pete's nice, but do you really think he doesn't

expect anything? You're my best friend in the world, and I couldn't stand it if something happened to you, like if you got pregnant," she said, hugging me tightly.

"You're my best friend too, MaryAnn," I said. "But don't worry. I'm not going to let that happen."

The graduation ceremony the next afternoon seemed to go on forever, even though there were only fifty-six graduates. When the speeches and diploma receiving were finally over, I found Mom in the gym with all the families and friends of the graduates. She hugged me and congratulated me, then said she had to leave, because Raymond had just gotten back from a long haul and she was meeting him at the truck stop for a drink. I changed from my dress into jeans in the restroom and waited in the hallway to meet Pete.

"I sure like this," Pete had said later as we headed out of Crossroads in his truck. "Me with the woman I love, hitting the open road."

"I like it too! Me and the man I love," I said, putting my head on his shoulder. We drove to the lake, and found a dirt road almost completely shrouded by a dense growth of bushes. Pete drove down close to the lake. He got a blanket out from behind the truck seat and a bag of sandwiches and sodas he had brought. We walked to a secluded area by the shore, and sat on the blanket.

"I love you, Meredith," Pete had said. "How much more perfect can a day be than this?" he asked, leaning over to kiss me deeply on the mouth.

I had felt my face get hot and pulled away from him, "This is as perfect as it gets," I agreed nervously. I reached in the bag and took out two sandwiches and handed one to him. "I love you, too," I said, taking a bite, "but I'm hungry and that's more important," I laughed. He gave me a look that made the risk I was taking sink in a little more. After lunch I said I wanted to wade in the water, so we rolled up the legs of our jeans and played in the lake. It was so cold we soon

got out and went to warm our feet on the blanket. I put on
a jacket and fell asleep in the sunshine, my head on Pete's
chest. Later on, in the evening, we built a campfire and I
made hamburgers with beef from the McBride's ranch.

"Now that was a good burger! Thanks for cooking!" he
said after we ate.

"You're welcome, Mr. McBride," I said politely.

"Meredith?"

"Hmm?"

"I'm not ready to get married yet. You know I plan to go
to college. I can work the ranch with my dad without going to
college, but my folks and I think it will be best in the long run
for me to get my degree."

"I know."

"But I hope someday you'll be my wife," he said, looking
into my eyes to see what my reaction would be.

"I hope so, too," I said, happier than I'd ever been.

"How many kids do you want?"

"I don't know, I never thought about the number, I just
picture myself with some."

"I picture myself with a whole troop of them. Three girls
and three boys, maybe."

"That's a tall order!" I laughed.

"And we'll run the ranch together eventually, because
my parents will want to retire someday. Our ranch is a good
place to raise a family, don't you think?"

"A wonderful place," I say. "You've decided for sure
then, that's what you want to do?" I had asked, remembering
the times he'd talked about maybe being a smokejumper or a
Marine.

"It's what I really want. I love the land, I love the animals, I love working with Nadia. I even love the weather
extremes. But what about you? What about your plans to be
a singer? And what are you going to do while I'm at college?
It's going to be terrible not seeing you every day."

"I don't want to sing professionally. When I have my own home some day, maybe some kids, I'm not going to be traipsing around the country going on tour, no siree. Except for vacations, I mean. For now, I hope MaryAnn and I can get an apartment. We've talked about it for years. I'll work full-time at The Serenade, so I'll still see Uncle Duck and everyone all the time. And don't worry; I'll miss you while you're at college, but being on my own for a while will be good for me. I just hope MaryAnn can leave her mom to do it."

"Well, I'll be done with school in four years. I hope you'll be ready to settle down and marry me then, because I'll be ready for you."

"Don't worry," I had told him, "I'll be ready."

We lay on the blanket on our backs for a long while, looking at the brilliant constellations of stars and talking about our future together.

When I got back home the next morning, I was locked out of the house. Raymond was at the window closest to the door, watching me. I pounded on the door for a minute until it was clear that he really wasn't going to let me in. I walked over to MaryAnn's in despair, and she called DeeDee at work and asked her what to do. "Mom wants to talk to you," she'd said, and handed me the phone.

"Meredith, I'm sorry for what you're going through, but of course you did make a poor choice by going on an overnight trip with Pete, so I don't blame your folks if they're mad about that," she said. "I know how easy it is to get carried away when you think you're in love."

"We just played in the lake and cooked hamburgers over a campfire," I said, which brought a sigh of uncertainty from DeeDee.

"Well, no matter what you did or didn't do, you have to have a place to stay until they let you back in, so you can stay with us—but if Raymond comes over and causes us trouble you'll have to find another place. I can't have him disrupting our home again," she said seriously, referring to the times he had stomped into their house without knocking to drag me home.

"I understand. Oh, thank you DeeDee," I'd said gratefully.

The twins went to sleep early that evening, when DeeDee was still at work. MaryAnn brought two steaming mugs of hot chocolate into her bedroom, and we sat on the floor leaning against her bed, sipping it.

"Thank you, MaryAnn," I said, suddenly welling up with tears.

"For what?" she said.

"For everything. For always sticking by me when things are rotten, for being happy for me when things are good," I said.

She put her mug down on the floor, then took mine gently out of my hands and put it on the floor too. She scooted close to me and put her arms around me, cradling the back of my head with her hand. "It's okay. Everything's going to be okay," she crooned, comforting me just as she did the twins when they were hurt or upset. She held me until I stopped crying.

"We've had a lot of good times together, haven't we?" she had asked. "Remember when we met?"

"Yep. Kindergarten. I remember all the kids were sitting around little tables and the teacher was giving instructions. I didn't understand what we were supposed to do, and I was scared. You were sitting next to me and leaned over from your chair when the teacher wasn't looking, and you told me what to do. And you've been helping me out ever since," I said.

"We've been helping each other ever since," she corrected me. "Like you helping me babysit, and when we got lost in the woods that summer."

"I try not to think about getting lost," I say. "But when I

do, I know you're the best friend I could ever have had."

"Same here." Suddenly she sat up straighter. "Remember when we talked about moving into the Greenway together?"

"Yes," I said.

"Let's do it! We're both out of high school—nobody can tell us we can't do it, if we have the money," she said excitedly.

I sat up and wiped my eyes with my sleeves. "You want to? I was just telling Pete that I wanted to! But what about your mom and the twins?" I wanted to get a place desperately, but I liked DeeDee and the twins a lot, and I didn't want to cause any problems.

"I'll still take care of the twins here, but I'll have to ask Mom for a little money. And I'll go home to our apartment every day when I'm done. Mom will have to ask Mrs. Embry to babysit if she works more than five days, because I need some time away from the kids," she said firmly.

"Sounds like you've been thinking a lot about this," I said.

"I have. I even called The Greenway and asked how much the apartments are. We can afford one, between your wages at The Serenade and what I would ask for from Mom. We won't be eating much, though."

"We don't eat much anyway. So that's okay with me!" I said excitedly. "Wow! We're going to get our own place! How many years have we been saying we would get our own place together some day?"

"I don't know, since we were ten? And Raymond locking you out will be the key to it finally happening!" MaryAnn laughed.

"Yuck, a reason to thank Raymond," I had said.

We got up early so we could talk to DeeDee about our plan while she was getting ready for work, before the twins woke up. I imagine she was a little disappointed that she wouldn't have a built in babysitter any more, but she had agreed that it seemed that since we had graduated, we should make our own decisions.

Moving day was one of the most exciting days of our lives, though I'm sitting here by the lake with Grant five years later, wondering what on earth we were thinking when we signed the agreement for the seedy little apartment. DeeDee came to look at it and was upset, but there was no other place to rent an apartment in town. I couldn't go on living at home, and I know she didn't want me to move in with them.

To get to the apartment, MaryAnn and I had to walk down a long dark corridor on the first floor, climb three flights to the top floor, then walk to the end of another long, dark corridor. The Persian carpeting on the corridor floor was frayed on the edges and threadbare in large spots, and the electric sconces, placed every twenty feet along the walls, cast a very dull yellow light, as though the bulbs in them were squeezing out their last watts. There wasn't any obvious trash lying around in the corridors, but the place always smelled bad.

Inside our tiny apartment, there was a two-foot-long crack, loosely in the shape of an L, in the tall, narrow living room window. It had been repaired with silver tape, so when we looked out to the street below we had to peer out one side of the crack, or crouch down to look through the approximately five inches of unobstructed glass below the L. In the same room, the gray speckled linoleum covering the floor was warped in the center, which reminded us of the sidewalk on MaryAnn's block, where tree roots under the cement had created small hills.

The tiny kitchen had a little white refrigerator on legs, similar to one I had seen in old Tippy's kitchen in the back of the market across the street from my house, and a two burner gas stove. Our apartment had a strange odor apart from the trashy smell in the corridors. I worried it might be a gas leak, but when I called Mr. Packard, the owner, he said I wouldn't be able to smell a gas leak, so there was nothing to worry about. I tried not to think about it, but I wasn't sure that Mr. Packard knew what he was talking about.

The plumbing was quirky, and the heat register either cooked us or didn't work at all. The place was a dump, but it was our sanctuary. We loved it. We loved walking in after we'd been somewhere together, tossing our purses on the little table, and sitting down to a cup of hot chocolate that we made in our own kitchen. Every day it seemed like MaryAnn became a little happier than the day before. She'd been so busy taking care of the twins while her mom was working, that she never had much chance for fun. But she appeared to be much more content when we moved into the apartment, and by the time Pete left for college in the fall, it seemed like I was living with the MaryAnn I knew before the twins came along.

I had not been expecting it to be so hard to live so far from Pete. I was ecstatic when he came home for Easter that April. But that was when I began to realize that something was seriously wrong with MaryAnn. I just couldn't figure out what it was.

Chapter 4

❧

"This is a red letter day, Grant!" I say, looking out the windows in the restaurant kitchen. "It's Midsummer, and the day of The Serenade's grand re-opening!"

"Midsummer," Grant says with a mouthful of cereal. "I don't know what that is, but I know what the grand re-opening is!"

"I'm sure you do know what the grand re-opening is, because we've been planning for it since we got here, but Midsummer is the day that is the longest day of the year," I say.

Grant munches while he thinks that over. "So I won't go to bed tonight until a lot later?"

"Tonight won't be how it usually is, but since it's our first day and we won't close until nine, you will most likely be up late. But Midsummer Day is the day of the year that stays lightest for the longest time," I explain, while Grant nods his head, accepting my explanation.

Grant is such a sweet kid. Ever since he began to talk, I have cherished our conversations and the little hugs with attached "I love you's" he gives me out of the blue. Now I feel a shadow of guilt following me around because I'm able to spend so little time with him. I used to have weekends off, but now the few minutes we have before he goes to bed every night are just about all we have together.

I didn't exactly plan our opening day to coincide with Midsummer, but when I realized that we could actually be ready by today, I had a five foot tall "Grand Opening—Midsummer Day!" banner stretched out across the front of the restaurant with the times of operation listed below. Around here grand openings of any kind are well attended, so we're all looking forward to a very busy first day!

Grant gets up from the table and takes his cereal bowl to the sink. "When are the people going to start coming, Mom?" he asks a little nervously.

"The banner out front says the restaurant opens at noon for lunch, so it won't be too long. We better get a move on!" Mona, Danielle and I invested a lot of time and elbow grease scrubbing floors, walls, and everything else in the huge industrial kitchen. All the hotel linens, towels, and kitchen aprons are freshly laundered. The shelves of the pantry, freezers, and walk-in refrigerators are stocked. Even Grant was anxious to be part of the hubbub, so yesterday he had the special task of polishing the stairs and banister of the beautiful hotel staircase. I showed him an old brochure that had been written about the hotel when Uncle Duck first opened it in 1946, featuring the staircase on the front, so he would know how important it was to keep the staircase polished. Crafted by a local artisan all those years ago, it's still breathtaking—usually the first thing new visitors comment on.

Jacob, who has proven to be a good hire, has gone over the premises with a fine toothed comb. Repairs included the meat slicer, bathroom plumbing, loose doorknobs, and wobbly tables and chairs. I think his work is quality, which is very important to me.

This morning Mona arrives early and catches me playing with the ends of my hair, an old habit from my younger years that sometimes flares up when I'm nervous.

"I know we're going to do just fine," she says, reassuring me.

"I know you're right. But I feel like there's a swarm of butterflies in my stomach, anyway!"

Shortly before we're due to open she gives me a big hug, and says, "They'll come in droves. And we're ready for them!"

"Right," I say.

"Right," Grant chimes in.

By eleven a large crowd is milling about on the restaurant deck. "You better go ahead and open the door!" Mona says. "We can't really expect them to wait until noon!"

I glance at her for strength, swallow hard, then walk over to the restaurant door and pull it open. "Good morning, everybody!" I say cheerfully, though the butterflies have multiplied. "Thank you all so much for coming to the grand re-opening of The Serenade. I want to let you know that, just like in the old days, you can seat yourselves at lunch, so go ahead!" I start shaking hands and greeting old acquaintances and friends as they file in. Grant stands by my side with a wide grin, his blue eyes twinkling.

Most of the customers are townspeople, I notice. The few I don't recognize I imagine are travelers who left the highway to get a bite to eat, unaware that they would be part of our big day. We don't have enough seating, and the benches on the porch and inside the door fill up quickly.

This big of a turnout is going to be tough on Charlie and Ralph, his assistant cook, so I go into the kitchen and put on an apron to help as the first orders trickle in. I smile when I see the old familiar house specials in waitress shorthand on the orders—Flapjacks with Serenade Syrup, Scrambled Eggs Just Ducky, the sloppy but delectable Bison Burger, and a new addition, sure to be a favorite on our children's menu, the PBJ (peanut butter jelly sandwich), which we make on homemade bread with locally made jelly.

"Ready for the onslaught?" I ask the cooks.

"Ready as we'll ever be," Charlie grumbles as he grabs the first ticket off the wheel.

All of us have been on our feet for four hours. My feet are on fire. I haven't been in a job that requires standing this long since the last time I worked here, and I had forgotten how much my feet had hurt the first few weeks. The heat in the kitchen is tremendous, and I make a mental note to ask Mr. Overgaard if 'operating capital' includes money for an air conditioning system. During a quick restroom break I look in the mirror and am dismayed to see what a mess I am — strands of long blonde hair have escaped from my ponytail and are plastered across my forehead with sweat, the little makeup I had on is nowhere to be seen, and my blouse is wet with sweat under the armpits.

"Meredith!" Charlie yells before I have time to fix myself up. "We're busy out here!"

"Okay, Charlie. Be right there," I yell back. I wash my hands, and scurry back to the kitchen, hastily tying my apron strings. Ralph pulls a ticket down and thrusts it at me, then grabs one for himself.

I start to read the ticket, then out of the corner of my eye I see movement at the back of the kitchen. I turn, stunned to see Pete coming in the back door!

I grab a paper towel and wipe the sweat off my forehead. "Pete!" I say excitedly, smoothing my hair back with my hands.

"Meredith!" he says, walking toward me, transporting me back in time to the first day I met him. "I know you're busy. Sorry for busting in this way."

"Oh, Pete!" I'm so happy to finally see him again that a few tears escape and roll down my face. "Did Jim tell you I would be here?"

"Yeah, he did. And I heard on the radio that you were opening The Serenade today, so I put in for time off."

"I'm so glad to see you! But I can't visit much right now, we're even busier than we expected! I can slip an order in for you, if you were going to stay for lunch?"

"I'm sure the food is great. But let's have coffee or something together later, okay? So we can talk?"

Charlie harrumphs loudly and shoots me a look, warning me to put an end to the idle chit chat.

"I'd like that very much," I say to Pete.

"I'm staying a few days at my folks' place," he says. "Let me give you the number." I quickly pull a pen and pad out of my apron pocket and write the number he gives me, even though I still know it by heart. "Call me when you get a chance, will you?" He flashes me a smile and heads for the door.

"I will!" I call after him. My face feels hot as I run to peek out the window by the back door to watch him leave. I notice Charlie and Ralph are looking at me, so I get back to work, but it's impossible to concentrate on work, with the sound of Pete's voice, and his face—how good he looked!— so fresh in my mind. "I'll be right back, promise," I tell Charlie and Ralph, as I go out through the swinging doors to the restaurant, to size up the atmosphere, get my mind back on business. I hear the steady loud hum of many conversations, and look out over the sea of faces, watching our customers eating and talking contentedly. I catch Mona's eye as she turns away from taking an order, and motion to her to come over to me.

"What is it?" she asks quietly.

"Pete came to see me!" I whisper.

"Are you kidding? How did he get by me?" she asks, clearly excited for me.

"He came in the back door! He asked me to call him!" I'm not whispering very well anymore, and Mrs. West, who has been the town librarian as long as anyone can remember, looks up from her plate to cast a disapproving glance at me. "Better go," I say. Mona smiles at me and gives me a thumbs up.

Between Pete's visit and how smoothly things are going for our grand opening, I'm on cloud nine for the rest of the day. There are a few minor mishaps—a plate knocked off a table by a child, and a water glass that slipped out of a busboy's hand. We run out of a few items—butter that we substitute with margarine and cream we substitute with milk—but we don't get any complaints over it. I hear people commenting throughout the day that they sure are happy to have this place open again, and my heart soars every time I hear it.

When it's finally my turn for a ten-minute break in the afternoon, I take Grant and go out the back door, remembering something my mother told me, when I was really young. She said that an old time Midsummer Day tradition told of unmarried girls picking seven different kinds of flowers to tuck under their pillows to sleep on that night, which would make them dream of who they would marry. MaryAnn and I loved the idea, and went out to pick the flowers once when we were about twelve. I remember we got a good laugh over telling our dreams to each other the next day. I dreamed of a chimpanzee that I had seen on TV, and she dreamed of a math test she needed to study for. I'm not a young girl anymore, but if there's even a shred of hope that picking a bouquet of flowers will help name my future husband, then I'm ready to try it again. I only tell Grant that I want some pretty flowers for the kitchen, so he goes right to work on picking a bunch. I gather my seven flowers quickly, then we go back inside. I get a vase for Grant's flowers, then sneak mine, stems wrapped in wet paper towel and foil, up to our room and under my pillow.

When the last customer leaves, sometime after nine that evening, I bring four bottles of chilled champagne out to the employees, who are finally relaxing in the booths and chairs around the dining room, some with feet up on adjacent seats. I get a tube of Dixie Cups out of the store room and put one for each person on a large round serving tray. Ralph and Charlie make a big deal of opening the champagne and shooting the tops across the kitchen before they pour it into the cups. I carry a cup of juice to Grant, who is nestled, bleary-eyed, up against Mona in a tall backed booth.

Charlie and Ralph carry the trays of cups around to each employee. "Everyone take a cup, we're going to have a toast!" I exclaim. There's lots of laughing and joking, even though everyone is exhausted. The idea of a champagne toast to themselves makes them proud and giddy.

"I don't know about you all, but I know my last job wasn't this hard," JoLynn, a pretty waitress says and laughs. Everyone good naturedly voices their agreement.

"I'm with you there," Mona shouts, making everyone laugh, since this was her last job.

"Okay, okay everybody," I say. "This has been an extremely busy day for all of us. We're dead on our feet and we still have cleanup. I just want to take a few minutes to thank you all and to let you know how very much your help means to me." I raise my cup of champagne, and everyone else raises theirs. "Here's to the grand re-opening of The Serenade, and to you all. Thanks for your efforts. I know Duck would have been proud."

"Hear! Hear!" everyone cries out, leaving their seats to touch their co-worker's cups. I raise my cup to Charlie and Mona, thanking them. "Grant? Do you want to do cheers with me?" I ask him, just as his head leans completely on Mona's shoulder and he lets out a soft little snore.

"Dead to the world," Mona chuckles. "About like I feel." Then, misty eyed, adds, "Duck would be really proud of you, Meredith."

"He would have been proud of all of us," I say, looking around the room. I look back on everything that happened here since early this morning, feeling that everything is right with my world.

Grant is asleep and I'm getting ready for bed, when there is a knock on the door of our suite. "Who is it?" I ask, throwing my robe on.

"It's Pete."

I open the door a bit, completely taken off guard. "Shhh..."I say, a finger to my lips, not wanting to wake Grant.

"I know I said I'd be in town a few days, Meredith, but one of the guys at the ranch got hurt today...not too seriously, at least, but he can't work, and they need me to take his place. I just wanted to see you again before I go."

"Come on in," I say quietly, thrilled that he's here, "but we have to keep our voices down. Grant is sleeping in the next room."

"Jim told me he met Grant that day at the store, and that he was a cute kid." Pete looks at me, and I can tell he's not sure what to say next.

"Oh yeah, he took quite a shine to Jim," I say, chuckling. "He was walking around with his thumbs stuck in his pockets for a few days after that, trying to be like Jim."

"That must have been funny. Grant's what, five now?"

"Yes, five. But hey, how did you know where I was staying, anyway?" I ask, changing the subject.

"Oh, that woman at the hotel desk, um, what's her name..."

"Cathy Olson," I help him out.

"Yeah. I knew she was an Olson—I remember in school she was always reminding everyone of that. Anyway, I asked her if she knew where you lived, and she said here in the hotel and told me what room. I hope that isn't a problem, that she told me, I mean."

"No, of course not. Normally I wouldn't want her telling anyone, but I'm glad she told you," I say.

"Good. So—Cathy also said you own the place now?

That's really something!" Pete says.

"It's been quite a ride," I agree. "It was a real shock to hear that Uncle Duck left it to me. In the first place, I didn't even know Uncle Duck was sick. I didn't know a thing about it until Sam Overgaard sent me a letter explaining everything, and Uncle Duck was already dead. He also sent a letter Uncle Duck had written to me about his will. It was terrible. I'd always meant to come back, let him get to know Grant. I feel awful about it."

"I'm sure you do," Pete says softly, knowing how much I cared for Uncle Duck, and how I had loved this place. "But he knew he could trust you, and you are obviously off to a good start."

"Thanks, Pete. I appreciate that."

"Oh, before I forget, Mom and Dad say 'hi'!"

"I sure miss them. How are they doing?"

"Well, Dad's health isn't too good anymore. He's got a lot of problems," he says downheartedly.

"Oh, no," I say, thinking of Matthew suffering. "How's your mom holding up?"

"She's doing the best she can under the circumstances. She's under a lot of stress, of course. She helps Dad with everything that he used to be able to do himself, so she has very little time for herself." he says. "But she always tells me she's fine, and that this is part of what love is."

"That's a beautiful thought," I say. "I would expect your mom to say something like that." I remember times when my home life had been particularly stressful; Evelyn had sat me down at her kitchen table with a cup of tea and asked me to tell her my troubles. She always listened intently, and the wisdom she shared with me never failed to raise my spirits.

"Do you think they'd be better off in town?" I ask Pete now.

"No, they don't want to leave the ranch. I hope it doesn't come to that. They really love that place. I can't blame them—I love it too."

"When you see them again please tell them I'm thinking of them, will you?"

"You bet," he says. "You know, it's strange, I never really imagined my dad having problems like he does now. I knew that he'd get old some day, but you can't be prepared for this. Mom and Dad aren't that old, you know? They're only in their mid-fifties! Remember how muscular Dad was? Now he's thin, and his hair is white." Pete sighs heavily, then adds, "He was always helping me figure out how to do things, and was always there to help me sort out my problems. Mom too, both of them have always been great, but now they need my help. It's hard for them to maintain the place on their own, so I try to get over here at least once a month. I fix things around the ranch, run errands for them, stuff like that, and I'm glad to do it. I'm just sad about the situation."

"I'm glad you're able to be there for them. I remember you planned to go into the ranching business with your dad after you graduated. So does this mean that you'll be taking over the business eventually?"

"I hope I can. Dad's running very few cattle; he just hasn't been able to handle it in the last few years. They've used most of their savings on his medical care already. He's been hospitalized so many times."

"I'm so sorry, Pete."

"Thanks," he says, then pauses before he goes on. "Meredith, the reason I wanted to see you today is that I, um, I just want to say I'm sorry for how things went when Grant came into the picture. I guess it was just too much at the time," he adds, his voice cracking emotionally. "I couldn't see how it could work."

"It was hard for me, too. But I'm okay now, and so is Grant," I say, wondering what he wants me to say, if he wants to be let off the hook.

He doesn't move, so I move close to him and put my arms around him, burying my face in his chest, letting him know that I care about all of it; Matthew's failing health, our shared past, and the inkling of a possibility of a shared future. I want to tell him I love him, hoping that knowing it will somehow ease his pain.

Pete puts his arms around me now, and we stand holding each other for a long time. Finally I look up at him and ask him to make love to me.

He answers in kisses down one side of my neck, then the other. "It's been way too long, Meredith," he says. "I love you. I don't want to live without you anymore."

"You don't have to," I say, gently separating myself from him so I can lock the door between Grant's bedroom and mine. I turn off the light and lead Pete to my bed.

When my head touches the pillow I feel a little lump. The seven wildflowers, I think with a smile. As Pete moves close to me, a lingering worry flashes through my mind. I know it's only right that I tell him about Raymond. But not now. This is not the right time.

I kept the bouquet of wildflowers under my pillow for a week, and dreamed of Pete every night. I'm sensible enough to know that dreams aren't made from bouquets of flowers, but I want to believe in the story Mom told me—that I have dreamed of the man I will marry. The memory of our lovemaking tantalizes me nearly every waking hour in the following days, making me ache for more. I wonder why I haven't heard from him again, but I remind myself that Pete is a cowboy, and telephones are probably not easily accessed on every acre of the huge ranch that employs him.

It would be wonderful to have Pete here with me today, to celebrate the Fourth of July, but I do have Grant, and I am anxious to show him a Crossroads Fourth, done up right. Next to Christmas, it's my favorite holiday.

At the fairgrounds Grant is a little shy about getting involved in the field games that have been organized for children, until we see John, (a boy we met through Roma),

on the field sidelines with his mom, Carolyn. When their
age group is called out over the loudspeaker for a foot race,
Carolyn and I nudge them out on the field. They horse around
during the race and almost come in last, but they have fun,
and are anxious for the next event to start.

It doesn't seem so long ago that MaryAnn and I were
playing the same field games, while our moms meandered
together through the craft booths. After the games we'd stop
at the corndog vendor and find a shady spot to sit for lunch.
The corndogs were delectable treats, and I longed for the
taste all year. After lunch we went downtown for the parade.
MaryAnn and I didn't much care about the noisy sirens of the
fire trucks, police and sheriff's cars, the high school marching
band, or the string of vintage cars. But we had to wait through
it all in order to see the spectacular Royal Court of the Crossroads Rodeo, crowned at the previous year's rodeo. Canter-
ing by on their highly decorated horses, these beauties of
the Royal Court wore glittering rhinestone tiaras and waved
graciously to the subjects lining the tiny parade route.

MaryAnn and I were in awe of not only their beauty, but
also their expert horsemanship, noting that they could have
a spooked horse under control in seconds. We commented
every year that the girls looked lovely but sad, because the
parade was nearly the last event of their reign. (This led us to
invent our game of Rodeo Royals, in which we wore tinfoil
tiaras and practiced waving in the mirror while discussing
possible decorations for our horses.)

Weeks ahead of the rodeo, the *Bugle* ran photos and bios
of the contestants, which MaryAnn and I mulled over until
we figured out who should be queen and why. Some of our
winners were chosen because of civic-minded activities, like,
"loves to help in the senior center," or "has adopted six pup-
pies from the animal shelter." But sometimes we had to go
with one because she just looked regal. Mom and DeeDee, on
the other hand, did not seem interested in royalty. I remember

being embarrassed during the rodeo once when mom leaned over to DeeDee and whispered, "Just right, nice and tight," and DeeDee laughed and agreed with her. It wasn't until I was much older that I began to take an interest in cowboys, but by then MaryAnn's dad had left. Her mom was managing the drive-in and MaryAnn had been needed at home to babysit the twins. I knew I wouldn't enjoy the rodeo without MaryAnn, so we watched the twins together instead. We still pored over the royal court information in the paper, but I didn't see the crowning again until the year I met Pete.

The Serenade is closed today, so everyone can enjoy the Fourth of July festivities. Mona and I will have to put in an hour after the parade to prep for tomorrow. Grant and I walk along the sidewalk downtown, looking for a place to put our lawn chairs to watch the parade, but most of the shady spots under the green and gold striped storefront awnings have been taken.

As we walk, I tell Grant about the businesses in the two-block downtown. I have to shout to compete with the blaring sirens of the fire trucks, signaling the start of the parade. I point at the bank across Main Street, and shout that Mr. Overgaard works there. It's a big, light-colored granite building erected in 1908.

We walk past Johanson's Department Store, and I tell Grant that Johanson's carries sturdy clothing for the whole family, like overalls and work shirts. People in Crossroads know that if you want any fancy or fun clothing, you better order from a catalog or head for the nearest large town. In Johanson's, the men's wear is on the first floor, and women's and children's is on the second floor mezzanine. On down the block there is the appliance and furniture store, a real estate office, an antique mall, (which is five little store fronts put together), and Rae Ann's Parlour of Beauty.

When I was a kid, Mom absolutely wouldn't skip her hair

appointments, even though we were on assistance. She said it was her God-given right as a woman to go to the beauty parlor every six weeks, and if someone didn't like it they could stuff it you-know-where. I wouldn't have cared one way or the other, except that Mom always insisted that I walk down to Rae Ann's with her and wait to walk back home with her, so I spent a lot of time in the tiny reception area waiting. Maybe she was embarrassed about spending money on her hair when we were scrabbling for food, and figured nobody would harass her about it if her child was sitting in the waiting area. But she didn't seem to have any qualms about joining Rae Ann and the other women gossiping about people who weren't there to defend themselves. It dawned on me over a period of years, that there was probably some juicy gossip flung around about us when we weren't there.

I couldn't tell if Rae Ann was really Mom's friend or not, but my intuition was well developed for my young age, and I suspected she was not. One afternoon, when I was about twelve, I was shocked and angry when I heard her ask Mom to send me to help her out. "She could start out just sweeping up and making appointments, you know, after school and Saturdays, and then after high school she goes to beauty school and then works for me doing hair!" Rae Ann had said.

"You mean it? You'd want my kid here helping you?" Mom had asked, thrilled with the idea.

"Yes! She's got that long blonde hair that would be fun to wear lots of different ways. That would be good for business, for the clients to see different styles we can create for them. Why won't she ever let me do something with her hair? But anyway, I'd like to expand the business, but I'd need someone in here with me. So I figure when she gets her beautician's license, then she could start working here, and we could add three chairs and three more dryers. There's no telling how much she could earn." Mom had flashed a big grin at me over the planter of tall fake flowers that separated the waiting room from the work stations.

"I heard everything you and Rae Ann said about me," I told Mom after we left Rae Ann's. "I'm not going to beauty school! There's no way I'm going to spend my life playing with hair and spreading gossip!"

Mom looked at me as surprised as if I'd slapped her in the face. "You ungrateful brat!" she said sharply. "You'll be out of school before you know it, and you'll need a job. To have her offer to take you on now is…"

"It's a prison sentence!" I had yelled, running ahead of her.

Ah, the good old days, I think, as Grant and I approach Rae Ann's. The place is closed for the Fourth, but I look in the window and see three styling chairs and three hair dryers Nothing has changed, right down to the fake flowers. I was able to escape the sentence, and apparently nobody else has succumbed to it, either.

Next to the bank are the coin-op laundry, a soda fountain, a little Christian bookstore, and the Crossroads Theatre, owned and operated by Old Man Nelson. He would never play a movie for us until we had at least twenty people to watch it, so whenever anyone wanted to see a movie, if we couldn't round up twenty people, it was just too bad.

When I realize that the only awning-covered stretch of sidewalk with space left for parade watching is across the street at the end of the second block, I take Grant's hand and cross at the next corner. We walk past the insurance agency and hardware store, and stop in front of Peterson's Bridle and Bridal. "Come in for a Bit," it says under the sign.

I'm disappointed that we have to sit in front of Peterson's. When Pete and I were engaged, my wedding dress had come from Peterson's. Seeing the place sends a pang through my chest. It's closed now for the parade, but a handwritten sign assuring people they'll be back in a jiffy is taped to the door. Though they were older than me by ten years, I had heard that Karl and Kirsten were all over each other in high school, and headed down the aisle as soon as they graduated. Soon after, with a down payment from their parents, they opened the store. Supposedly they wanted to work side by side, but his passion was for all things horses, and hers was for weddings. Nobody thought it would work for folks to walk into a store with reins, bridles, and saddles on top of hay bales on one side, and a flurry of tiaras, heart shaped accessories, and plastic draped wedding and bridesmaid's dresses hanging along the walls on the other. But, as with Johanson's, the locals know that if they don't want to buy their tack or wedding supplies here, they have to order elsewhere or drive quite a ways. The Peterson's have been successful, but just seeing their storefront takes me down a lane of memories I don't want to go down. I unfold our chairs so Grant and I can sit down to watch the parade.

"Would you like a balloon animal?" I ask him when some clowns get close to us. It's tradition for the rodeo clowns make balloon animals for the all the kids waiting along the parade route.

"Yes!" Grant says. I wave to the closest clown and he weaves his way between the groups of people until he's next to us.

"What'll it be?" the clown asks Grant.

"A tiger!" Grant shouts out. The clown blows up a long skinny orange balloon, then does some well rehearsed squeaky pulls and tugs. Finally he pulls a black magic marker out of a pocket and draws some squiggly whiskers and stripes and hands it to Grant.

"Grrr!" Grant says, pretending the tiger is nibbling my arm.

"Thanks," I tell the clown. I give Grant a look that reminds him to say thanks, too, which he does.

Soon the American flag is carried by in front of us, and I tell Grant that we need to stand to pay tribute to it. After

Old Glory, the high school band goes marching by, playing "When the Saints go Marching In." It's the same lineup that I have witnessed every time I've been at the parade. Some folks might call that boring, but I call it comfortable, like eating in a favorite restaurant where you know what to expect. I look as far down the block as I can, hoping to see Pete riding Nadia, but I don't see him anywhere. I thought for sure he would be here.

"The Fourth sure brings back memories, huh?" Mona says, startling me.

"Yeah, it sure does. I was hoping to see..."

"I know what you were hoping. But tell me, why are we sitting in front of Peterson's?"

"It was the only place left in the shade," I explain.

"Well, it's a public sidewalk," she says. "Hey Grant, what do you think of the parade so far?"

"It's fun! Look, a clown made me a tiger!" he says, showing off his balloon.

"That's a scary looking tiger!" Mona says.

"Yeah, I'm going to show John this tiger later," he says.

The pooper scooper clowns jog by in zigzag patterns in the street, wheeling their little carts, just stopping long enough to mime their displeasure in their stinky jobs and scoop up the horse manure with shovels before bowing to their cheering audience. Grant is thrilled with the long procession of antique tractors and other farm machinery that rumbles by next, some on trailers and some under their own steam, black coils of smoke billowing out their stacks.

"Let's go in Peterson's," Mona says as the parade comes to an end. "Just see what it looks like in there these days. We have a little time before we have to get back."

"I don't think so," I say firmly. I stand and fold my chair up, then help Grant with his.

Suddenly Kirsten Peterson is standing next to us. "Hey Meredith! Mona!" she's unbelievably bouncy, as always. "How wonderful to see you both! That was some parade, wasn't it?"

"It was. I always love our little parade," I say, trying to look too busy collecting our belongings to look at her.

"I'm so happy that you waited until I got back to the store so we could visit. You've been gone so long, Meredith! We have a lot of catching up to do!" she says, like we were old pals or something. She turns to unlock the door of the store and looks back at me quickly with a half smile.

"I wasn't waiting for you, I was watching the parade. Why would I be waiting for you?" I ask.

"Oh, Cathy Olson told me about you and Pete," she says with a wink. I'm beginning to think that Cathy has a very big mouth.

"What, that he came to see me the day we opened The Serenade?" I ask, hoping that's all Cathy had said.

"You know what I mean," Kirsten says secretively, drawing a look from Mona. I'm going to talk to Cathy about this as soon as I see her, I think. My blood pressure is on the rise when Kirsten says, "Well, since we're all here, come on in and see what's new! Do you still have the wedding dress I sold you?"

"Of course not," I say.

"I was just going to tell you that you could bring it in and exchange it for one of better quality. You're a business owner now, and that cheap dress you bought really won't do this time around."

"What are you talking about?" I snap back.

"From what Cathy said, it sounds like you and Pete are a couple again! I think it's just super!" she says.

"Cathy isn't really in on it," I say. "Pete and I have only spoken once since I've been back, so please don't jump to any conclusions. If I need your services, I'll let you know," I add coldly, taking Grant with one hand and fumbling clumsily with the chairs with the other.

Mona steps in and picks up the chairs, then says to Kirsten, "'Scuse us, but The Serenade's waiting. You know how it is, running a business that's making money hand over fist. It won't take care of itself!" Then she turns to me and says, "Let's go, Meredith." I allow Mona to lead me and Grant away. Halfway down the block I realize I hadn't even mentioned Grant, which I hope doesn't hurt his feelings. I'm sure Kirsten already knows quite a bit about him, since she's been talking to Cathy.

I don't usually hold a grudge, but I guess I haven't let go of the one I've felt toward Kirsten since the day I went to her shop to look at wedding dresses when Pete and I were engaged. I had fallen in love with a beautiful white dress that Kirsten had on display in the window. I had asked if she would please get it down for me to try on, but instead, she asked when our wedding date was.

"We haven't set a date," I told her. "We're just in the planning stages." I told her that Pete and I wanted a big wedding—one that people would remember fondly. I wanted bridesmaids, groomsmen, a three-tiered cake, a big buffet, dancing, and an album full of photos.

"You know it's tradition for the bride's parents to pay for the wedding," she had said in a snotty tone, knowing full well that my folks weren't going to pay for anything.

I wondered why she would say such a thing. "We want to do this ourselves, so we'll have to save for a while. But I want to look at dresses now."

"Well," she asked, "where's your engagement ring, if you don't mind me asking? You aren't really engaged if you don't have a ring."

"I don't have one yet. We decided not to buy one just yet. I'll get a diamond ring later."

"The date will be set later, the ring will come later? Are you sure this is a real engagement?"

I was so hurt that I left without saying anything, and told Pete about it as soon as I saw him. Giving me a peck on the cheek, he told me he had an errand to run and that he'd be back pretty soon. When he returned he was wearing the smile that had hooked me from the beginning.

"I had a little talk with Kirsten," he said. The dress is too big for you, so it will be at the alterations shop. You need to go over there tomorrow and try it on for them. It's bought and paid for, baby," he said with a grin. "Now don't worry about Kirsten anymore. She's just one of those unhappy folks who take their misery out on other people."

I didn't know if his parents paid for it, or if he took money out of his bank account, or what, but I was thrilled. Three weeks later I had the dress, and then it hung, unused, in my closet in my apartment at the Greenway, and in two more closets in Oregon, before I finally gave it to a co-worker at my last job.

Last night I shooed all the employees out of The Serenade early—a little early Fourth of July treat—knowing full well that I would be doing dishes today because of it. This dishwasher makes a lot more racket now than it did when I was a teenager, and it was pretty noisy then. I need to replace it soon, I think. Mona sidles up to me as I'm spreading silverware around the large flat tray to go into the washer.

"What the heck was Kirsten talking about, that stuff about Cathy and Pete?" she asks.

"It was opening day. Remember when Pete came in the back door of the kitchen? He asked me to call him in the next few days so we could get together. But then he got called back to the ranch that evening because a coworker got hurt, and he had to be at work in the morning to take the other guy's place. He wanted to tell me, so he came back here to the hotel, and Cathy told him that Grant and I had a room upstairs. So he came up for a few minutes," I explain.

"And nothing happened in your room?" she asks, although we both know it's none of her business.

"I'm not saying nothing happened, but I don't want to tell the whole town!"

Mona's eyes twinkle as she asks, "I hope it was worth all the gossip it no doubt started!"

"Oh yes, it was worth it," I laugh.

"That sounds like progress," Mona laughs, then adds, "but you better give Cathy a talking-to. She's out of line."

"Yeah, I know. I will."

That night when Grant is tucked in and lightly snoring, I go downstairs to talk to Cathy. There are a few guests lounging quietly around the fireplace, not far from the check-in desk. "Listen, Cathy," I say, keeping my voice low. "At the time, I didn't mind that you told Pete my room number, but I should have come down right then and there and told you it was inappropriate. But I didn't, and that was my mistake."

"I'm sorry, I thought you wanted…,"

"I'm not finished," I say. "I ran into Kirsten Peterson today at the parade. Apparently you said something that made her think there's something going on between Pete and me, and that I might be in the market for a wedding gown. None of that was any of your business. I'm sure you realize you shouldn't have told anyone that he was even there," I chastise her sternly.

"Maybe I accidentally let something slip," she says, her tone transparent.

"Consider this your only warning. If you need another one, I'll have to let you go." I hate saying that, but I have no choice. She assures me it won't happen again, and I hope she's right.

Chapter 5

The five members of the Mountain Silver Band, a country band that will be playing here in the bar on some Serenade Nights, started playing together ten years ago as seniors at Crossroads High School. They've achieved a certain amount of local celebrity in several counties, and they aren't easy to book, especially on short notice. When I was in high school, Uncle Duck used to be able to call them up on a Saturday and have them there that night, but things have changed, and I'm happy for them.

It's our first Serenade Night, two weeks into July, and I'm feeling pretty nervous. Not only have I been wondering all week long if our customers will enjoy Serenade Night like they used to when Uncle Duck was here, but tonight I'm also going to be subbing for a barmaid who called in sick. I'm glad I spent most of the day in the office pushing paper instead of doing a lot of physical work, or I'd be tired already. Mona is upstairs with Grant in our rooms. I had asked her earlier if she wanted to work in the bar tonight, since she used to enjoy it. But she says she's too beat from working today and would rather babysit than barmaid.

"What?" I had asked with a laugh. "You'd pass up the

chance to do some major derriere swinging? Think of your admiring audience! Think of the tips!"

"Yeah, it's a shame, isn't it?" she says, chuckling. "But honestly, I've done my time in the bar. It's a better job for a single gal, anyway. I couldn't enjoy myself in there anymore, holding myself back like I'd have to, being married and all."

"I can't believe what I'm hearing! Mona saying she's not fit to flirt?"

"You'll never hear me say any such thing, no matter how old or married I get. I'm just sharing the glory with you, is all. Now git!"

"Okay! Okay! I'm going!" I kissed Grant goodnight and went downstairs to try to take Mona's place as the queen of curves, knowing I couldn't possibly measure up.

When I walk into the darkened bar carrying my drink tray, Ryan, the lead singer in the band, let's out a loud, "Ewwww Doggie!" I guess he approves of the outfit I'm wearing. Mona cooked these up for the barmaids—white western cut shirt, white leather skirt, vest, hat, and boots, all with contrasting red accents. Mona said I would look good in it for those times I had to work in the bar. Little did we know that I would be wearing it so soon! Ryan, who's pretty good to look at, grins at me as he walks through the bar, offering the microphone to anyone who wants to sing.

I'm happy to see that Ryan has a taker. A young man takes the mic and sings, badly, to the young woman with him. Ryan signals to the rest of the band members up on the stage, who strike up some chords to accompany the singer. This singer is pretty entertaining, off key and messing up the lyrics, but it doesn't matter. He and the woman are enjoying it, and when he's finished, everyone in the bar cheers. I feel like his success is my own! I make my way through the bar, delivering drinks as Ryan goes back up on the stage. Suddenly he says into the mic, "I know a purty little lady right here at The Serenade who loves to sing! Let's get Meredith up here to sing for us!" He grins as he points at me with the mic.

I'm balancing a cocktail tray on one hand and holding a drink in the other so all I can do is say, "No, no," and shake my head. Many of the people here tonight know me, and are shouting out, encouraging me to do it. I'm not prepared at all to sing; I haven't sung in public since I worked here with Uncle Duck. but then I realize it will be better for business if I'm a good sport about it. Danielle suddenly appears, whisks away my drink tray, and shoos me toward the stage. I'm not sure I can come up with the lyrics to anything popular right now. I dig around in my head trying to come up with something I'm sure of, when the customers start shouting "Rodeo Man! Rodeo Man!"

"Thanks for the request," I say into the mic. "I love that song, because it reminds me of working here when I was younger. I wrote it after one very special Fourth of July here in Crossroads, when I was a teenager. It's about two things I love to watch: cowboys at the rodeo, and the parade!" Everyone cheers and the band strikes up the music.

"Sing with me!" I say into the mic, just before I jump into the first verse.

Lookin' in the mirror put on my new hat
A tiny bit crooked, I like it like that.
Snap the pearls on my favorite shirt
Give a little tiny tug to my blue jean skirt.
It's parade day, but I'm thinking 'bout him.

Walking down Main, blockades on Tenth and First
Thinkin' bout that cowboy who landed in the dirt.
He didn't place first in bustin' or ropin'
But he's first in my heart and you know that I'm hopin'
That I'll see him again
Who was that ha ha ha ha hot rodeo man?

People are singing along with me, but by the verse when the cowboy is thrown from his horse and lands at my feet, they're really shouting. Cheers, whistles and applause go up all over the room as I get down off the stage. When I start taking drink orders again, several customers ask me if I'm going to start singing in the bar as a regular. I thank them for asking, but tell them the live music we'll have every Serenade Night will probably be more entertaining. It's funny how things change. Time was, I was chomping at the bit for Uncle Duck to let me sing in the bar, and now, although I am flattered by the attention I'm getting tonight, all I want to do is get upstairs to Grant.

I just finished helping the hotel maids clean rooms, and now Grant and I are polishing the stairs and banister. He loves to help, and now I pay him a quarter a day if he really makes an effort. He's saving his money for a special robot toy that twists and turns into another creature. I can afford to buy it for him, but I think he'll appreciate it more if he has to earn it.

It's noon and none of today's reservations have arrived yet, so we can still get a little more work done. I love the smell of the polish on the pine wood. It takes me back to the days when Jenny was here, living in the room next to the suites Grant and I have now, when I used to clean her room for her. "Did I ever tell you about Jenny?" I ask Grant as we work.

"Who's Jenny?" he asks.

"I'll tell you. The first time I ever walked into The Serenade when I was about fifteen, I was amazed at how big it is in here. Remember what you thought the first time you saw it?"

"Yeah, it was so big I was scared!" he says.

"That's kind of what I thought too. I looked all around the lobby, at those huge beams up by the ceiling. I remember the fire in the fireplace was flickering and throwing strange shadows on the walls. Then I looked around at the sofas and chairs around the fireplace, and I saw just one person in the whole huge place."

"Was that Jenny?"

"Yes. Jenny was a good friend of Uncle Duck's. I didn't know it at the time, but later I learned that she used to love to sit out in the lobby and just watch people. So here was this little old lady, so tiny in the big old chair she was sitting in—that one right down there," I say, pointing at a red overstuffed chair near the fireplace. "Uncle Duck had taken me to lunch here in The Serenade that first day. After we ate he had to leave right away, but he thought Jenny and I would get along, so he introduced me to her. Mona brought us a pot of peppermint tea and two pretty china cups and saucers with roses on them. I had never used a pretty teacup and saucer before, and it made me feel very grown up."

"How did Mona know you wanted peppermint tea?" Grant asks.

"I had never seen Mona before that day, either, so she didn't know what I liked to drink, but she did know that Jenny just adored peppermint, and those pretty cups and saucers. Oh, peppermint! Peppermint tea and peppermint candy, she just loved it!" I explain. Grant nods in understanding.

"As far as I knew, Jenny was probably the oldest person in the world. But she had a sweet look on her face, and her voice was sweet, too. She told me there was plenty of room for me to sit beside her. I remember she scooted over and patted the empty half of the chair. Uncle Duck nodded to me that it was okay, so I sat down next to her. I found out right away that she even smelled like peppermint! She asked me if she'd seen me in The Serenade before, and I told her that I'd never been there before.

"Do you live here in Crossroads?" she had asked me.

She was surprised when I answered, "Yes, in the pink house near the market on Sixth Street. I've lived there all my life," I said.

"My goodness!" she'd said. "That house is full of stories. Do you know that the Jonsson family built that house? That's a very special house to me. Why, the Jonsson's daughter, Anna, was my dear friend!"

"I was amazed to hear that," I tell Grant.

"Why, Mom?"

"Because I had never really thought about how old my house was, or who might have lived in it before me."

Grant is silent for a few moments—he's a little young for the concept of houses built that long ago. "Where's Jenny now?" he finally asks.

"Well, she was pretty old then, although she wasn't the oldest person in the world, like I thought when I was a kid. So I don't know, she might not be around anymore. I would have loved for you to have known her. She was so friendly and funny, and also full of information about things that happened long before you and I were even born."

"Even before you were born?" he asks me.

"Yes."

"Wow, that's a long time ago!" I chuckle. It's the first time I've been referred to as old, in so many words.

"Do you know anything about Jenny?" I ask Mona later in the kitchen. "I mean, what happened to her? I think about her every time I have a reason to go in her old room upstairs." I don't admit that I've been afraid she'll tell me Jenny is dead, so I'm relieved when Mona says she saw her at the beginning of May.

"When Duck got sick he had no choice but to put her in a home. He felt awful about it, but he was in pretty bad shape himself, so he had to. It's an adult care home that opened up about five years ago, about a half hour drive out of town. It was the only place close enough that he could go visit her—and getting out there was hard on him, too. Sam and I took turns driving him out there every week, except at the last, when he wasn't up to it. It's a depressing place, as far as I'm concerned. I don't know how she could like it there, but she hasn't complained about it to me."

"She never was one to complain," I say, then add, "Poor Uncle Duck. I know how much he cared about her."

"Well, she didn't look too bad, at least, the last time I saw her. But she talks about Duck every time I see her. She isn't over it."

We're silent for a few minutes before I ask, "Do you know how they met? Uncle Duck and Jenny?"

"I don't know how they met, I just know they're old family friends. Here," she says, handing me a paper towel she just wrote something on. "It's the directions to the place where Jenny lives. She'll be thrilled to see you, whenever you can get out there."

Grant and I are sitting on metal folding chairs in the commons room of Jenny's care home the next Saturday, waiting for a staff member to bring her in to us. When she is led into the room, I'm surprised to see that her white hair is all wispy and thin, and that she is slightly stooped and leans on a cane with one hand. My heart falls, but when our eyes meet, I know that her memory is still sharp.

"Oh my goodness, Meredith!" she says loudly, her voice strong and clear. "I cannot believe my eyes!" I jump out of my chair to wrap my arms around her, her face burrowed into my chest. We hug for a long minute. I feel Grant standing next to me, his hand hesitantly touching me. "And this must be Grant! Duck told me all about you! I have been hoping you two would come see me some day!"

"I wish we could have come sooner, Jenny," I say, hugging her again.

"Well you're here now, and that's all that matters. Let's move over here to this table where we can have tea together," she says, directing us. "Now Grant, you're certainly a grown up and handsome young man," Jenny says, her eyes sparkling.

"Thank you," Grant says politely, blushing.

"Ah, your mother has raised you with good manners." She nods approvingly. "Let me see you, Meredith," she says, eyeing me closely. "You still haven't put on any weight. How many times have I told you that you are too thin?"

"Oh, by current standards I'm about right," I tell her. She's from another line of thought: that a little extra weight is a good thing. She just shakes her head.

"We brought you some peppermint candy," Grant says, handing her the box we bought for her before we left town.

"I absolutely love this kind of candy! Thank you!" she says happily. I'm going to go ask someone to bring us some peppermint tea to go with it!" She rises slowly from her chair, leaning on her cane.

"Do you want me to get it?" I ask.

"Heavens, no," she says. "I need all the exercise I can get. I rarely get to go outside, even for a breath of fresh air, and the so-called activity coordinator just wants us to sit around tables and make things out of Popsicle sticks and balls of yarn. We never do anything that requires moving! So I'll go," she says, walking gingerly toward the office door.

Several other old folks are watching us, but none of them say anything.

"Mom," Grant whispers to me, "why are those people looking at us?"

"Probably because they don't get many visitors, so they want to enjoy Jenny's visitors too," I whisper back, confident that we're out of earshot.

"That's sad, Mom," he says very quietly, as Jenny comes back in the room.

"They'll be bringing the tea in soon!" she says, smiling brightly.

In a little while we're sipping our tea and eating peppermint candy. I had forgotten how wonderful the combination was. Suddenly, Jenny looks around and notices the other occupants of the room watching us. "Grant," she says, "kindly take the box of candy and offer some to these other folks."

Grant is happy she noticed the problem, but his shyness keeps him from hopping right up to do what Jenny asks. "None of these old folks will bite, dear. Most of them don't even have teeth, so these hard peppermints are just perfect for them. They can just suck on them."

"They don't have teeth? Where are they?" Grant asks.

"Well, a lot of people, when they get real old, have to get artificial teeth. Fake ones. Because their own teeth finally wore out. Oh, it's just the way of things," Jenny says with a sigh.

"They can't bite with the fake ones?" Grant asks, the worry obvious on his face.

"No, most of them leave their teeth in their bedside table drawer," Jenny says, making us all laugh. She hands the box of candy to Grant and he gets up and begins to offer it to the elderly people around the room. I watch, relieved to see a lot of happy faces now, and bursts of conversation. These people are really enjoying having Grant here, and he seems to be enjoying the attention.

"Oh, I remember the first day we met," Jenny says to me in a lilting voice. "We got along fine, didn't we, Meredith?"

"We really did. From the first. You told me about…"

"The house you lived in. I remember! I've thought of that day many times. But how have you been? I know you've been living over in Oregon. Now don't just tell me you've been busy—all mothers are busy!" she laughs.

"I've been fine. I …I don't know if you heard that Uncle Duck left me The Serenade in his will? I was completely shocked! First I was shocked that he had died, and then to find out that he left me The Serenade…" I force back tears, not able to finish my sentence.

"I know, it's been terrible, losing Duck. I don't know that

I'll ever get over it. I never thought I would outlive him," she says, looking at her lap. "It just doesn't seem right. I expect to lose people who are old, like I am, but I don't expect to lose someone so much younger. I think it would make him happy, though, if we remembered him as healthy, happy, and hard working, not frail and sick."

"That's how I do remember him, Jenny! And I always will!" Jenny and I are clinging to each other when Grant comes back with a nearly empty candy box. He sits back down in his chair and looks at the two of us curiously.

"But yes," Jenny says, clearing her throat and wiping her eyes with a tissue. "I knew that he left you The Serenade. Isn't it wonderful? I was thrilled that he left it for you. He worked so hard at making it successful, and when it came time, it was terrible for him to shut it down. There were some real estate investors trying to buy it, but he knew they planned to split the property up into several lots to sell off for condos or strip malls! He wanted The Serenade to go to someone who loved and would care for it, and who better than you?"

"Thank you so much, Jenny. It's wonderful to own it. I promise to do my best to take care of it."

"Jenny?" Grant asks timidly.

"Yes, dear?"

"Do you still have your own teeth?"

I burst out laughing as Jenny smiles widely and shows Grant her choppers, the vintage gold fillings gleaming in the light. "The same ones God gave me," she assures Grant. "I take care of them, and I would advise you to do the same with yours!"

"I will, Jenny. I promise."

I'm happy that Grant and Jenny seem as comfortable together as she and I had always been. I hope eventually we'll have more time to spend with her, and they can get to know each other better. But today I had only a short time open on my schedule, and it has already flown by. When I reluctantly say that I have to get back to The Serenade, Jenny's eyes reveal her disappointment, but she quickly picks up her cane, pushes herself up, and leads the way out to the big front porch.

"Bye, Jenny!" Grant says, hugging her around the waist.

"Good bye, Grant. I'm so glad to have met you," she says.

"I'm glad I got to meet you, too!" he answers. "I'll come back to see you again, okay?"

"That would be wonderful! Now, you'll be a big help to your mother, won't you?"

"I always help. Right, Mom?"

"You're a big help," I agree. "For one thing, he keeps the staircase polished!" Grant smiles at my comment, but he clearly wants to get going. I'm sure this place seems strange and sad to him. We've only been here an hour and the place is just plain depressing. The only laughter came from us and what Grant got out of the old folks when he was passing the candy around. Pretty much the only other sound is the drone of daytime television. Many of the old faces simply look vacant.

"Oh, that beautiful staircase," Jenny says. "I remember when I met the man who built it. He was a small man, and he needed help transporting the logs that were used for the railings." She notices Grant hurrying toward our truck, and adds, "But you have to go now, so I'll tell you about it some other time."

"We'll come back soon," I say, "but I can't plan it ahead. My schedule changes from day to day, depending on if someone calls in sick."

"I understand. Thanks for taking care of The Serenade so well," Jenny says. "And thanks for coming to see me." We hug and say goodbye, and I turn to walk down the porch stairs.

"Meredith, wait!" Jenny says, her voice suddenly panicky. "I don't want to be here! I don't like living here one bit!"

I call Grant back up on the grassy area in front of the building, then help Jenny sit down on a bench on the porch. I sit down next to her. One more look in her eyes and I know what I have to do. I make a quick calculation of space on the first floor in The Serenade that could be made into a suite for Jenny, panicking a little myself, thinking about taking care of Jenny along with all my other responsibilities. "Jenny, would you move back into The Serenade, and live with us?"

Jenny is so happy that she starts to cry. "Will it really work? I don't want to be a burden," she says, clinging to my arm with both bony old hands.

"We'll make it work. But it will take a few weeks to get your room ready," I say. "And Jenny, there's no way you could ever be a burden," I add firmly. "Now, don't mention anything to anyone here, okay? I'll call the manager here in a few days after I get everything figured out, let them know what day you'll be leaving. When your room is ready, we'll get your things moved over, and soon you'll be living back in The Serenade!" She thanks me profusely, which I don't need after all she has done for me in the past.

The next morning, over coffee, I tell Mona that Grant and I went to visit Jenny.

"Well, how'd she seem?" Mona asks, and I tell her Jenny isn't happy, and will be moving in here, after I figure out how to get a suite built for her.

"Well, here's Jacob, just when you need him," Mona says with a laugh as he enters the kitchen.

"Whoa, why are you two gals talking about me?" he asks in mock fear. Lately there has been a lot of harmless flirting going on in the kitchen.

"We talk about you all the time, don't we, Meredith?" Mona bats her eyes at Jacob.

I laugh, then tell Jacob about Jenny moving in and my remodeling plan so she can live at the back of the first floor of the hotel. "I need a room for her within two weeks," I explain. "I know it isn't really what I hired you for, but would you consider it? I can hire someone else if you don't want to try it," I add.

"I need to take a look at the plan first, to see if it's feasible," he says. "And if it is, I'd be glad to do it."

"Thanks! I really appreciate it," I say.

We finish our coffee, then Jacob and I go down a long corridor to the back section of the building where all the hotel and laundry supplies are stored in six large walk in closets.

Jacob goes from one little room to another, pursing his lips, figuring. I enjoy watching him. "Well, what do you think?" I ask as he surveys the last closet.

"It'll work. This is what I see..." he says, explaining how he'll remodel it to accommodate Jenny's bed, a bookcase, dresser, closet space, small sitting area, and bath. "Sound good to you?" he asks.

"Yes, it sounds great. Do we need to hire more help or can you do this alone within two weeks?"

"Well, let me get started, and if it looks too big for me to do it all, I'll let you know. Okay?"

"Great, then. Please keep me posted," I say, as we both head for the doorway.

"After you," he says with a wide sweeping gesture. I smile at his chivalry, and as I move to pass him, he puts an arm on my shoulder and turns me around gently to face him.

"Meredith," he says, "I want to tell you something."

"What is it?" I ask, moving out into the hallway, a few steps from him.

"Don't you think there could be something between us?" he asks, his eyes sincere.

"You're an attractive, interesting person, but there's another man in my life," I say.

"Pete?"

"Do you know him?" I ask, surprised.

"I remember you two were engaged a while back. It was common knowledge. But I didn't know you were a couple again," he says apologetically.

"I really don't know if we could be classified as a couple yet, but I want to give it a chance. I hope you understand. We better be getting back to the old grindstone," I add, walking down the hall to the kitchen before he can say anything else.

During my weekly financial meeting with Mr. Overgaard, I tell him that Jenny will be moving in. He raises his eyebrows and says, "Taking Jenny in is a very noble gesture, but it's also an enormous responsibility. Especially because she's elderly and has special needs. Have you considered the investment of time that will require?"

"I know it's going to take a lot of time," I reply.

"Where do you hope to find all this time?" he asks with concern. "By the numbers it looks like you're doing a fine job with The Serenade, but I know that's because you spend so much time working."

"I don't know, Mr. Overgaard. I just know I have to squeeze the time in somewhere. Jenny isn't happy in that place, and I have to help her out. She was always so good to me — she's kind of like a grandmother, you know?"

"I know how you feel about her. Well, if you have your mind set on this, you're going to need to hire help. You make time to see her every day for a bit, visit with her, but leave the rest of her needs to an assistant you're going to hire. Jenny isn't destitute. She can pay you for room and board," he says.

"She offered, but I can't let her do that!" I say quickly. "I don't want to take her money. She should save it, just in case I can't take care of her some day and she has to go back to the home."

"It's generous of you, but really, let her pay her own way."

"No, I won't feel right about it. Please let me do this," I plead.

"Well, okay, if you feel that strongly about it. You should still be able to manage on your income from The Serenade, without even having to touch the acreage. Just be thrifty in your personal life. Don't take any grand vacations or buy a new car, that sort of thing."

"Oh, you mean keep living the way I've lived my whole life?" I ask with a laugh.

Mr. Overgaard finally smiles a little. "Okay, okay. Now, how skilled of a person do you think is needed to take care of Jenny properly?"

"Just moderate daytime help. It seems like her mind is strong. The only thing I noticed is that she's a little stooped over and uses a cane now. But I'll put a phone in her room so she can get help whenever she needs it."

"Good. So you'll take care of hiring someone then?"

"Yes, I will."

"You're ready for her to move in?"

"We're getting there. I asked Jacob to build her a suite on the first floor so she doesn't have to go up and down the stairs," I say. "He's converting six walk in closets."

"That sounds resourceful. Let me know when it's ready, and when you've hired your help, then I'll arrange to have her things moved over. I'll pick Jenny up myself. It will be good to see her—it's been a while."

"Thanks, that's real nice of you," I say, walking to the door. "I have to get back—I'm expecting an exterminator. There's some kind of critter in the hotel, up in the attic. The customers are starting to complain about the noise, and a musty smell. Grant and I have been noticing it too, so I don't blame them."

"That doesn't sound good," he says. "Let me know what has to be done, and the cost estimate."

"I will. Thanks for your time, Mr. Overgaard."

"I always have time for you, Meredith," he says.

When the exterminator comes to my office, he announces that a colony of bats is in residence in the attic.

"Oh, jeez! Bats give me the creeps! Can you get rid of them right away?" I ask.

"In this case, no. You need to call someone who preserves the critters that are removed. Bats are good critters, no matter how you feel about them. They eat lots of bugs! If we didn't have bats there would be so many pests around here you would never want to go outside all summer. But just to warn you— you might have to wait until the end of September, to make sure the baby bats will be old enough to fly," he says.

"You mean I have to live with bats in my belfry that long?"

He laughs. "Maybe. But call Bats Be Gone and ask them. They'll do the right thing. I've always heard good things about them. You can find them in the book."

"Okay, thanks, I will," I say. I call Bats Be Gone as soon as the exterminator leaves, and schedule a preliminary evaluation visit, then tentatively schedule the removal for September twenty-fourth. At first I'm dismayed at the wait, but then I realize that it might actually be better because I have no hotel guests scheduled after the twenty-first. I don't want anyone to be here for it, including the employees, Grant, Jenny, and myself. I keep imagining hordes of big black bats flying through The Serenade, getting caught in everybody's hair and biting people, giving them rabies! I imagine Grant being attacked by bats, which spurs me to decide that I'll relocate Grant, Jenny, and myself for a few days, and close the restaurant and bar down early for a day so the place will be empty.

I shudder, then try to get back to the business at hand, which is my search for a person to help with Jenny. I place ads in the Bugle, and a few newspapers in California, Oregon and Idaho, because I don't want to end up with just a few locals whose only work experience is from the place Jenny is leaving. I hope Jenny will feel she made a good trade—that depressing place for this batty one.

Chapter 6

ଓ

The Serenade has been a hive of activity since the Fourth of July, and we're making a profit! I'm thriving on the hustle and bustle of it.

Grant has plenty to do in his corner in the kitchen, and when the weather cooperates, he likes to play outside behind the building where he's made a fort and a series of trails though the scrubby, pungent juniper grove. But I've been concerned that he doesn't usually get to play with other kids, like he did at his babysitter's house in Oregon.

Then last Sunday, John, the little boy Roma introduced us to, and his family had lunch here in the restaurant. John is also five, so he and Grant will be in Roma's kindergarten class in the fall. Carolyn and I chatted a little, then she asked if Grant could come spend a day at their house, which is where he is today. It feels strange not to see him at least every half-hour or so, but I'm glad he has found a buddy. Actually, it's a good day for him to be over at John's. I'm so busy right now that I would barely have time for a word with him if he were here.

Mona and I had finally compromised on the waitress uniform, though she had wanted shorter, tighter skirts. I'm wearing it this morning—flared denim calf length skirt, red and white gingham blouse, and cowgirl hat and boots, as I scurry through my station to take breakfast orders. Suddenly I hear a man's voice behind me say, "Ma'am, more coffee, please," from a booth I just passed. I know that voice, I think, and turn around. It's Pete! He takes his cowboy hat off as I walk back the few steps to his booth. I'm happy to see that he's alone.

"Pete! I'm so glad to see you!"

"Me, too," he says. "I'm here for food this time," he says with a grin, reaching out to hold my hand. "I already ordered from Mona. But I wanted to ask if you and Grant can meet me at the park tonight for a picnic supper? Don't worry about the food; I'm taking care of it."

"Well, thank you!" I say.

"And uh, I'm in town for three days to fix some things at my folks' place, and I was wondering if you might have a little free time in the next evening or two?" he asks.

"Yes, to both. A picnic would be fun, and Grant can feed the ducks, which he dearly loves to do," I say. "But we'll meet you there. I'll bring some bread for the ducks."

"Okay then, how about six o'clock?"

"That will be great!" I say, thrilled. "I have to get to these customers now, though," I tell him quietly. He nods and gently squeezes my hand. When I run into Mona in the kitchen later I ask if she'd be able to take Grant the next night, and she says yes.

"Makin' hay while the sun shines?" she asks playfully.

"Shh! I don't want everyone to hear!" I whisper.

"Okay! Sorry!" she whispers back.

But I'm nervous all afternoon, knowing that I have to lay it all out on the line for Pete tonight. I can't in good conscience string him along without telling him what he has a right to know if we're going to get serious about each other.

When Grant gets back from John's house I tell him about the picnic and that he is going to meet my special friend, Pete.

"I've heard about Pete," he says.

"Yes, you have. I've talked about him before. I've really missed him so it's nice that we get to see him," I explain.

"Are you going to marry him?"

"Well, if he asked me I probably would, but that's a big if."

"Why, Mom?"

"I guess because we haven't been around each other much for a long time, so we don't know each other very well anymore. You need to know somebody well before you marry them, and you should also love them."

"Maybe you can get to know each other at the park," Grant says, "while we're feeding the ducks. If it's supposed to happen, it will."

I laugh. "You remember everything I say, don't you! Now will you please help me pack the food?"

When my shift is over, we go straight from The Serenade to the park, so we're there ahead of Pete. Grant starts feeding the ducks the stale bread. He has a few favorite ones that seem to be more affectionate than the others. I think they may have been domestic pets at one time.

"Hello!" Pete calls when we've been there about a half-hour. He's walking toward us at the duck pond.

I wave to him. "Grant, that's Pete. I'll introduce you when he gets over here."

Instead, Grant surprises me by running up to Pete. "Hi Pete! Do you like ducks?" I hear him ask.

Pete says, "Yes, I do. Did your mom tell you we used to come here all the time to feed the ducks?"

"Mom," Grant says, "Did you come here with Pete to feed the ducks when you were little?"

"We weren't exactly little, but yes, we did feed them when we were younger," I laugh.

"Were the same ducks here then?" he asks, pointing to his two favorite ducks.

"No, I don't think so," I say.

"I don't remember them either," Pete says, "but I do remember the monkey bars over there at the playground. Do you like the monkey bars?" he asks Grant, then turns to me and asks quickly if it's okay if he takes Grant to play.

I nod yes, as Grant shouts, "I love the monkey bars! Me and John go the highest on the monkey bars. His mom tells us we get too far up and makes us come down a ways," he says excitedly.

They head for the playground together while I walk to a nearby picnic table and open the basket Pete brought. I spread the red and white tablecloth out as I listen contentedly to Pete and Grant playing. In a perfect world, this is how it could be, I let myself think for one fleeting moment.

The picnic was excellent. I hadn't had time to eat more than a few bites all day, and I was ravenous. "That was excellent chicken, whoever the cook was!" I say.

"Well...my mom fixed it," Pete says. "I remember how you loved my mom's chicken, so I asked her to do it. When I told her it was for you, she got right to it," Pete says.

"That was nice of her. I always did like your folks," I tell him. "Please tell her thanks."

"I will," he says.

"Mom, what are folks?" Grant asks.

"I just meant Pete's parents," I explain.

"Oh. Do you like my mom's folks?" Grant asks Pete.

"I didn't get to know them much," Pete says.

I mouth my thanks to Pete over Grant's head. He smiles and nods his head slightly.

Grant asks to go back to the playground, so Pete and I sit together at the table, watching him slide and climb.

"He's a great kid, Meredith," Pete says, his eyes straight ahead on the playground. "I'd like to see more of both of you, if you think it would be okay."

"Why the change of heart?" I ask, even though his words are what I've been hoping to hear.

"People change." he says. "I've grown up, I guess. I'm not apologizing for my decision five years ago—that's where I was at that time in my life. But now, I'd like to get to know Grant, and you, all over again, if you'll let me."

"I've missed you every day since I left, and every day since I've been back." I say.

"Meredith," Pete says, "When we split up, I was numb. I was dead inside. But I thought I was doing the right thing. Then, I don't know if anyone told you, I tried to start over. I got married about a year later to a woman I met in college. I didn't want to wait for graduation. I was desperate to be close to someone! We were married for two years. I finally realized that I didn't love her. I kept trying to make it work, but finally I had to tell her that our marriage wasn't fair to either of us. I didn't tell her that she was just a substitute for you, but that's the truth of it." He reaches out to me and takes both my hands in his.

"Before we got married, Patricia—that's her name— said she was fine with my plan to go into business with Dad after graduation, but the second year we were married, she said there was no way she was living out in the country on a ranch. She'd have to commute miles to any job she might want. It just didn't work out," he says. "But what about you? How were things going for you in Oregon?"

"I had a job, paid the bills, kept us fed and clothed, but I didn't ever meet anyone I was interested in, or who was interested in us," I say. "In the back of my mind I was always holding out for you. I'm glad I didn't know back then that you'd gotten married, or I'd have given up!"

"I'm glad, too," he says.

At that moment I decide to put everything on the table. "Pete, if we get any more involved, there's something I need to tell you about Grant," I say, hesitating.

"I already know MaryAnn was Grant's real mother," he says.

"Yes, but there's more. Something that I didn't know about until after you and I broke up," I say. I want Pete back so badly, and I dread telling him this, but Pete deserves to know the true nature of Grant's birth if he's going to be a part of our lives.

"Okay, what is it?" he asks nervously.

"I found out in MaryAnn's journal. Her mom sent it to me after I'd had Grant about three years. She'd read the first page and didn't want to read the rest, but she offered it to me as a keepsake of MaryAnn if I wanted it. At first I wasn't sure I wanted to read it either, but I finally decided maybe it would help me understand MaryAnn's last years better, and also I thought maybe Grant should have it when he grew up. So I took it.

"I don't remember it word for word, of course, but I remember the basics of it. Something like:

'Meredith and I were best friends since we were old enough to cross a few streets to visit each other. When we were little we loved playing house, and dress up and tea party with things our moms had stored in closets. By the time we were twelve, we were talking about boys, and experimenting with each other's hair and make up. We talked about our dreams, too—of what we wanted to be someday. She wanted to be a country singer, and I wanted to be an interior designer. Sometimes she'd be singing a song she'd written, while I was decorating interiors of grand homes I had drawn with my colored pencils and crayons.

We looked nothing alike. I'm short, dark-haired and dark-eyed, and at that age I was beginning to get busty, and Meredith has always been willowy, blonde and green-eyed. We were confused that our moms said we were joined at the hip like Siamese twins, but we loved being compared to sleek, beautiful cats.

Life took a surprising turn when we were fifteen. My par-

ents had twin baby girls, Denise and Cherise, and my father left eight months later. He went out for cigarettes one night and just didn't come back. We heard about him occasionally over the years, but never saw him again. I missed him, but I know it was more peaceful since he was gone, because my parents had done nothing but fight after the twins were born. Dad never paid child support, but I think Mom would have had to go to work even if he had. When she found a job, she hired an older lady to baby-sit during the school day, and when I got home from school I was in charge of the twins until whenever Mom got home, which was usually after nine o'clock. In the summer I had them all day, and since Mom was the manager of the drive-in, her hours could be very long.

Right after Meredith turned sixteen, she got a job wait-ressing at The Serenade after school and full-time in the summer, but she still helped me with the twins when she was off. I was so jealous of her. I desperately wanted to wear a pink uniform dress like she had, so she let me wear it at home sometimes, even though my big bust threatened to pop the buttons off.

Babysitting was a lot of work, but when Meredith was with me it was fun. Each of us would choose a baby that would be 'ours' to look after for the day, and we pretended we were their moms. But when they started walking, just after their first birthday, we discovered that keeping up with two toddlers was twice as much work as looking after crawlers. And when I was alone, it was overwhelming. The house was so much messier when they started walking. I was always cleaning up a mess on them, a mess they had made, or feed-ing them, which led to more mess. I'm a tidy person, and all this messiness made me feel very out of control. I decided that keeping the twins in matching outfits might make things appear tidier, so if one got messy, I'd change the other one's outfit to match even if she didn't need it.

Looking back I see that was when I stopped having fun. Even when I wasn't babysitting and Meredith came over, I just didn't feel like designing anymore, chatting about girl stuff, or watching our favorite TV shows. I didn't want to walk to Tippy's Market for a treat, go to the indoor pool, or to the library to check out books. Meredith could choose to come visit me or she could stay away when she had free time, but she usually chose to see me, even though I know I wasn't the same friend she used to know.

Finally, when we finished high school, Meredith and I rented an apartment in the Greenway, an old three-level brick building. A stone sign at the entrance said "Erected 1880," so it was one of the older buildings in town. It was creepy the first time we went in the Greenway. I felt like it might be haunted by the ghosts of the people who had lived there back in the eighteen hundreds. But the owner said the rent on this particular apartment was only two-seventy-five a month, so we took it. It was affordable with our incomes—Meredith was waitressing full time at The Serenade and I was babysitting the twins full time. I didn't want to babysit anymore, but Mom couldn't afford to pay anyone else what they asked, and I couldn't let her down.

You get what you pay for, and that's how it was with our apartment. It was very small and there was nothing pretty about the peeling, faded cabbage rose wallpaper and dingy gray counters. There was a tiny living room with a threadbare carpet, a galley kitchen just big enough for one person to turn around in, a bedroom, and a little semi- private alcove we could either put a cot in or use for an eating area. I volunteered to use the alcove as my room for a while, then we planned to switch places.

The bathroom was just large enough to accommodate an old porcelain sink, toilet, and clawfoot tub. The first night we moved in we were both pretty tired, so we just opened a big can of spaghetti and meatballs and heated it for dinner. We didn't eat all of it, and some got washed down the kitchen sink instead of going in the garbage. The next morning, when I went in the bathroom to take a bath, I was shocked to see the spaghetti that had gone down the kitchen sink was floating around in a shallow pool in the bathtub! Meredith and I had a good laugh over it. We called the landlord later in the day and asked if he could fix the plumbing, and also the broken front door lock, which we had not been able to lock the previous night. He assured us he would call the plumbers and he would put the lock on his list of things to repair. The plumbers came in the next few days, but I lost track of how many times we asked him to fix the lock, though we weren't too worried about burglars in Crossroads.

It wasn't long after we moved into the apartment that I began to feel much more lighthearted, like I had back before the twins were born. I still had never dated a boy! I just hadn't had time in high school, but I hoped maybe I could catch up now.

I was alone in the apartment one Saturday night. It was spring break weekend, and Pete was home from college for a few days, so he and Meredith had gone to The Serenade to go dancing. I was lying on my cot reading, when I heard the door open. I called Meredith's name out, but nobody answered. I got up and peeked around the corner of the alcove and saw Raymond. He and Meredith's mom had recently gotten divorced, and I couldn't imagine why he was here—I knew Meredith certainly wouldn't want to see him. I immediately thought of the times he'd gotten drunk and walked right in my house without knocking to take Meredith home. He was really awful to her when he was drunk. He'd knock her and her mom around pretty badly. I smelled booze as soon as he walked in the apartment, and I was scared. I called out from the alcove that Meredith wasn't home and asked him to leave, but he came over and sat down on my cot! I was shaking all over. He asked me why I wasn't out on a date, a pretty thing

like me, and I said I didn't have a boyfriend. I remember I
was strangely thrilled, even though I was scared, to hear him
say I was pretty. Then he stood up and shook his head and
said it was a shame that my parents had those damn twins so
I never got a chance to go have any fun. I love the twins, but
in my mind I agreed with him at least a little. Anyway, I told
him it wasn't so bad, and he didn't need to worry about it.

I wanted him to leave, but he said he just wanted to talk
to someone. In a little while it dawned on me that he was
actually handsome. He had black hair and pretty deep blue
eyes. I am ashamed to say that at that time I put my friendship with Meredith in the back of my mind. I didn't protest
at all when I knew we were going to have sex. I was excited,
and I wanted it! I was scared, but I needn't have worried.
He wasn't rough at all. In fact he was very gentle. But I kept
it pretty quiet, because I ended up pregnant! I didn't tell
Raymond. I never wanted to see him again. I hate myself for
betraying my best friend! When we were little kids we spent
quite a bit of time coming up with plans to get rid of him for
treating Meredith and her mom so badly, and then I go and
sleep with him! I don't think Meredith would ever forgive me.
I don't think I can forgive myself.

Mom took it hard. She said she couldn't support the baby,
financially or any other way. When I told her that I didn't ask
for a baby, either, that I already had the twins to take care of,
which I'd done forever, she just started crying. She quit her
job in a few weeks and moved us all to Oregon to be close to
her sister.

I had the baby three months ago, and named him Grant,
after Mom's grandpa.

"That's about it," I tell Pete sadly after I recount what
I can remember. "The police said the witnesses reported
that she drove her car off the cliff on the coast highway,
and it appeared to be intentional. When DeeDee asked me

to take Grant I didn't know Raymond was his father."

"The whole thing is terrible," Pete says, shaking his head. "It seems strange that DeeDee could just give her grandchild away like that. Did you legally adopt him?"

"I tried, but I was told that because I was single, too young, and didn't have enough income, I couldn't adopt him. I went out to Oregon and got myself a place to live, and Grant moved in with me, but on paper, he was still living with DeeDee, not with me. When Mr. Overgaard wrote to me about inheriting The Serenade, and asked me if I wanted to come back to manage it, I told him about Grant and that I wasn't his legal guardian and didn't think I should leave the state with him. So Mr. Overgaard sent me to a lawyer in Portland, and the adoption went through pretty quickly. It was a huge relief to get that taken care of!" I say.

It's getting dark, and Grant is still playing on the playground equipment. Finally, Pete clears his throat and says quietly, "That must have been terrible, finding out that Raymond is his dad. You know how I feel about that guy," he says.

"Yes, I do, and I want you to know I still appreciate that you stood up to him. And you're right; it was terrible, finding out. I started dwelling on it, looking for signs of Raymond in Grant, wondering if he would develop Raymond's mean streak. But then I realized thinking like that gave Raymond a certain kind of power over me. After I thought it over, I decided to start looking for good signs, things that remind me of the way MaryAnn was before all this happened. "

"I don't know what to say," Pete says. "I admire your courage, I always have."

"Thank you," I say.

"But this is a serious problem," Pete says, "because we both know that Raymond will find out that Grant is his son some day, and then he'll be right here, trying to get some level of custody. Imagine having to share Grant with Raymond, or worse, losing him to Raymond altogether! Weirder things have happened in court rooms," he says.

"I've imagined it happening many times," I say, "and it scares me to death."

"If we got married, we'd have to go to the authorities and tell them the situation, and do whatever they said."

"If we got married," I say, amazed that we're even using the 'm' word, "Nobody would be told about Raymond being Grant's dad. I don't even know where Raymond is these days for sure. He doesn't know about Grant, so why should we tell him and risk Grant's safety?"

"It has to be legal," Pete says.

"No, in this situation, legal means I'll no longer have control over what happens to my son," I say defensively. "And I'm not letting that happen!"

"He wouldn't just be your son if we got married," Pete says. "We'd have to decide these things together."

"It sounds like you've already decided it has to be done your way!" I say angrily. "I'm not going to allow things to happen that are going to jeopardize Grant!"

I can't remember Pete ever using the icy tone he takes as he says, "I can kind of see where we're headed as far as raising Grant together, and it doesn't look good. It's going to have to be fifty-fifty if I'm going to help raise him! I have to get going now."

"Wait! I'm sorry! Can't we discuss it any more?" I ask in a panic.

"I don't know, can we? Is the topic open for discussion?" he asks.

I don't reply. A melancholy feeling washes over me as we scoop up the picnic gear. Pete stops by our truck, helps Grant get in, and tells him it was nice to meet him, then surprisingly opens my door for me.

"Tell your parents hi for me," I say, wondering if this is goodbye forever.

"I will," he says, and turns to go.

"Is this..." I start to say, then think better of it.

"I don't know what it is," he says, and heads for his truck.

"Pete!" Grant yells out his window. Pete is across the parking lot and turns to look back. "Do you know my mom enough to marry her yet?"

It's too dark for me to see Pete's face clearly when he yells back, "That's a tough one," in answer to Grant's question.

Grant pulls his head inside the window and looks at me deeply and silently. I can see that even at his young age, he is aware that I am very hurt.

Chapter 7

❧

"Jenny is coming today!" I tell Grant a few days after our picnic with Pete. "Mr. Overgaard is going to bring her over pretty soon." Grant's been looking forward to having Jenny here ever since he met her at the care home.

I hired a woman to assist with Jenny. She moved here recently from Los Angeles, because she was tired of city life, particularly the traffic jams and dirty air. She had visited Glacier Park a few summers back and decided that she was going to live somewhere near there, so she could go there often. Her name is Jean, she's a certified nursing assistant, and I'm guessing she's in her mid-thirties. I had six qualified applicants, but Jean's personality is wonderful. She's funny and smart, and I think I can tell from just that one interview that she really does enjoy working with the elderly.

She's so easy to talk to that we got off business and just sat there shooting the breeze for a few minutes. She told me that she met a wonderful guy out at the truck stop right after she moved here. I told her about Serenade Night and suggested that she and her new guy might enjoy coming here to dance, and she said she'll ask him to. She's got a place over at The Greenway (I didn't tell her I hope she can find another place to live), and she will start full time tomorrow.

I'm still reeling from the unhappy ending of my last conversation with Pete. I keep replaying it in my mind, mystified by how men think. To me, he is clearly wrong about how to handle the Raymond issue. I feel terrible that we were getting so close again, and that Raymond is once again causing so much trouble. But I can't dwell on the situation. I have Grant's happiness to think of, and if I'm not happy, Grant won't be, either.

Grant comes bounding into the kitchen shortly after noon. "She's here, Mom! Jenny's here!" He had posted himself at my bedroom window when I told him to start watching for Mr. Overgaard's silver car and a small moving van, and now they're finally here.

I wait while Mona issues a few instructions to the waitresses on duty, then Grant, Mona and I go greet Sam and Jenny in the parking lot.

"I'm so glad to be back!" Jenny says, sounding close to tears, as we all welcome her home. I nudge Grant, who is carrying a tin of peppermint candy. He holds the candy out to Jenny.

"Here's a present for you, Jenny," he says.

"Oh, you shouldn't have!" she says excitedly, "but I'm very glad you did! Oh Sam! Open it for me, will you?" Mr. Overgaard smiles and takes off the plastic wrapping, then opens it for Jenny, who wastes no time in popping one in her mouth. "This is the best kind, Sam, have one!" she says, and Mr. Overgaard takes one. "Have one, Grant. It's so good! Grant, do you think we can get some peppermint tea to go with it?"

"Mom? Do we have peppermint tea?" Grant asks, looking up at me.

"Yes, but let's show Jenny where her room is, then we'll go to the restaurant and have lunch and peppermint tea. How about that, Jenny?" I ask.

"Oh fine, that's fine. I can't wait to see where I'm going to live! So it's on the first floor? Where ever did you find room?" she asks.

"This way," I say, getting in front of the group so I can lead them down the corridor.

Mr. Overgaard, bringing up the rear, says, "This is the first time I've been in The Serenade in nearly a year. It sure feels good to be back."

"Same here, Sam," Jenny says.

Mona and I agree that we're glad they're here too, then I stop the group in the corridor by Jenny's rooms. "Here we are! Come in, Jenny!" I usher her into the first of her rooms. "Ta-da!" I say with great fanfare.

"Ta-da!" Grant mimics me and laughs as everyone files into the room.

"Oh, it's lovely!" Jenny exclaims, running a hand over the wallpaper, a rich textured antique rose pattern in pinks and reds. I had hoped decorating the walls this way would bring warmth and friendliness to the room, and I believe it has.

"The movers will set up your furniture while we have lunch," I explain to Jenny. "And after lunch you can come back and see it all put together. Let me show you the sitting room before we go," I say, leading her into the adjoining room.

"Oh, it's just perfect!" Jenny says, clutching her chest. "You did all this for me?"

"I told our handyman, Jacob, what I wanted for you, and he came up with it. So mostly it was Jacob's doing," I say.

"He did a nice job," Mr. Overgaard says, which is important to me because in matters related to The Serenade, he is an important liaison between Uncle Duck and me.

We sit down in a large booth I reserved earlier and study the menu, except for Grant, who has already announced that he is having a 'PBJ.'

"For old times' sake I'm going to order what Duck always fixed for me himself: an Eggs Just Ducky scrambled egg sandwich," Jenny says.

I like Jenny's idea, so in memory of the first time Uncle Duck and I ate together, I order a grilled cheese sandwich, French onion soup, and a salad, asking JoLynn to make sure there are lots of cherry tomatoes on top. It's wonderful to be here with people who loved Uncle Duck. We spend at least an hour talking, eating, laughing, and reminiscing. Jenny directs plenty of the conversation toward Grant so he doesn't get bored.

"Unfortunately, I have to leave this party," Mona says. "I have a few waitresses that I need to keep an eye on. But it was great seeing everyone. Sam, I hope it won't be this long before we see you again," she adds.

"Yes, it has been too long, hasn't it?" Mr. Overgaard agrees, standing when Mona does.

I see that Jenny's eyes are red rimmed and weary. I'm sure she's happy, but it has been a very busy day for her already. It's time for me to wrap it up, so I excuse Grant from the table.

"When will I see you two men again?" Jenny asks Sam and Grant.

"I'll try to come see you next week," Sam says.

"And I'll see you every day, right, Mom?" he looks up at me for verification.

"That's right. There's no escaping us now, Jenny," I laugh. We all say goodbye to Mr. Overgaard, then he walks Grant to the restaurant door and shakes Grant's hand before he leaves.

In Jenny's room we're pleased to see that the movers have done a nice job of setting her furniture up. I show her the phone and the list of important telephone numbers I wrote in a notebook.

"Do you want to lie down?" I ask her.

"I think so. It's been wonderful seeing everyone, but I am quite tired out," she says. I find her blankets and sheets in several boxes, then get her settled in for a nap. "Oh, would you please fold that blanket up just so it fits over the end of my bed?" she asks, pointing to a worn out faded white blanket that I had intentionally left in a box because of its shabby appearance. I wonder about it, but I just do as she asks.

"I'll help you unpack and organize your things later," I say, turning to leave.

"Please sit down for a minute with me, Meredith," she says, patting the bed next to her. I'm happy to oblige. When she used to live here in the hotel, and I was working here, I would often bring her a snack in the evening before she went to sleep. She'd pat the bed and I'd sit down next to her, and she'd tell me a story of when she was younger, or we'd just chat about things. I know it helped her relax so she could sleep better, but it also made me feel needed and wanted.

"We haven't had time alone to talk yet," she says.

"No, it's been a pretty busy day," I say.

"Meredith, I've been wanting to ask you a question," Jenny says.

"Go ahead, ask me anything," I say.

"Are you happy living back here in Crossroads? After having had a taste of city life?"

"I love it here, and of course being with you and Mona again. But truthfully, not being with Pete was getting to be easier when I was gone. I saw him the day I re-opened The Serenade, and it seemed like we were going to get back together. But the next time I saw him we had a big blow up, and now things don't look so good. So it feels like I've lost him all over again," I explain, a lump rising in my throat.

"May I ask what you argued about?"

"I don't know if you want to hear it," I say.

"Go on. I've lived a very long time and I bet you can't shock me," she says.

I wonder for a few moments if I should say anything more, then I just blurt out, "It has something to do with Grant and Raymond."

"I already know that Raymond is Grant's father," she says softly, patting my hand. "Duck told me about it, shortly after MaryAnn's mother gave you her journal, when you called him about it. Please don't be angry—he needed to tell someone, just like you did," she says.

"No, I'm not angry," I say. "I guess I never thought about Uncle Duck needing someone to unload on. I guess I gave him plenty of stuff to unload!"

"You had a rough upbringing, and Duck and I were both glad that we could be here for you," she says.

"Thanks," I say. "But about the argument—I had just told Pete that Raymond is Grant's father, which shocked him, I'm sure."

"Yes, I'm sure it did," she agrees.

"So, Pete said if we got married, then we'd have to go to the authorities and tell them about Raymond being Grant's father, so they could decide if he should have any custodial rights!"

"At least the subject of marriage came up!" she says.

"But it went right back down. I got pretty mad, and told him we wouldn't tell anyone about Grant and Raymond. Raymond doesn't even know he's Grant's father, and I can't bear the thought of him having any rights at all! They could give him full custody! Like Pete said, stranger things have happened in court!"

"It's understandable that you're arguing over it. But look at it from what Pete's perspective might be. First of all, you two were engaged, and then you took on a baby on your own. Pete was taken by surprise, and broke off the engagement. Five years later, he sees you again and you both think of starting over, but you tell him that the child he would be helping to raise is fathered by your ex-stepfather! Now the poor guy is reeling with uncertainty. What would you do, put in that situation?" Jenny asks me seriously.

I think for a minute, trying to imagine myself in Pete's shoes. "I guess I'd panic," I say.

"And no doubt he did, too. Raymond's involvement could make your lives very difficult. Pete isn't scared of Raymond physically, as we know, but he's scared that he might cause a lot of upheaval in your family life if he marries you.

"Yeah, I guess you're right. I was worried that when I told him about Raymond being Grant's dad that there would be some fireworks—I just wasn't expecting him to say what he did. I can't see the answers right now, but then I haven't seen Pete since then, so maybe he won't be in the picture anyway."

Suddenly I'm overwhelmed with fatigue, and I don't want to think anymore about this problem right now. I sigh at the thought of the full afternoon of work ahead of me.

"I'm sorry, Jenny, I have to get back to work. But before I go—did Mr. Overgaard tell you about the lady I hired to help us out? He said he was going to tell you about her on the way over here."

"You mean Jean? Yes, he told me she'll bring me most of my meals, help me bathe and dress, go for walks and errands with me. It sounds like it should be fine! And I'm willing to pay her wages, and room and board, too," she adds.

"No, none of that, now. You need to hang on to your money. I might not be able to have you with me some day and if that happens, you'll need to be able to pay for your care."

"Alright, Meredith, but if you change your mind…"

"I won't. Now, Jean's phone number is also in the notebook by the phone," I say, standing up to tuck her in again.

While Jenny's napping this afternoon, I need to lend a hand in the laundry. I don't mind it at all—in fact it's a nice breather from what I usually do. I sort the items to be washed into different plastic bins: kitchen towels and aprons, guest towels, washcloths and bedding.

Jenny's sweet face comes to mind as I work, and I think of the stories she used to tell me. There was one in particular about a man who went to California during the Gold Rush in the 1840s. He didn't do well as a miner, but he was very intelligent and saw that he could make a lot of money by selling supplies to the miners. Eventually his store developed into quite a large, popular business, and as he and the woman he later married were very thrifty, there was a lot of money left to their only child, a son, upon their deaths. I was not much more than a child when Jenny used to tell me this story, and I wondered what it would feel like to have an inheritance, but now I know.

Every once in a while Grant asks me if Pete's coming back, and I tell him I don't know. I've been wondering myself. I know that he's busy—he has a job and he's worried about his parents, but it seems he would at least give me a quick call, if he's interested. I'm not moping around, waiting for him. I've kept plenty busy myself these two weeks since we met at the park. I'm waitressing today, for instance. I'm balancing two plates up my left arm and carrying a coffee pot in my right hand, as if this had always been my destiny. My customers look approvingly at the aromatic food I deliver to them, and thank me. I go back in the swinging kitchen doors and see Jacob taking a break, sitting on a tall stool by Grant's play area. Grant has become attached to Jacob since he's been here. I feel kind of strange about it, because I don't really know Jacob, but Grant seems to enjoy being with him.

"How big are the fish that you catch?" Grant is asking Jacob as I hang another order on the wheel in front of Charlie.

"They're pretty big fish, usually. Pike, mostly," Jacob answers. "I know some great fishing holes. Maybe we can go fishing together," he says.

"Wow! I want to catch some fish, Jacob!" Grant exclaims.

"Ask your mother if you can go with me, and let's ask her to go along too," Jacob says.

Grant surprises me by saying seriously, "Mom won't want to. If Pete came here and we went away with you, he might not know where we were! But I think I can go without Mom." I don't like where this is going, but I have to take syrup out to a customer, so I can't wait in the kitchen to hear what Jacob says.

"Mom!" I'm back in the kitchen to pick up a fresh pot of coffee, and Grant comes up behind me, something he knows he isn't supposed to do to me or anyone else. "I'm going fishing with Jacob! Jacob knows a place where we can catch really big fish!" I can see it's going to be difficult to get out of this gracefully—he's so excited.

"First of all," I say as I put my coffee pot back down, "you broke a safety rule. Don't ever come up behind me or anyone else in the kitchen. Someone could turn around and run right into you. What if I hadn't known you were behind me and I had turned around quickly? I would have spilled hot coffee on you! And maybe on me, too! Do you understand? You're supposed to be in your play area when you're in here," I remind him.

"I'm sorry, Mom," he says, but adds quickly, "Jacob wants me to go fishing with him!"

"It's my fault," Jacob says, coming toward us. "I got him thinking about fishing and made him forget the rules," he says.

"Thanks, but I know Grant is smart enough to remember the rules no matter what," I say firmly.

"I really do know some great fishing spots," Jacob says with a big smile. "I think Grant will love it. You might, too."

"Can I go Mom? Please? Pleeeease?" Grant looks up at me eagerly.

"I'm sorry, Grant, but you can't go fishing without me, and Jacob and I haven't had any time to get to know each other," I try to explain to Grant in a way that won't hurt Jacob's feelings.

"The same thing again," Grant says dejectedly, confusing me until he adds, "Pete didn't get to know you well enough at the park, so he didn't come back. Now you don't know Jacob well enough, so I can't go fishing." His words cut me like a knife, and I give in.

"Well, maybe we can both go, for a little while. Thank you for the invitation, Jacob," I say with formal politeness. "Grant hasn't gotten to go fishing before, so he'll probably enjoy the experience. I'll check my schedule to see when we can go."

"Thanks Mom!" Grant gives me a big hug around my waist and grins at Jacob. I ask him to go outside to play for awhile. He goes out the back door, the screen door slamming shut behind him.

"We should really go early in the morning, for the best chances," Jacob says.

"That's going to be tough," I say. "I'm on the breakfast shift for the next two weeks. I have to be in the kitchen at seven. That doesn't allow much time for fishing," I add, relieved to have an out.

"No, it'll work. If we leave at five, take a half hour to get there, fish for an hour, and a half hour back, you should be fine," he says with a grin, his obvious interest in making this more than a fishing trip irritating me.

"Fine. I'll meet you in the kitchen at four tomorrow morning," I say, then turn and grab my coffee pot again.

"Great!" Jacob says.

I sleep poorly, tossing and turning, first dreaming that Pete and Jacob both turn up in the morning to go fishing. But in another dream, my arms are around a pair of wide, muscled shoulders, but I know it's Jacob, even though I don't see his face. Just as we're about to get intimate, I hear Grant shouting that he has caught a fish, and I wake up. I get out of bed, trying to shake off the dream, but it hovers close by while I dress, making me feel strangely guilty.

I suddenly recall the tension of those few moments with Jacob in the corridor near Jenny's rooms. He had made me feel very uncomfortable that day, and I felt the same way yesterday with him. I sit on the edge of my bed thinking for a few minutes before I wake Grant up, and come to the conclusion that only one thing attracts me to Jacob—he's physically very sexy. But I don't really like him. His charm seems fake to me. I feel like Jacob is only interested in me for the possibility of sex, and nothing more. But I need more from a man, and I want to see more in a man. If I'm going to have a man, I want it to be Pete. I miss the closeness of having him so much I can almost taste it. Since that night with him here in my room, the thought of not having him in my life breaks my heart over and over again.

I'm going natural on this fishing trip. It's too early and I'm too tired to bother with makeup. Just a good hair brushing will have to do, which is what I'm doing when I wake Grant up. "Come on, out of bed, little fisherman. We're going fishing, remember?" I say, shaking his shoulder gently.

"It's morning?" he bolts out of bed and runs to the window, which looks out over the parking lot with the main highway through Crossroads just beyond. I've never seen Grant move like that this early in the morning. "It's still dark, Mom! It's not morning!"

"It actually is. But it's very early, which I guess is when the fishing is best. People are still sleeping, so you need to be quiet, okay? Now get ready and we'll have oatmeal before we go," I say, wishing I already had a cup of coffee in my hand.

"I'll be ready real fast," he whispers, and today it really looks like he will be.

I want to drive because I don't know if Jacob's a good driver, but I'm exhausted from a busy day yesterday and not sleeping well last night. When Jacob arrives, I tell him I'm too tired to drive.

"I'll drive. I was going to, anyway," he says in a surprised voice.

"Okay. I just didn't sleep well last night," I explain.

"No problem," he says, opening the passenger door of his truck. I think for a second of cancelling the whole thing, but then I see the excitement on Grant's face. Grant climbs into the truck and I buckle him up between Jacob and me. I ask Jacob the area we're going to, and then I relay the location to Mona, just in case. She knows to expect me for my shift at seven.

When we get out on the road I try to keep my eyes open, but the motion of the truck lulls me to sleep in minutes.

I wake up with the sun shining in my face. When I look at my watch I see it's six-ten already! I sit up to stretch, then I see Grant about fifty yards away, perched on a big rock by the shore of a little lake. He's holding a fishing pole with both hands, the line apparently submerged. I start unbuckling my seatbelt, panicked at seeing him alone by the water. Suddenly the other truck door opens, startling me. It's Jacob.

"Why didn't you wake me up?" I ask angrily.

"You fell asleep the minute we got on the road," Jacob says defensively. "I know you put in a lot of hours yesterday, and it sounded like you didn't really want to fish, so I let you sleep."

"You walk away, leaving my five-year-old next to a lake?" I demand.

"Relax, will you? It's about six inches deep for at least fifteen yards out. He's fine."

That calms me down a bit, so he adds, "I like you with no makeup." I turn away, uncomfortable to know he's been studying me.

He sighs, still standing by the open truck door. Looking at his watch, he says, "We should go if you're going to get back on time."

"We don't have to go quite yet, if it only took a half-hour

to get here. I want to go down by the lake for a few minutes," I say.

"I come here pretty often," Jacob says. "It's one of my favorite places. I like to sit by the shore and think while I fish," he says.

"Oh really?" I ask as we walk down to the shore.

"Yeah, and lately all I've been thinking about is you," he says.

I sigh and say quietly, "Please don't talk like that with Grant right there. I don't want him to think there's something going on between us."

"There could be, if you'd stop…"

"No, there couldn't. So you please stop!" I hiss, hoping we're still out of Grant's earshot.

"Want to see my fish, Mom?" Grant asks proudly when I get up next to the rock he's sitting on.

"You really caught some?" I ask.

"Yep! Two big ones. They're in the cooler! Do you want to see?" he asks again.

"I'll see them at home. I'll bet they're just beauties, but there isn't time to get them out right now. I have to help Charlie and Ralph with the prep work, so we need to head back in a few minutes. It's time to hop down now." He understands that when I say I need to get to work, there can be no delaying, so he hands the pole to Jacob and jumps off the rock onto the shore. When we get back to the truck. Jacob hurries around to the passenger side and opens the door, then steers me by my arm so that I'll get in the truck first.

"No, Grant will sit between us again," I say, pulling back from Jacob and lifting Grant up on the seat.

"Suit yourself," Jacob says stiffly.

Grant looks at me, then Jacob. I know he realizes that something is wrong.

"That was a lot of fun!" he says nervously.

"I'm glad you had fun," Jacob says. "I wish your mother had," he adds.

"I'm sorry, I'm just not into fish," I say.

Grant laughs and looks at me. "Not into fish? That sounds funny, Mom. How would you be into fish?"

I smile at him. "I just meant that I'm not interested in fishing," I tell him.

"Are you interested in anything?" Jacob asks.

"Yes," I reply. "Right now I'm interested in getting to work."

We ride in cold silence. Grant looks up at me to try to read my face, then holds onto my arm with both hands and leans against me. Jacob stares stone faced at the road and I seethe all the way back to The Serenade.

Chapter 8

The customers in the restaurant this Monday morning are primarily people staying in the hotel who want to get an early start on the road. I'm savoring the smell of bacon and coffee wafting through the air, waiting for Grant to finish getting ready for school, which has been in session for two weeks. It sounds like he's playing in the employee restroom, singing and splashing water in the sink, and I'm across the kitchen where I'm peeling and dicing onions.

The bus horn honks, and Charlie goes to the restroom door. "Get a move on, Grant," he shouts in a no-nonsense tone. "The bus is here and they aren't going to wait for you!"

Grant comes running out of the restroom, grabs his lunch sack off the break table, and runs to me. I bend down, give him a kiss on the cheek and gently remind him not to run in the kitchen. I pull a paper out of my apron pocket and hand it to him. "Here's a note for the teacher that says I'm going to meet you today after school to pick you up, so don't get on the bus after school. Remember, we talked about it last night?" He needs a new coat, and I just haven't had time to take him downtown until now to buy one.

"Okay! Love you Mom!" he shouts as he runs out the door.

"I love you too! Have a good day!" I call back. I thank Charlie for helping me get Grant out the door one more time. He just grunts an acknowledgement, his back turned to me.

That afternoon I'm getting out of my car at the school to pick Grant up when I see a man get out of a white sedan across the street. As he starts to cross the street toward the school, I immediately feel sick to my stomach as I recognize Raymond's unmistakable swagger and build, and his dark hair. There have been newspaper articles in several counties about The Serenade, and of course my name is mentioned as the new owner. I wonder if he saw a copy of it and has come back to make trouble for me.

I stand by my car, waiting to see what he's going to do. I don't want to talk to him, but I'm worried that he's found out about Grant and is thinking of taking him! I decide I have to confront him, but as he approaches me I break out in a cold sweat.

"What do you want?" I ask him, my voice shaky. "Why are you here?"

"I followed you from The Serenade. I want a word with you, without an audience." His breath reeks of old booze, something I had hoped never to smell again.

"I don't have time to talk." I say rudely.

"That damned Steve Maddocks—I know he left you The Serenade, and some property," he sneers.

"What about it?" I demand.

"I should own part of that!" he glares at me, his blue eyes angry.

"That's ridiculous!"

"All the time I'm raising you, feeding and clothing you, you're running off to him and that stupid Serenade. It made me crazy, a grown man having you over there all the time! I should have turned him in! And he had the nerve to threaten me for knocking you around, threatened to turn me in!"

"Yeah, my luck changed for the better after I met him.

You hardly ever beat me up anymore after that," I say, turning to leave.

"I never beat you up!" he sneers. "You got spanked like any kid that needs it. So you go running all over town telling people you got beat up, then I always have to watch my back because of your lies."

There's no way to reason with a drunk. "You should have been in jail a lot more than a few days for everything you did to me. If Mom had ever pressed charges you would have been."

"Don't even mention her, the bitch. Running off to Florida! You women are nothing but bitches! Oh, forget it! I want half of what Maddocks gave you!" He steps right in front of me, blocking my path.

"Get out of my way," I say loudly. I throw my shoulders back and raise my head to make myself look bigger as I push past him and walk across the street to the school. Here I am—a mother, a business owner—yet when I get near Raymond I'm shaking with fear.

"I'm not through with you, Meredith!" he shouts, heading for his car. "By the way, I hear you give me a grandkid! And I want to see him!"

"You stay away from him!" I yell. "He's not your grandchild!" Raymond scowls at me, then gets in his car and speeds away.

I'm shaking all over as I enter the school. I give Grant a big bear hug when I meet him in the doorway of his classroom.

"Oh hi, Meredith," Roma says when she sees me. I was hoping not to have to talk to anyone other than Grant, I'm so shaken up. I look down at the floor and raise my hand to my mouth to cover a fake cough.

"Hi," I say.

She moves closer to me and says quietly, "Listen, I'm having a Lady in Love party at my house Saturday night at seven. I'm inviting all of the women from our class who still live here—it should be fun. Tressa Swanson just started selling the product line, so I thought I'd help her get her business off the ground by having a party. Would you like to come?" she asks.

When I don't reply right away, she looks at me closely, and sees the fear on my face. "Meredith! What's wrong? Come in the room, here, sit down at my desk," she insists. Grant follows behind as Roma leads me into the classroom. The other kindergarteners, all lined up in two rows at the door to be walked to the bus or to waiting parents, stare at me with worried eyes. I'm sorry that I'm upsetting them. Roma asks her aide to take the bus children out, then asks, "What is it, Meredith?"

"Grant, honey, it's okay. Please go wait with John. I'll be right there and then we'll go downtown," I say, forcing a smile for him. He reluctantly leaves my side, and I tell Roma that Raymond was harassing me in the street.

"I'm calling Dave," she says, picking up the receiver from the classroom phone on the wall behind her desk. "Did you get a license number?"

"No, but I can describe the car," I say. I will myself to stop trembling, telling myself that I can't allow Raymond to interfere in our lives. I take a few deep breaths, then Roma tells Dave what I said. She gives me the phone for a description of the car Raymond was driving. "What should I do? Give Raymond some money? To get him off my back?"

"I don't recommend it," Dave says firmly. "That man has been bullying you for years. Why reward him for it?"

"You're right. And Uncle Duck wouldn't want any of his money to go to Raymond either."

"I can vouch for that."

"But how do I keep Raymond from bothering me?"

"I think you should consider a restraining order barring him from coming in contact with you or Grant," he says. "At least that will let him know that the authorities are aware of the problem. Come to my office tomorrow. I'll get the paperwork for you."

"I didn't think he was living here," I say. "I've heard that the house is vacant."

"It is vacant. I didn't think he was around here either. He must have heard your name attached to The Serenade and decided to come back to collect," Dave says.

"I was afraid to move back because of him. I never wanted to see him again, and I didn't want Grant to have to deal with him either," I say disgustedly.

"He's a blight," Dave agrees. "Well, I'll see you tomorrow."

"Okay. Thanks, Dave."

"You know I'm as close as a phone call, Meredith. Take care now," he says, and hangs up.

"Thanks Roma," I say when I get off the phone with her husband. "I think I'm okay. Not as shaky, anyway. You mentioned Saturday night? A Lady in Love Party at your place at what time again?"

"Seven," Roma says. "Are you sure you're okay? You can sit here as long as you need to," she says, concerned.

"No, I'm fine now. Thanks for your help, Roma."

"You're entirely welcome. Call me, will you? I mean, if you'd like to talk," she says.

"Thanks. I'll see you Saturday night if I can get a babysitter," I say, taking Grant by the hand.

I'm sure Grant is wondering what just went on, but I have to be careful with my explanation. I don't want him to have to worry about Raymond all the time like I will be. He only needs enough information to stay safe. I decide if Grant doesn't bring it up, I'll think it over and talk to him about it later.

"I missed you today, honey," I say. "Did you have a good day?"

"Sure! Mrs. Bunsen took us outside to draw pictures of clouds. That was fun. And John brought a tyrannosaurus in his lunch bag!" he says excitedly.

"He did?" I ask in pretend amazement. "That must have been some huge bag!"

"Oh Mom," he says laughing, "you're so silly."

"If I can't be silly with my son, who can I be silly with?" I ask. "Well, let's go find you a new coat. Pretty soon the real winter weather will be here. Do you know what color you want if we can find it?"

"Yeah! Red with black lines, like a spider!"

"Yuck! I don't think I could look at a coat like that!"

"Okay, red and blue like one of my super hero guys?"

"That would be much easier to take."

The next morning I drive over to the police station. I read and then sign the papers Dave Bunsen has for me on his desk.

"I guess I'm worried about some kind of retaliation," I say.

"It's possible," Dave says. "I've called the school principal and told him to alert the staff, and you'll have to be vigilant, like I will. The police department needs to know immediately if he shows up at The Serenade, so tell your employees to contact either the police department or you immediately if they can identify him and see him on the premises. I told Sam about it yesterday. Hopefully, when Raymond knows that we're watching him, he'll see that there's no point in continuing with these threats."

"I hate to be a pessimist," I say, "but this is Raymond we're talking about."

I've been feeling pretty nervous since my run-in with Raymond day before yesterday, but I don't think anyone notices. Grant is at the break table eating his after-school snack, and I'm having a cup of coffee while I sit with him for a few minutes before getting back to some paperwork I left unfinished in my office.

Mona comes in the swinging doors and glances at the clock before pouring herself a cup of coffee and sitting down next to me. "I think I'll have me a little java while it's quiet out there," she says. "How's it going, Grant? Mrs. Bunsen keeping you busy at school?"

"Uh huh," he says, licking jelly out of the V between two fingers. "Sometimes too busy!"

"That's good. You'll keep out of trouble that way," she says with a chuckle.

"What trouble?" he asks, his face suddenly concerned.

"It's just an expression," I tell him. "It's just something people say."

"Like after while crocodile?" he says quickly.

"Exactly!" Mona says. "Just a funny thing to say."

"I didn't think it was funny," he says seriously.

"Okay, we'll try not to say it anymore," I say. "All done? Want to go outside?" He nods yes and hops down, then goes in the restroom to wash his hands before going outside.

"He sure comes up with some funny stuff," Mona comments.

"Yeah, he does. It reminds me of one day, when I was at my last job, my boss told me he was going to be gone for a week—he had business in Seattle. So on the way home from picking Grant up from the sitter, I said, 'Mr. Hopewell is going to Seattle, so next week will be easy for me.' And he says, 'Who's Attle?' It struck me so funny, I just cracked up. Of course that hurt his feelings, but when I stopped laughing, I explained it to him. I spend a lot of time explaining. But I think that's a good use of my time," I say.

"You seem to be cut out for motherhood," Mona says. "I love my daughter—you know I do, but when she was growing up, my motto was, it's up to her teacher to teach her!"

"Oh, really?" is all I say. I won't tell Mona that that is exactly the way my mom was, and I'm determined to give Grant more.

"Hey, since Grant's outside, I've been wanting to talk to you about something," she says. "You've been acting kind of like you're not really here. What's going on?"

I tell Mona about seeing Raymond and the restraining order. She says she'll talk to the waitresses about it, and I tell her I'll talk to the rest of the employees. Of course some of them wouldn't know him from Adam if he walked in anyway, like Jean, since she just moved here.

Suddenly Grant bolts in through the back door. "Mom, I forgot to ask—who's going to stay with me when you go to the party on Saturday night?"

"What party?" I ask, remembering as soon as the words are out of my mouth.

"The love party that Mrs. Bunsen 'vited you for," he reminds me. Jacob, who has just come in and is rummaging through a supply cupboard, turns and gives me an inquisitive look.

Ralph, who is making a batch of sloppy buffalo joe sauce, lets out a big belly laugh, and Grant's face turns red.

"I was happy to be invited to the Lady in Love party," I say loudly enough so everyone can hear it, "but I don't think I'll go."

"Because you don't have a babysitter?" Grant asks, coming over to my side.

"Well, that, but also I don't really need any of the things that will be sold at the party," I tell him.

"Yes, you are too going," Mona says behind me. "Grant can come to my house for the night."

"Oh, I don't know, Mona. What if he gets scared during the night, and wants to come home?" I ask.

"So we'll bring him home."

"What about Jenny? I'd be leaving her alone here in the hotel," I say.

"You'll probably be home long before this place closes

up for the night," Mona says. "Or she can come to my place too, either way."

"Do you think Evan will be okay with it?" I ask.

"I know he would be fine with it," she assures me. "Grant, wouldn't you like to come out to my house to spend Saturday night with me and Evan? I have a bedroom that my grandkids use when they visit, and there are plenty of toys. Then in the morning you can help Evan milk the cows," she adds.

"I want to go! Can I, Mom?" Grant asks me excitedly.

"Well…"

"Would you just go to the darn party!" Mona insists.

"Okay. If you're sure about this. I'll talk to Jenny and see what she wants to do. Thanks a million, Mona," I say.

"You're welcome!" she says in pretend exasperation. "Grant, you can go home with me after work Saturday. So pack your overnight bag," Mona says.

Grant thrusts a hand out to Mona and says, "It's a deal, pardner."

"Deal!" she says. Ralph calls out that an order is up, and Mona hurries over to the plates waiting under the hot lights to carry them out to the customers.

"Can I go see Jenny, Mom?" Grant asks.

"Yes, but be sure to knock on her door and wait for her to invite you in. And please don't wear out your welcome. I mean, only stay for a short visit. We don't want to tire Jenny out."

"Okay!" he says as he leaves by the corridor to the hotel.

Ralph says he's taking five for a smoke and goes out the back door, and the other waitresses on duty both grab coffee pots and head out to do warm ups.

I tense up when I see Jacob walking toward me. "I've been wanting to talk to you privately since the day we went to the lake."

"What about?" I ask.

"I just wanted to say it's too bad that we got off on the wrong foot, but I think we can start over," he says, rubbing my upper arm slowly with one finger.

"There's nothing to start over. I'm not…" I start to speak, but he interrupts me.

"I bet they do have something for you at the loving party," he says. "I bet you'd look terrific in everything they sell." He tries to get me to meet his eyes but I look the other way.

"You don't give up, do you?" I ask, embarrassed but flattered.

"Why would I? I like what I see too much to give up!" he says, his voice serious.

"I…" I begin, but then I realize I'm not sure what I want to say. I want Pete back—I'm sure of that. But Jacob, in his obnoxious confidence, stirs something in me that is hard to ignore. "I'm in love with Pete," I say, gathering my resolve. "I don't know if he's coming back, but I'm not ready to give up on him! So please, Jacob, let's put this to rest. Excuse me. I have some paperwork I have to get back to," I say, and turn to leave.

"We'll see," he calls behind me.

I just shake my head and sigh.

I'm looking forward to spending this evening at the Bunsen's for the Lady in Love party. Mona took Grant home with her, and he didn't seem worried at all, so I'm trying not to be. Jenny opted to stay in her suite, so I wrote down the Bunsen's number in the notebook by her phone, just in case of an emergency.

On my way to the party I realize that I'm actually excited that tonight I'm going to see some people I went to school with. There were a few girls other than MaryAnn that I used to enjoy being with, and I haven't been in touch with any of them since I left. It will be good to catch up on their news.

When I enter the Bunsen's house, I'm taken by surprise.

An array of sexy panties, bras, and negligees dangle from the small chandelier over the dining room table, and more hang from the drapes and walls. There are about twenty folding chairs in a circle, five of them already filled with chatting women. Our class was small, so of course everyone knows everyone here.

"This looks pretty risqué, ma'am," I say, stone faced, to Roma as I step inside. "Somebody call the police!"

"It's all legal, don't worry," Roma says. Everyone laughs, and she adds, "Lots of food on the kitchen table, girls. And there's wine and soft drinks—you can have them in the living room while Tressa gives her presentation."

Tressa is one of those genuinely nice people, so I'll probably buy something from her tonight even if I won't use it. I mill around, holding a glass of Chardonnay, sipping and chatting. It's a rare luxury, this feeling of freedom I have tonight. Between Grant, The Serenade, and my new tenant, Jenny, I have forgotten how it is to be responsible for just myself for an evening.

"Everyone find a place to sit," Tressa calls out. "Let's go around the circle and introduce ourselves. And if you're a Lady in Love, then tell us who you're in love with! If it's okay to tell, that is!" Everyone laughs. At that moment the doorbell rings and Tressa walks over to answer it. "Hi Cathy! Come in, we're just starting. There's a seat next to Meredith," she says. I look behind me and see Cathy Olson, carrying a large photo album and a camera. I haven't talked to her much since I warned her about giving out my private information. I'm surprised to see her, but she was in our class, so I shouldn't be.

"Roma, since you're the hostess, why don't you be the ice breaker?" Tressa says, no doubt using suggestions she learned when she was in training. "Oh, and introduce yourself too, why don't you?" There's a lot of laughing over that, since there's no need for introductions, but Tressa is going by the book.

"Hi, I'm Roma Bunsen," Roma begins. "I am the kindergarten teacher at Crossroads Elementary. I love kindergarteners, quilting, and I am in love with Dave Bunsen!" Applause and squeals of delight go up all around the circle.

"Well I just know there are some items here that will make Dave a very happy man!" Tressa says, laughing with the rest of us. "Cathy, since you're the first on this end, you go next, then we'll go this way," she says, as she makes a sweeping gesture around the room, making me next.

"Hi everyone, I'm Cathy Olson, which you all know, and, as fate would have it, I work at The Serenade now. And if that isn't strange enough, Meredith is my boss! Strange, how things go, huh?" she laughs. I see other people fidgeting uncomfortably, wanting to move on. "And I know Meredith so well now that I can probably tell you anything you want to know about her! Just see me after the party!" she winks, then continues, "As far as a love interest goes, I don't have one right now, but I have my eye on the hot looking handyman at The Serenade. So if any of you see him, he's mine!" she says, drawing some wild comments and laughter from the circle, and an unexplainable feeling of jealousy from me. Then she adds, "Oh, I brought my scrapbook—there are old pictures and mementos from school in it. I thought you all might like to see it. And I was hoping to get some pictures tonight to add to it, if that's okay with all of you?" The other women all express their interest in her album, then Tressa tells me it's my turn to speak.

"I'm Meredith Larsson," I say a little nervously, "and I'm happy to be back in Crossroads after a long time in Oregon. I reopened The Serenade, and I love working there. I'm kind of in limbo about the love interest, so I'm just crossing my fingers for now," I say, sitting down to scattered applause.

The next three women talk briefly about themselves, then Carolyn, John's mom, says, "I'm Carolyn Anders, and I keep busy with my three kids. John is my oldest, and he is in

Roma's class, along with his new buddy Grant, who is Meredith's son! We just love Grant. He is such a doll," she says sincerely. Apparently not everyone was aware that I had a son yet, because this information draws a flutter of comments. I smile and mouth 'thanks' toward Carolyn and get ready for the questions about Grant I'll have to field after the presentation.

When the last of the women speak, Tressa goes back to the center of the circle and holds up a pair of red bikini panties in one hand and a matching baby doll negligee in the other. Cathy snaps a photo of Tressa holding the panties in the air. "Who wants to have this beautiful, sexy ensemble?" she asks playfully, answered by a chorus of "I do's!" Then she turns to Cathy and says, "I don't want that photo being passed around just anywhere, Cathy," Tressa says, obviously annoyed. "My husband knows about my job, but people who don't might get the wrong idea about me if they see that picture out of context. Please hold off on your photography until after my presentation."

"Oh, it won't be shown to anyone but all of us, Tressa! Please don't worry about it," Cathy says.

"Thanks," Tressa says coolly, returning to her spiel. "Any of you may qualify to own this sexy ensemble absolutely free, just by hostessing a Lady in Love party, and by having three hundred dollars in sales at your party! Talk to me about it tonight, if you're interested in getting this gift, and others, absolutely free! Now this next item comes in midnight, red or black. It's for those special nights when the kids are over at grandma's and you don't have to worry about anyone disturbing you…"

It's kind of fun to see all the things Tressa holds up in front of us. Just listening to all the women laughing out loud at some of them, and imagining myself wearing some of them, is funny. But there are some really lovely classic nightgowns that I would like to have, so I fill out the order form for two of them. After Tressa's presentation some of the women are still thinking over what they want to buy, and some, including me, head for the refreshments.

I finish my glass of wine and pour my glass half full again, which is all I will allow myself since I'll be driving. Two women join me at the refreshment table. I see Cathy chatting with Roma across the room, but she's so loud I hear her say she's going to sample the refreshments, so I know she'll be butting in soon.

"So you have a son! That's great!" Lei, an attractive woman of Chinese heritage, says.

"Thanks," I say. "I'm glad to see you here, but I'm surprised! You were a senior when the rest of us were freshmen—you were my math tutor!"

"Yes, I live right next door, so Roma invited me even though I wasn't in your class," she explains.

"I'm glad she did," I say. "Do you have kids now?"

"I have two," she says, "a five-month-old boy and a three-year-old girl."

"I don't envy you those sleepless nights," I say.

Lei laughs, and says, "Yes, especially when I have to get up for work!"

"That's for sure!" I agree.

"I have twin boys, two years old," Christie, the other woman, says, then pats her swollen stomach. "And two more on the way!"

"Oh my gosh, Christie, you're a saint!" We all laugh. Cathy has just reached our group. She catches the tail end of our conversation and laughs loudly, drowning out the rest of us.

"Talking about kids, it sounds like," Cathy says. "I don't have any yet, but I'm not married, so of course I don't. You're all so lucky, to have found that special man. Oh, sorry Meredith, that was thoughtless of me."

"What do you mean?" I ask.

"Well, you were married, but now you're divorced," Cathy says, as though she's surprised that I didn't know what she meant.

"I wasn't married," I say.

"Oh," Cathy says. "Well, these things happen." Apparently Lei and Christies' embarrassed silence was the reaction she was looking for, because she suddenly says," If you'll excuse me, I'm going to find the little girls' room," and leaves us. I'm not going to tell anyone about MaryAnn and dishonor her memory, so I decide it's best to leave before anyone asks more about Grant's father.

"It's been great seeing you again," I say to Lei and Christie. "I better be going. Lots of work to do still tonight."

Christie says goodbye and moves away toward another group of women.

"Don't leave already, just because of Cathy," Lei says.

"Thanks, but I deal with her every day, and truthfully, if I had thought she would be here, I wouldn't have come. It just didn't cross my mind that she would be here," I explain.

"I understand," Lei says. Well, it was nice seeing you again."

"Same here! Drop in and see me at The Serenade if you have time, okay? Lunch on me?"

"How nice! Maybe I will!" she says, genuinely pleased.

I'm in a low mood when I get back to The Serenade and start up the stairs to my suite. Then I hear faint singing from the bar—it's the last Serenade Night of the season—and I feel even worse, being alone on my first night out in a very long time. I walk down the corridor to see if Jenny is awake, but I see no light under her door, so I go back to the lobby.

I sit down in a chair and stare up at the animal heads high above me on the walls. "Hey guys," I say, "what's happening?" I get up and walk to a closet in the back of the lobby where bottles of wine and hard liquor are stored. "How pathetic. Talking to stuffed animal heads," I mutter as I unlock the closet. I rarely drink, but tonight I've already had a little at Roma's, and now I take a bottle out to the kitchen and pour myself a glass, then a few more. I think of how much fun it used to be to dance with Pete. I miss him so much. I'm so lonely, I'm thinking, as I wobble out the hotel lobby door and walk around the building to the bar entrance. I sit down on the bench on the porch, suddenly realizing that I shouldn't go in if I can't walk straight. But I want to dance. The juke box is playing a slow song that Pete and I used to dance to. Despair flows through me, and everything that's wrong in my life comes rushing to the forefront. In seconds tears are rolling down my cheeks.

"Meredith, what's the trouble?" I look up to see Jacob standing in front of me.

"Oh, great," I say, wiping my cheeks with my hands. "I really want the employees to see me like this."

"What's going on?" he asks with concern, sitting down next to me. I don't resist when he takes my hands in his.

"I don't know, I'm just—a mess, is all. I miss Pete, and I'm lonely, and that's a song we used to dance to all the time."

"I'm sorry you're having a bad time," he says. "I thought tonight was the loving party," he says, borrowing Grant's phrase.

"It was. I went. But that Cathy was giving me a hard time, so I left early."

"A hard time about what?"

"Oh, she was talking like I was a moral backslider."

"What did she say?"

"Oh, something about me having a kid and no husband."

"Oh, she's one of those. Doesn't she know they sell clothes at that kind of party that could lead to moral backsliding?" he asks with a chuckle. "You could have told her that."

"I should have, but I didn't think of it. That's not my style anyway," I say.

"She's probably a backslider, herself, so I wouldn't worry about it," he says.

"Don't be nice to me. I don't deserve it!" I say, the tears starting up again.

"You don't want me to be nice? Okay, woman," he says, pulling me off the bench, with pretend roughness. "I'm taking you inside." He looks at me in the porch light and wipes my cheeks with his thumbs. "It won't do for the owner of the place to come in with black rivers running down her face," he says. When we get inside he stands with his arm around me.

In a few minutes Jacob nabs a table near the center of the room that a couple is just leaving. When Danielle, the barmaid, comes over to take our drink orders, she looks surprised that Jacob and I are together. I'm relieved that she only asks what we'll have.

"Two coffees," Jacob says. Danielle nods and leaves.

The band has come back from break, and starts up the set with a loud, lively song. Between that and all the loud conversations in here, there isn't much chance for Jacob and me to talk. To add to the confusion, there must be some kind of celebration going on here tonight—there are cheers and flashes of lights going on a few tables away from us.

Danielle brings the coffees in short order, and we sit silently sipping them for a few minutes. The next song is a slow one, and Jacob takes me by the hand and leads me to the dance floor. I feel drained. I don't think I have it in me to dance right now, but when Jacob gathers me to his chest and puts an arm around me, I change my mind. He moves us fluidly around the floor, which can't be easy with me right now. He touches a finger under my chin and draws my face up, then leans down to me, his mouth nearly on mine. There are more lights flashing and cheers from the party table. I'm confused and drunk. Then Jacob kisses me, stirring something deep inside me. I know in my heart that I love Pete, but right now it's Jacob who is making me feel like a woman.

In the morning I wake up glad that Jacob is off until Wednesday. Now that my head's on straight again, I realize letting him take control last night probably led him on unfairly, which I'm going to have to apologize for. My cheeks burn when I remember that just the other day I'd brushed him off again, and last night I started it myself.

"Hi, Mom!" Grant says at about noon, entering the kitchen from the corridor. "I'm home!" Sundays are extremely busy, so I lead him over to his play corner where we can talk and be out of the way.

"Did you have fun with Mona and Evan?" I ask, hugging him tightly.

"Yeah! I helped milk the cows! Flossie and Fauna," he says.

"We had a great time," Mona says. She has come in right behind him with his gear. "We better do that again some time!"

"Yeah!" Grant shouts.

"How was the loving party?" Mona asks.

"It was okay," I say, not wanting to talk about last night in front of Grant. "I ordered a few things."

"You did?"

"A couple of long nightgowns."

"Lady in Love sells flannel?" Mona asks with a grin.

"No, smarty pants, I got real classy nightgowns," I say.

"Can I go see Jenny?" Grant interrupts.

"No, honey, she's having lunch right now. Maybe in a while," I say, then add, "Grant, Mona and I were speaking when you interrupted."

"I'm sorry," he says quickly, and keeps talking. "Mom, when I was with Jenny yesterday, I met that new lady, the one who helps out."

"Jean," I tell him, exchanging smiles with Mona. She knows I try to get him to mind his manners, but it doesn't always work out.

"Jean's nice," he says.

"That's one of the reasons I asked her to come help with Jenny," I say.

"Oh yeah, I forgot to tell you something," he adds, climbing onto a chair at the employee table. "Jenny wants you to come to her room."

"She asked you to tell me this yesterday?" There's no need to panic, I'm sure. Jenny has both my number and Jean's if she needs us, but I still don't want her thinking I don't care about her. "Okay, I'll fix you a sandwich and then I'll go see her." I make a sandwich, pour a glass of milk, and get an apple out of a box in the walk in, then put everything on a tray for him. He follows me as I carry his food to the little table in his corner. "All set?" I ask him as he sits down.

"Yep!" he smiles and takes a bite of his sandwich.

"Thanks so much for having Grant all night," I tell Mona. "That was so sweet of you and Evan."

"It was fun—let us have him over again some time," she offers.

"If he really was fun to have over, then I'll take you up on it sometime," I say, relieved that he wasn't a problem.

"No, he was perfect. It worked out fine, and he didn't wake up during the night wanting to go home or anything!"

"I'm glad to hear it. I better go see Jenny, but I'll be back in a little while. Do you have to leave now?" I ask Mona, hoping to get a chance to tell her about last night.

"I should. I have to go grocery shopping and run a bunch of errands. So I'll see you tomorrow."

"Well, thanks again," I say. "Grant, I'm going to go see what Jenny needed. You stay and finish your lunch, please. Then you may go outside if you want to."

"Okay," he shouts from the corner.

I knock on Jenny's door a minute later. "Who is it?" Jenny calls out.

"It's Meredith," I say in a singsong voice.

She unlocks her door. "Hi, Jenny! I stopped by last night around nine to see if you wanted to chat, but your light was out," I say.

"Yes, I went to bed early last night," she says. "I'm sorry I missed you! I didn't think you'd be back that early."

"That kind of party isn't very long," I say. "Grant just told me that you asked me to come by yesterday. I would have been here right away, if he had told me sooner," I apologize. "Probably better not send any important messages with him. He's a little too young for a lot of responsibility."

"Oh, it wasn't urgent. But it's a little troubling. It's probably nothing, but yesterday when Jean was here—oh, by the way, I really like Jean. She's as nice as can be."

"I know, she really is," I say, happy to hear that Jenny thinks so. "But you were saying?"

"Oh, yes. Jean was here when Grant came to see me. She said she didn't recall knowing anyone with such beautiful black hair and blue eyes until she moved here, and now she knows two people with them!"

I wait for Jenny to pour some water from the antique tumble up set on her night stand. "She wasn't going to elaborate, so I asked her who the other person is, and she said it was her boyfriend. Grant asked her if her boyfriend's name is Grant, like his. She said, no, her boyfriend's name is Raymond."

"Oh jeez," I say. "I was hoping never to see him again, but he turned up outside the school just the other day and told me he wanted me to give him part of my inheritance, and now this? It can't be the same Raymond!"

"Oh dear, I hope that inheritance isn't going to be more a curse than a blessing," Jenny says in a worried tone.

"No, it isn't, Jenny, don't worry. But I can't imagine Jean with Raymond!" I say. "It wouldn't surprise me to see Raymond with someone much younger like Jean, but the personality differences!"

"We don't know if it is him," Jenny reminds me. "There are probably other men named Raymond in town. And he could act entirely differently to other people than he did to you and your mother," she adds.

"Another Raymond with black hair and blue eyes in Crossroads?" I ask, thinking how strange it seemed for a person named Larsson to look like him in the first place. "If it's him, I don't know how I could stand to have Jean here."

"Oh, I hope she doesn't have to go. I really like her," Jenny says in a worried voice.

"I don't know how I could work with a woman who— well, let's just hope for the best. I'll have to talk to her about it. Thanks for letting me know. I better get back to work now."

"I'll cross my fingers that it's a different Raymond," Jenny says.

"Me too," I say as I open the door to leave.

Later in the day I run into Jean in the lobby. I remind myself that I am the employer, so the butterflies in my stomach are uncalled for, but that doesn't help. "Jean, may I talk to you for a minute?" I ask.

"Sure," she says.

"Let's go into my office," I say, turning to lead her down the corridor. I sit down at my desk and motion to her to have a seat. "I don't know how to approach this subject, so I'm just going to cut right to the chase," I say, drawing a quizzical look from her.

"I was talking to Jenny earlier, and she said you mentioned your boyfriend's name is Raymond?"

"Yes," she says. "Is there a problem?" she asks in a worried voice.

"Well, I hope not. I know that there may be many Raymond's in this town—let me just get this out of my system. Is his last name Larsson?"

"Yes, it is. So you know him?" she asks, her brows knit.

"Well, if he has a trucking business and also drives a

white sedan, then it is probably my former stepfather."

"Small world, huh?" Jean laughs. I can see she is re-lieved.

"Where does he live now, if you don't mind my asking?"

"We live on Sixth Street. It's a big old pink Victorian across from a little market."

"Oh," I say quietly, as visions of Raymond in that house shoot through my mind.

"What's wrong?" Jean asks.

"I thought he had sold that house and moved away," I say, while I search for the right way to tell her about him. "That's the house I was raised in."

"He did say that he had been living in Great Falls for a while, and that the house was rented out while he was gone. He asked me to move in with him about ten days ago, and I didn't want to live in that crummy Greenway any longer."

"I'm curious—have you told him you work here?" I ask.

"No, he wasn't really interested in my job, so other than saying I take care of an elderly lady, I haven't talked to him about it. But then, I'm not really interested in trucking either," she says.

I'm nervous about bringing this up to her, but I feel like I have to. "You wouldn't have any way of knowing about Ray-mond, so I'm going to tell you. My mom married him when I was a kid. He was a long-haul trucker then, too. When he was home he drank a lot, and he was a mean drunk. My mom and I have the scars to prove it."

Jean looks at me like I've lost my mind. "Raymond has been wonderful to me!" she says defensively. "He'd never hurt me!"

"I thought you might say something like that," I say, thinking of how shocked I was when I had read MaryAnn's perception of Raymond. "I have to do what I think is right, and I thought you should be warned about him. If we didn't like you so much it would be easy to fire you, because truthfully, it's going to be very hard for me to ignore that you're with the man who caused me and my mom so much trouble. But I'm going to try, so if you want to stay on, you can. On a few conditions. I don't ever want to hear about him, and please don't talk to him about me or anything to do with me. And when he finds out that you work here, he'll be mad, and you better watch out!"

I wait for some kind of response, but Jean remains silent.

"There's one more thing. He threatened me recently about wanting me to hand over some of an inheritance I got, and I have a restraining order against him. He is not allowed on the premises of The Serenade."

Jean rubs her forehead with a hand for a moment, then asks, "Why would he threaten you like that?"

"He was drunk, and he can't control himself when he's drunk. There's no telling what he'll do."

She sits for a few moments, thinking, then says, "Raymond loves me. I know he does. He's been so good to me. I have no reason not to believe you, but I have to stand by him. But I'm staying on here. I enjoy working here, and I'm really fond of Jenny already. In fact, I'm fond of a lot of people here, including you! I'll make it work," she says. "But let's not talk about it anymore now, okay?" she says, clearing her throat and wiping a tear from her eye.

"Just be aware of the awkwardness this could cause for us. I mean, pretty much everyone in town knows the history," I explain.

"I'll deal with it," she says.

I nod as she leaves my office. I hope she doesn't make the connection of the blue eyes and black hair that both Raymond and Grant have. I also hope she doesn't have children with him. I doubt Jean would be the same kind of mother my mom was, but I can't believe Raymond would be any different. I'm angry that Jean wants to stick by him. When she leaves, I go into the kitchen and tell Mona that I told Jean about Raymond being my stepfather.

"What'd she say?" Mona asks.

"She said that Raymond has been good to her, and that she doesn't believe he would do anything to hurt her," I say, shaking my head in disbelief. "She's going to stand by him, she said."

"Sounds like a song," she says, making me laugh in spite of myself.

"She says she wants to stay on here anyway. She really likes Jenny and wants to keep working with her. I know Jenny wants her to stay, too. But I asked her not to talk to Raymond about me or the business, and she says she won't."

"That's not always going to be easy. Evan and I always talk about what goes on at work. How's she going to avoid that?"

"She can't, not really. He'll find out she's working here, and the you-know-what will hit the fan."

Mona says, "You're right. But you've done what you could now, short of letting her go, so we just have to wait and see what happens, okay?"

"Okay," I say, glad to have her steer me away from the subject.

Chapter 9

I'm having a cup of hot chocolate when the image of dear old Tippy comes to my mind. He owned the market across the street from my house when I was a kid. The market is still called Tippy's, even though he's long dead. Mom used to send me over there for things she ran out of between regular shopping trips. Before MaryAnn's baby sisters came along, she and I spent plenty of time in Tippy's after school, dawdling around the candy displays. Tippy, a gentle old man, let us take our time. Whenever we took a particularly long time to choose our candy, Tippy would say, "I'm not in a hurry. I'm not going nowhere until—oh, I'm not going nowhere at all. I live here!" We would all laugh, because we knew that he lived in the rooms at the back of the store with his two black cats, Licorice and Pepper.

In October, the year I was thirteen, Raymond married Mom and moved into our house on Sixth Street. One night, towards the end of that first winter, Mom and Raymond got drunk, which had become a regular thing by then. This particular evening, Mom looked at the clock and said it was only eight-thirty, and Tippy's would still be open for another half-hour. She said they had the munchies, so I was sent to get some chips and dip. It was cold—there was a thin layer of snow on the ground—so I grabbed my jean jacket for the quick trip across the street.

I chatted with Tippy a bit, and headed back home with a bag of chips and dip, only to find the door locked. I pounded on the door, but I guessed Mom and Raymond must have gone upstairs, because nobody came to let me in. I tried the back door but it was also locked. I desperately wanted to think that they thought they would hear me knocking when I got back. It was pretty cold outside. The jean jacket was no match for the weather, and I started crying. I ran the several blocks to MaryAnn's house, but there were no lights on and the door was locked. Then I remembered that her aunt was visiting from Oregon, and they had all gone to Great Falls to visit some cousins.

The only other person I knew well in the neighborhood was Tippy, so I walked back to the market, which I was dismayed to see was now dark and closed for the night. I went around to the back of the store and knocked for a few minutes on the back door as loudly as I could. Finally I heard Tippy shuffling across the linoleum in the beaded doeskin moccasins that he always wore. When he opened the door and took a look at my tear-stained face and runny nose, he said, "Meredith! What's wrong?" I was so overwhelmed I couldn't talk, so Tippy took my arm and, pulling me gently inside, said, "You were my last customer of the day and now you're first in line for tomorrow! Come in!"

He led me through the first cozy room, which had a big upholstered easy chair with a little table beside it, and a massive bookcase crammed full of all shapes and sizes of books. Then we walked into a tiny kitchen with a small Formica-topped table and two metal chairs with red vinyl seats, an old black cast iron stove, a strange refrigerator on long legs, and a big porcelain sink. To one side and beyond the kitchen through a partially closed door I could see the head of his bed, a red and white quilt rumpled over it. He went in his bedroom to get the quilt, and wrapped it around me.

"Here, have a seat by the stove. I'll stoke it up again so it'll really put the heat out. Then I'll make us some hot chocolate. Nothing like hot chocolate on a cold night," he said, moving faster than he usually did. I watched him as he gathered up a bundle of kindling from a milk crate next to the kitchen door that led into the store. He opened the front of the stove and tossed in the kindling a few sticks at a time, then crumpled a few pages of an old edition of the *Bugle* from a stack of them in a bin by the kindling crate. On top of that he put a wedge of split firewood which had been sitting on the floor by the stove.

"Warming up?" he asked. I nodded that I was, but my teeth were still chattering.

"What happened, Meredith?" he finally asked as he sat down next to me.

"I got locked out. I knocked on the door as long as I could but nobody let me in," I said, and started crying again. Licorice and Pepper wound curiously around my ankles as I sobbed.

"It's alright. Old Tippy's going to take care of you," he said, taking my hands and rubbing them together in his. The loose, papery skin on his big old hands was foreign to me, but a great comfort at the same time.

Soon Tippy got up to make the hot chocolate, and when it was ready he poured us each a mug. I began to feel better as we sat together, blowing on our mugs and sipping. When I finished mine I thanked him and told him it was the best hot chocolate I'd ever had. I stayed overnight at Tippy's, sleeping in the easy chair which I helped him drag to the kitchen so I would stay warm next to the stove. Licorice and Pepper curled up in my lap and purred me to sleep. In the morning, before he walked me home, Tippy and I ate toast and grape jelly, and drank leftover hot chocolate. To this day, I think of

Tippy's warmth and caring whenever I drink hot chocolate.

"Hey, we're moving into our new place this week," Mona says while we work in the kitchen. "And I know you don't want to be here when the bat guy comes, so I was wondering if you guys would like to stay in our old trailer when the bat guy is here?"

"That sounds wonderful! Thanks!" I say, relieved to have a solution to that problem. "Evan won't mind?" I ask.

"No, we know you're responsible. I'll leave the bed that Jody and Frank use when they're here and the kid's beds..." Mona says, thinking out loud.

"I'm sure Jenny will be fine with the idea, but I want to pass it by her. I want to give her a say in whatever we do as a family."'

"Jenny's such a sweet lady. Whatever you think will make her happy," Mona says. Then she tilts her head to one side and says, "You know, if you hadn't come back, Jenny would most likely have lived the rest of her life in that home, and she wouldn't have been happy. It's funny with Jenny and me. We've always gotten along, but we just don't really connect. Every time I visited her in the home I asked her if she wanted to come stay with me for a few days, but she wouldn't. Here you go out there the first time, and you bring her home permanently!"

"I know she likes you, Mona," I say reassuringly. "She's told me lots of times. And she really appreciated you visiting her. She must have told you."

"Oh sure, she always thanked me. I know she enjoyed my visits," Mona says.

"I think Jenny and I are so close because I met her when I was so young, and I was having such a bad time with Raymond. She wanted to help me. How old were you when you met her?" I ask.

"I guess it was when Jody was little, but I can't remember exactly."

"But you were already an adult. You didn't need her like I did," I reason. "She's like a grandmother to me," I add.

"Yes, and you're lucky to have her," Mona replies. "Well, we both are."

Now that I'm older, I know that Jenny is a rare, beautiful bird. There are other people I care deeply for, but Jenny is different even than those. I didn't tell her anything about Raymond and Mom until I had known her for months, but Jenny must have come up with a fair assessment of my background from my appearance, my poor grammar, and my lack of manners. She began to correct and instruct me, but she was never condescending. I realize now that I would not have had the self-confidence to manage The Serenade without Jenny's attention in my youth. Once, when I was a senior, I remember I was sitting next to her on her bed. I had just brought her a scrambled egg sandwich Uncle Duck had made for her. My hands were folded in my lap. I had been feeling low, and Jenny must have sensed it.

"What's the matter?" she had asked.

"Nothing, I'm okay," I answered, not wanting to bother her with my problems.

"I'm glad you've never mentioned wanting to be a movie star, because you can't act!" she said with a laugh.

"I can't do anything," I said.

"I was just teasing," Jenny said. "What's the problem?"

"Today in homeroom the teacher announced that college-bound seniors should see her about the SATs, you know, the test you have to take if you're going to college? So I stopped at her desk, along with a bunch of other kids. She handed out a slip of paper to all the others and told them to hurry so they wouldn't be late for their next class. They left, and other kids were coming in for the next class. Then she asked me if I really thought I was college material. A few boys who were passing behind me right then laughed and made fun of me. I was so embarrassed that I just left."

"She should never have spoken to you like that in front of other students. I can imagine that she really hurt you by saying it."

"She did," I said.

"Every time I've asked you about college, you've said you weren't interested. So why did you go to the teacher's desk when she asked for college-bound seniors to come up?"

"I guess because I wanted to fit in, and I didn't want to look dumb," I said.

"Did all the other seniors go to her desk?" Jenny asked.

"No."

"Why not?"

"Well, some of the other kids already have plans, like Cindy wants to be a beautician, Carl is going to work with his dad on the farm, a few are going into the military…" I paused, thinking of other things I'd heard my classmates talk about.

"I don't think those are dumb ideas," Jenny says. "You've told me before what you want to do after high school, and that didn't sound dumb either."

"I want to move out of the house and live with MaryAnn for a few years. Then I want to marry Pete, and a few years after that I hope we have some kids."

"That's a very nice idea," Jenny said, which made me smile.

"I love singing, but I don't really want a career doing it."

"Why don't you ask Duck to let you sing here at The Serenade sometimes?

"Do you think he'd let me?" I asked excitedly.

"I think he would," she said. "You know, those students going to college may need to go to be teachers, scientists, doctors—whatever they need to do to fulfill their dreams. It's important for everybody to fulfill their dreams," she added.

I hugged Jenny tightly and told her that I would do whatever it took to fulfill my dreams, too.

The creaks and groans coming out of the old dishwasher tell me it is in the throes of death. I head to my office to call a supply house to order a new machine. I'm trying to keep my mind on business, but I keep thinking of the apology I finally gave Jacob yesterday. I explained to him that I felt foolish for drinking too much in the first place, and for letting him think I was falling in love with him on top of it. As I expected, he was pretty upset, and tried to convince me again that he is the one for me.

Suddenly Cathy throws my office door open. "You're never going to guess who's here to see you!" she squeals.

I'm in no mood to deal with Cathy's rudeness today. "Please don't come in without knocking," I say stiffly.

"But Pete's here!" she squeals again. "He's out in the lobby! I'm sure he wants to see you! I didn't tell him where your office was, Meredith. I've really been careful about what I say since our little talk," she says.

"Oh, for the love of…" I start. "Pete's welcome in my office!" I say in exasperation.

"You're kind of hard to read, Meredith, so I'm just being very careful," she says, raising my hackles even more. I walk quickly down the corridor, trying to smooth my hair, but the dishwasher steam has pretty well ruined my look.

"Pete! It's great to see you!" I say warmly. I make a quick survey of the lobby and see there are no guests who might overhear us.

"New hairdo?" he says, laughing. Cathy laughs too, which annoys me.

"I was just attacked by the dishwasher," I say with a smile.

"Is it that same old dishwasher?" Pete asks, referring to when I worked here for Uncle Duck. Pete used to stop in toward the end of my shift and help me with my prep work, like filling salts, sugars and napkin holders, and sometimes filling the dishwasher for its last run of the day. Nobody minded if he was in the kitchen as long as he was helping out.

"The same one," I reply.

"That thing didn't even work too well back then," he chuckles. Then he surprises me and backs away from Cathy, turning to walk down the corridor. I follow him into my office and he shuts the door behind me. He leans down to me and kisses me on the mouth, then my neck. I push his chin up gently and kiss him. The taste of his sweet breath, and the smell of his clothes still thrill me.

"I've been thinking about that night in your room," he says.

"What have you been thinking about it?" I tease.

"That I'd like to repeat it," he says, nuzzling my neck.

"I think we can arrange that," I say, straightening up and attempting to smooth my hair down again. "Hey, mister, are you ever going to give me a warning, or are you always going to just pop in on me like this?"

"Sorry I haven't been in touch. The last time—the things you said at the park—just took me a while to think through. I love you, Meredith, and we're going to have to work out our different opinions about important things," he says, hugging me tightly.

"I love you, too. That's why I'm willing to work on it," I say.

"I was going to call you when I got to my folks' place later today. Nadia hurt her leg and they're keeping an eye on her at our ranch, so I'm going out there to check on her myself. You know how I feel about that horse. Anyway, Cathy called my mom and left a message for me to stop by here the next time I was in town. She said she had something for me. Do you know what she's talking about?"

"No, not at all," I say, growing angry at the thought of Cathy calling Pete's mom.

"Do you think you can get someone to watch Grant tonight?"

"I'll check with Mona and see if she can. I'll call you and let you know after I talk to her. I guess we have to go back out there so you can find out what Cathy has for you," I say, reluctantly opening my office door.

"I'd rather stay in here with you," Pete says, pulling me close for one more kiss.

Back in the lobby, Pete asks Cathy why she wanted him to stop by. I cringe, wondering what it could be.

"Wait a minute," she says, reaching under the lobby desk. She pulls out the photo album she had brought to the party at Roma's.

"Cathy," I say, annoyed. "You called Pete to see photos of Roma's party?" I ask in disbelief. Pete gives us both questioning glances.

"No, no," Cathy says. "I took pictures of Jim's birthday party here at The Serenade. I thought you might like to see them since you couldn't get off work. Jim told me," she says.

"Oh yeah," Pete says. "He invited you to his party?"

"No, I just happened to be here for Serenade Night, and saw him and his friends. I asked if they'd like some pictures from his birthday party and they all said yes."

"You came here after Roma's party?" I ask her as she flips through the album to the last pages.

"Well, I didn't have anything to do, so I just came by to have a drink, see if anyone wanted to dance," Cathy replies. "Here's a good one of Jim and Wes. They were having a pretty good time," she says laughing, as she holds the album up for Pete.

"Looks like they were," he says. "Thanks Cathy," he says, turning toward me.

"Oh here's another good one," she says, moving slightly in front of Pete. She holds the album up near his face so that he can't help but see it. "I mean, they were feeling no pain!" she says gleefully. "Look at them!"

Pete looks and laughs, then looks again, more carefully.

"Who's this, behind them?" he asks quietly. Cathy takes the book back from him and looks closely at the photo.

"I'm not sure. Oh wait—that's you, Meredith! With Jacob! I didn't know you were there too! It was so crowded in there I could barely find a place to sit!" Pete takes the album back from her. I follow the movement of his eyes from photo to photo. Cathy leans over his arm and points to another photo. "Look at Jim—I just got a bit of his goofy expression in this one. Hey, there's Meredith and Jacob on the dance floor behind Jim. Kissing?" Cathy looks up at me faking innocence. "I heard you and Jacob broke up after that fishing trip! I'm sorry, Meredith. I would never have said I was interested in him at Roma's party if I had known."

Pete thrusts the album at Cathy. "Jacob and I are not going together," I say. "We never were. He offered to take Grant fishing and I wouldn't allow him to take Grant without me," I explain for Pete's benefit. I try to lead Pete away but he isn't moving. "And that night in the bar we danced one dance and he kissed me. I didn't kiss him." Pete takes a deep breath, gives Cathy a disgusted look, and heads for the door. I follow him outside, asking him to stop so I can explain. When we get to his truck I say, "I was lonely. I had a few drinks, and Jacob happened to show up. I didn't kiss him!" I say again. "He kissed me!"

"Meredith, it's been hard, knowing you're this close and I can't see you every day. But every time we manage to see each other, another problem comes up. I know Cathy went out of her way to show me this, and that was really low of her, but..."

"Why can't you believe me?" I ask in desperation.

"The thing is," he says, shaking his head sadly, "is that I was just starting to get over losing you the first time, and now you're back, but with all these strings attached," he adds as he opens his truck door.

As his truck pulls away from me I shout in anguish,

"Pete! I love you!" but my words are vaporized in the billows of dust swirling around his truck. I turn and trudge up the hotel steps, then collapse on the bench outside the lobby door. I sit for a few minutes, coughing the dust out of my lungs and trying to compose myself, then go inside to the desk where Cathy is pretending to do paperwork.

"Come with me," I say angrily to her, heading down the corridor.

"What are you doing?" Cathy asks, moving quickly to keep up with me. She follows me into my office.

"Shut the door, have a seat," I say curtly. I know how much her paychecks are, so I grab my checkbook, dash off a check and rip it out of my book.

"Are you firing me?" she asks, sounding surprised.

"Yes," I say, thrusting the check at her.

"On what grounds?" she asks.

"On the grounds that I shouldn't have hired you in the first place," I say.

"Come up with something better than that, or I'm going to report you for unlawful firing," she threatens. "It will be your word against mine, and who do you think anyone is going to believe around here: someone from your family, or someone from mine?"

"I really don't care," I say. "If there are penalties, they'll be worth it if you're out of my sight. And furthermore," I add, "you are no longer welcome in any part of this establishment."

"You only have yourself to blame for this," she says.

"What? How can you say that? You took those pictures of me with Jacob intending to show Pete! Why would you do that?" I demand.

"Because I had just said at Roma's party, not an hour before, that I was interested in Jacob, and then I see you two hanging all over each other on the dance floor. Why did you do that to me?" she asks.

Her voice does not ring true, for some reason, but it's nothing to me if she knows exactly what Jacob and I did. "That business you pulled on me that night." I say in disgust. "I left Roma's party feeling pretty bad because of it, so I had a few glasses of wine. I was sitting outside the bar when Jacob came along. We had coffee and one dance, and that's when he kissed me. And for that you called Pete and asked him to come by. Too bad this is a small town, because I really never want to see you again," I say.

She takes her check and leaves, without a word.

When Cathy's gone I close my office door, sit down and put my head down on the desk. I thought I had cried myself out over Pete, but Cathy just proved me wrong.

"She had it coming to her," Mona says to me early Saturday morning while we're scrubbing the kitchen floor.

"I know." I'm on my hands and knees, working my scrub brush into a corner. "I just don't know why I've felt so guilty about these last few days, but I do."

"It won't really get any easier, either. Duck didn't fire many people, but the ones he fired deserved it, like Cathy did. It was always hard for him to do, no matter what," Mona says, slowly pulling herself up with the help of a counter edge. "I don't know about you, but my knees have taken all they're taking for today."

"Yeah, me too. Let's sit a little while before we change," I say, standing up and stretching. "Thanks for helping me with these chores," I add.

"Hon, I've scrubbed these floors more times over the years than I care to say. A few more times isn't going to matter, but I won't cry if you get somebody else to do it next time either," Mona says as she pours two mugs of fresh coffee.

"So you're saying you won't miss this when you quit?"

"You got that right, sister!" Mona says with a laugh, letting out a raspy cough at the same time. Suddenly we hear footsteps moving quickly down the corridor. "I guess that could be Jenny, but she doesn't usually walk that fast," I say, getting up to investigate. "I just hope she remembered to put her robe on," I add, thinking of a recent evening when Jenny had gone out in the hotel lobby with just a lightweight nightgown on. Cathy and one hotel guest had been in the lobby at the time. Cathy came running to tell me in the kitchen, and seemed disappointed that I took it pretty calmly, reminding her that Jenny was pretty old, so a little slip up now and then was to be expected. The guest, a middle-aged woman, was very understanding about it, though I realize not everybody would be.

Now I walk down the corridor a little ways expecting to find Jenny, but instead I run into Jean rushing in from the hotel lobby.

"Jean! It's your day off!" I say, surprised. "What are you doing here?"

"Do you mind if I just get a cup of coffee?" she asks, her voice tense.

'Go ahead," I say. When we get back in the kitchen I invite her to sit at the break table while I get her coffee.

I put a steaming mug down in front of Jean, and Mona, catching my eye with a questioning look, asks, "Cream and sugar, Jean?"

"No thanks, this is fine," she says, taking a sip, but not looking at either of us.

"Everything okay?" I ask. Just then there are loud footsteps on the back porch, and I look up to see Ralph taking the last drag on a cigarette before he comes in the kitchen.

"Morning, Ralph," I say with a quick smile.

"Morning, Meredith," he says, motioning that he wants to speak to me privately. I go out on the back porch with him and shut the door.

"Raymond just parked out front and he's coming in through the hotel lobby," Ralph says.

"Are you sure it's Raymond?" I ask, my heart pounding.

"How long have I lived in Crossroads? Yeah, I'm sure," he says without skipping a beat.

I guess I look as scared as I feel, because Ralph, a well-muscled young man, goes back in the kitchen to the door that opens into the corridor and braces himself there like a cement wall.

In seconds, Raymond has come in through the lobby. I'm petrified as I hear him running down the corridor.

"Move, damn it!" he shouts, trying to shove Ralph aside.

"No can do. Somebody call for help," Ralph yells, and Mona runs to do it. "I'm sure you know that Meredith has a restraining order against you," he says to Raymond. The two men are about the same height, but Raymond's build can't begin to compete with Ralph's.

"I ain't here for her, and that's none of your business anyway," Raymond says.

"Yeah, it is," Ralph says. "You're threatening these women," he says. "And I can't let you do that. Just turn around and head on out the way you came in," he says.

Raymond shouts at Jean, whose terrified eyes look from me to Mona and back. "I told you, you ain't working here no more! Now, come on!"

Jean gets up and runs into the restroom, locking the door behind her.

"Get out of here!" I shout at him.

"No woman of mine is going to work for you!" he screams at me. "You're a bitch, just like your mother! You already owe me big time, and I haven't seen a cent of it yet. I told you I want half of it! Where is it?"

Ralph is doing his best to keep Raymond slightly out in the corridor so he won't have a chance of getting into the kitchen. Raymond's face goes to deeper shades of angry red, then purple, as he strikes at Ralph, landing a few punches. It seems to make Raymond even angrier that Ralph is so secure in his strength that he doesn't strike back, but just continues to block him from entering the kitchen. I'm terrified by the scene, fearful that there will be serious injuries soon.

Finally I see Dave Bunsen enter the far end of the corridor just as Raymond lays a skin-splitting blow on Ralph's face. In that instant Ralph's head turns toward us from the force of the blow, and drops of blood splatter yards away from him from a gash above his left eye. Ralph reels, and Raymond runs over to the bathroom door and starts pounding on it. Then he sees Dave, and dashes outside. Dave can't match Raymond's speed, but he runs out the back door after him. Mona and I run behind the row of ovens to get out of the way.

A few seconds after Dave and Raymond are gone, I lead Ralph to the table and press a cloth to his split brow. "This is deep—it's going to need stitches," I say. "Ralph, I'm so sorry."

"It's okay, Meredith. It doesn't hurt that much. I could have stopped his punches, but if I had, I would have really done some damage," he says.

Jean has come out of the restroom. "Thank you for not doing it," she says quietly, but nobody responds.

We hear the police siren start, and I ask Mona to stay with Ralph a minute while I go check on Grant and the hotel guests to see if anyone heard all the commotion and wonders what's going on.

"Sure," Mona says, taking my place with Ralph. I walk quickly down the corridor to the lobby. There aren't any guests in the lobby, which I take as a good sign. I go upstairs to check on Grant, grateful that it's a weekend so he was sleeping in, instead of in the kitchen with me.

"Mona," I say when I get back in the kitchen, "would you please drive Ralph to the hospital? I'll stay to cook. I'm pretty sure I can handle everything on the breakfast menu. I just won't be as fast as Ralph! I'll try to call in another waitress to take over for you, but I don't want to call Charlie in to cook. He was sounding pretty tired yesterday."

"We're on the way," Mona says, pulling her keys and cigarettes out of her purse. She lights a cigarette and takes a drag. I don't say anything, though, because I see the tension written all over her face.

Jean gets a bucket of water and some bleach and rags, and starts cleaning blood off the floor that Mona and I had just scrubbed. When Mona and Ralph leave, I go over to her.

"What happened?" I ask her quietly. "Did he just find out that you work here?"

She nods a yes, but doesn't speak for a few moments while she pulls herself together. Finally she says, "It came up just this morning, when he was getting ready to leave for a week on the road. He was so angry! I told him I love him, but that I'm still going to work here because I like this job, and that I like you and Jenny," she says.

"Just how I figured it would go when he found out," I say.

"I didn't want to believe it," Jean says, taking an apron from a hook on the wall.

Before she has a chance to put it on, I pull out a chair at the table and say, "Thanks for cleaning the floor, but please sit down. I'm making you a cup of tea. And while the water boils I'm going to make a few calls, see if I can get a waitress to take Mona's place for the rest of the morning."

When I have Mona's replacement taken care of and Jean settled with a cup of tea, I put on an apron and start cleaning stove tops, even though it was done last night. I have to keep busy. I wish the first customers would get here, get me going on breakfast orders so I wouldn't have time to imagine what scenes might be playing out with Dave and Raymond right now.

By the time Dave comes back, breakfast has been underway for about an hour and I've cooked about twenty orders, including Jenny's usual breakfast, which Jean has taken down the corridor to her.

"I lost him," Dave says quietly to me. "I'll have another officer close by here today, just in case he comes back."

"Okay, thanks," I say.

"What's the story?" he asks, and I tell him everything that happened since Jean came in this morning.

When Jean comes back to the kitchen, her face goes white when she sees Dave.

"Where's Raymond?" she asks nervously.

"I don't know. I lost him," Dave says. "I need to talk to you in Meredith's office, please," he says, motioning for Jean to go first down the corridor. In a little while they come back to the kitchen, and Dave asks me if I can keep Jean here a few days.

"Yes, of course, but there's no telling what crazy thing Raymond will do when he finds out she's staying here," I say.

"Hopefully we'll catch up to him soon," Dave says, "and he won't have the chance to cause any more trouble."

"But what's going to happen, even if you catch him?" I ask. "All those times he mistreated me and Mom, he only got a few days in jail here and there. He was always back pretty soon, and the aftermath was sometimes worse than what he was put in jail for." I look at Jean, her face streaked with tears. "I'm sorry, Jean," I say. "You must be feeling just awful over all this." I reach in my pants pocket and pull out my ring of master keys. "Here," I say, taking one off and handing it to her. "You can use this room as long as you need to stay away from Raymond's. Why don't you go up now and rest a while. When Charlie gets here, I'll get some of my clothes together for you so there's no need to go back to Raymond's to get your stuff yet."

"Thanks Meredith. I really appreciate this," she says, and leaves the kitchen.

Dave turns to me and says, "When we find him he'll

end up with a stiffer sentence this time because he broke the restraining order."

"I hope so," I say, though I think it will be just a little harder slap on the hand.

"I'm really sorry about all this," Dave says. "I was hoping you'd have a fresh start when you came back."

"Yeah, me too. I'm beginning to think coming here was just plain stupid. I had a job and a little apartment—true, we didn't have much else, but at least I didn't have to worry about Raymond," I say, my voice heavy with despair.

Dave is silent for a few moments. "I guess you're the only one who can decide if everything you came here for is worth it. And you can go whenever you choose, if it's not."

"You're right," I say. "I just have to find out if it's all worth it."

Chapter 10

I get a call from Terry Dennison a few days later. He's a beer distributor—a nice guy who needs a room for a few nights. He used to be on a regular route through here when I worked here as a teenager, but he says he's retired now, just helping someone out this week.

"I have a man coming to get rid of a colony of bats in the hotel attic," I tell him. "I scheduled it for when I didn't have any hotel guests, so nobody would be disturbed by it. I'm living here in the hotel. but I was going to leave for a few nights too. Bats really creep me out," I say.

"They're nothing to be afraid of. It's rare for a bat to hurt a person," he says.

"It doesn't really matter how many people tell me great things about bats," I say. "It's not going to change how I feel about them!"

"Sorry, I won't mention bats again!" Terry laughs. "But can't you help me out? The old guy at the Greenway will probably rent me a room for a few days, but those rooms are terrible!"

"I would like to give you a room," I say, "But I don't think I can." I don't want to be here when the Bat Be Gone guy is working and I can't very well leave if I have a hotel guest. "The bats have a strange smell, and they're noisy sometimes. You might not get enough sleep."

"Well the Greenwood smells funny too! It's not that noisy, in fact it's pretty dead, but it does smell!" he laughs, trying to convince me.

"I know you're trying to guilt me into this, but you can't tell me anything about the Greenway that I don't already know. I used to live there!"

"No kidding?" he asks.

"Yeah, that's where I lived right after I got out of high school. How many apartment buildings do you think there are in Crossroads, anyway?"

"Oh, yeah, I guess that's the only one."

"Hard to believe it used to be a grand hotel, and people came from miles around to stay there. As a matter of fact, Mona and Evan stayed there on their wedding night, but they said it was already pretty shabby by then. They got married at Christmas time, so it was really cold. The place was still a hotel then, but it was on its last legs, and the heating system wasn't working."

"It was their honeymoon? Then they probably enjoyed keeping each other warm!" Terry says, and we both laugh. It's good to joke around a little; let go of the stress I've been dealing with—Raymond, who is still evading police, and Jean, who is staying here with us.

"Actually, the bats are really not my biggest concern," I say, before telling Terry about Raymond and Jean. "The police haven't found him yet, and who knows if he'll show up here again. So it's not just bats that are worrying me right now."

"I've been carrying a weapon every day and night since Viet Nam," he says. "You won't have to worry while I'm there."

"Maybe to you Raymond wouldn't be much of a threat,

but I'm scared of him. Every day and night I wonder if he's going to break in, and I have my son to worry about too, not to mention everyone else who comes and goes around here! Thank goodness I don't have any customers right now."

"This Raymond person will think twice before trying anything with me," Terry says, making me feel a little better.

"Thanks," I say. "But I don't know if it'll work out. I have to rearrange some plans on this end. I'll call you back to let you know."

In a few hours I have it all set. Jean and Jenny will stay in Mona and Evan's old trailer for a few days, and Grant will stay with Mona and Evan at their new house.

"Thanks Mona," I tell her on the phone. "I'll add this to the list of big fat favors that I owe you."

"Just wait until I call all these favors in! I've been sitting around thinking up ways you can repay me for everything!" she says with a chuckle.

On the afternoon of September twenty-fourth, the day the bat removal is scheduled to take place, I help get Jenny and Jean settled in at Mona and Evan's trailer, which is only a few hundred yards from the new house. Grant is happily playing with Mona's grandkids' toys, even though I brought a box of his toys for him. On the drive home, in spite of my worry about the more urgent matters at hand, I think of how relieved I'll be to have the bats gone...for that smell to start fading and the noises to disappear. When I return to The Serenade, the hotel looby desk phone is ringing. It's the man from Bat Be Gone.

"Hey, uh, my wife has gone into labor—we'll be going to the hospital pretty soon," he says, "so I'm going to have to reschedule."

"Oh," I say, trying to conceal my disappointment. Of course this takes priority over getting rid of the bats, but it means I'll have to plan our hotel exodus again when he can reschedule. "I understand," I tell him. "Good luck and congratulations to you and your wife!" I add.

"Thanks. I'll call you in a few days," he says.

I sink down into one of the comfy lobby chairs, and just sit there for a few minutes. Terry isn't due to arrive for another few hours, so there isn't much reason to stay in the deserted hotel. I can't sit idly for long—my mind will start racing with a million thoughts—so I go down to the kitchen to help out until Terry gets here. He's a talker, full of jokes and stories about all the little towns and customers on his route. He likes shooting the breeze over a beer, and I'm looking forward to catching up with him.

I've just peeled a huge container of potatoes for home fries when the kitchen phone rings. I instantly think it's Mona calling to say that there's something wrong with Grant, so I run over to the phone on the back wall of the kitchen.

"Hello?" I ask nervously.

"Meredith?" a man's voice says, confusing me.

"Terry?" I ask, suddenly recognizing his voice.

"Did I pull you out of the north forty?" he asks. "Sounds like you're out of breath."

"Oh, sorry," I say. "I thought it was going to be Mona," I start to explain, then add, "never mind. What's up?"

"Unfortunately, I'm broken down in Havre, so I won't be getting to The Serenade tonight. I won't know until tomorrow how long the repairs will take. They might have to order parts," he says disgustedly.

"Wow! You and the bat man were the only ones I had scheduled for today and you both cancelled!" I say.

"Him too? Wow, I'm really sorry," he says. "I know you went to a lot of trouble for me."

"Don't apologize. It's not something you could have planned for," I reassure him. "I'll wait to hear from you then. Thanks for letting me know."

"Okay. I'll call you tomorrow," he says, and hangs up.

I stand by the phone a few seconds after I hang up,

amazed at how my day has gone.

"Meredith, are you here to help, or what?" Charlie yells. I can always count on him to get my feet back on the ground. He's getting behind on filling orders, so I grab one to work on.

At closing time I go over to assist Gabe, who has been helping out washing dishes. He's not used to kitchen work— he's been relocated from the hotel desk job for the off-season—and he looks pretty tired out. I decide to wash the pots and pans while he finishes with the things in the dishwasher.

"What do you think of this new machine?" I ask him.

"This is new?" he asks, surprised. "From all the noise I thought it was a dinosaur," he says.

"You should have heard the old one," I say, laughing. "It's not a fun job, I know. I've done it a gazillion times. But at least this one won't break down all the time. And you won't always be stuck doing this job while you're working here," I assure him. "You can move around to other positions. We'll talk to Mona about it. She's in charge of the work flow in the kitchen and restaurant."

"Okay, thanks," he says.

I have a policy that nobody leaves in the evening until everyone's tasks are finished, and that means that everyone pitches in to help, even with tasks they don't usually do. I tell them when I hire them that sooner or later there will come a day when they find themselves behind in their work, and having everyone else pitch in at closing will be a blessing. It works with everyone except Charlie, who leaves as soon as he cooks his last order. A little after nine I say goodnight to everyone at the front door, and thank them for their hard work, then I go make sure the bar is closing down. I had told the bar employees that we would be closing early tonight and it wouldn't be fair to ask them to stay later now, just because the man from Bat Be Gone cancelled.

I lock up and walk down the corridor to the hotel,

debating whether I should stay here overnight or go to Mona's and sleep on her couch, but I'm so tired I'm not sure I should even get behind the wheel to drive. I'd have to be here at four in the morning to start kitchen prep work for breakfast, and Grant isn't expecting me until tomorrow afternoon, so I decide I'm just going to go to our suite, lock the door and go to bed. I get ready for bed and turn on my radio, blocking out most of the skitters and flutters coming from the attic. I tune in to the Phone Pearl Show that broadcasts from several hundred miles away on a station that only comes in clearly in the evening. Pearl has a good sense of humor; she's good to listen to for a few minutes in the evening.

"Hello caller, welcome to the Phone Pearl Show. This is Pearl," says an old lady's voice.

"Hi Pearl," the caller, a young woman, says. "I'm calling because I have this problem with my husband..."

"Hmmm...is this suitable for a family program?" Pearl asks.

"Yes, it's not that kind of problem," the caller says with an embarrassed chuckle.

"Oh, shucks. No, seriously, out with it! What's the problem?"

"Well, my husband is normally the breadwinner in our household, and I have stayed home to take care of our two small children," the caller explains. "But recently, he got laid off. So I've been working while he looks for another good job."

"You're lucky you could do that," Pearl says.

"I know," the caller agrees. "But you see, when my husband was working, he'd come home at night and want me to have the kids in their pj's, already fed and in bed. He wanted to eat his dinner and watch TV with no interruptions because he was tired after working all day. I was tired too, but not earning any money of course, so I did my best to accommodate him."

"Oh, so he's a knuckle dragger?" Pearl asks.

"In some ways, yes," says the caller. "But now I'm the one who's at work all day. When I come home I need a little peace to eat dinner and relax before I start in with the kids," she says in a frustrated voice.

"This is just temporary until he finds another job, right?"

"Right."

"You need to unwind just as much as he does, so you should just swing by a fast food restaurant for your dinner, sit in their parking lot with your music on and relax until you feel like going home!"

"I might just try that."

"Good! Call me and let me know how it goes, will you?" The caller says she definitely will, thanks Pearl, and hangs up.

"That was pretty easy," Pearl says. "Does anyone have a tough problem? Call the Phone Pearl Show and let me know!" I laugh and turn off the radio, get the novel off my bedside table, then read for however long it takes to finally drift off to sleep.

FIRE! I wake up to a loud crackling sound, and the smell of smoke. I pick up my phone and call for help, but my voice is drowned out by a loud explosion. I shout my information and pray they heard me, because I can't hear them. Through the windows I catch a glimpse of a person wearing something long and light colored dashing across the parking lot below. I hope whoever it is will get help.

In the bathroom I grab a few towels to wet at the sink. I get the flashlight off my nightstand and go to my bedroom door. Holding one towel over my mouth and nose I reach up and turn the doorknob. It's warm, but I pull the door open—I have to get downstairs!I crawl out in the hallway a few feet. The sprinkler system is raining on me, and now I can hear the upstairs smoke alarm over the roar of the flames. I begin to stand, but a succession of explosions downstairs sends a burst of heat up the staircase, scaring me back down to a crawl-ing position. I crawl as far as a few yards from the edge of the staircase, where I look through the railings and see to my horror that the left half of the lobby is engulfed in flames. I'm terrified and shaking, but I know I have to get down the stairs before they burn through.

I hold the towel tightly to my face and run toward the staircase, but my vision is obscured with the smoke, and I don't notice one of Grant's toys until my foot slides on it and I overshoot the top stair. I fall halfway down the stairs, ending in an agonized heap. My left ankle throbs with excruciating pain, and the smoke and panic barely let me breathe. I try to pull myself up by the stair rail, but I can't stand. I get down on my hands and knees, crawling sideways down the next few stairs. Gasping for breath and strength, I will myself to go on. The fire's roar is terrible, and the heat and smoke are getting more intense. My eyes hurt too badly to keep them open, and now I'm feeling my way blindly. Suddenly, in the midst of the chaos, I hear someone shouting my name. I feel myself being scooped up in strong arms and carried out of hell, just as I lose consciousness.

I dream that I see Pete's face through a haze. I try to sit up, to hold him, but my body is leaden and I have no strength to move.

"Don't, Meredith. Lie still," I hear him say, but it sounds like he's a million miles away. I keep dream-waking, seeing his face over and over, but I never speak. "I love you," he says. It could have been seconds or years until I hear him say again, "I love you." Then he disappears.

"Meredith?" I hear a pleasant voice that I have heard be-fore but can't identify. "Meredith? Can you hear me?" I open my eyes and see Lei, my high school math tutor, who I saw at Roma's party. I can't imagine where I am or why she's here. I feel so out of myself, my mind is floating around.

"You're probably wondering what's going on," she says softly. I try to tell her she's right, but I can't seem to get any words out. "You were in a fire," she says. I immediately think of Grant. I can't remember where he is, and raise my head off the pillow as far as I can in a panic, but she reads my mind. "Grant's fine. He's with Mona, just where you left him."

I put my head back on the pillow, relieved.

"Your left ankle is broken, and there are second degree burns on your legs and hands," Lei says. "But Doctor Anderson, who has been taking care of you, says you'll heal."

"I'm a psychologist," she says. "I work part-time here at the regional hospital. I told your doctor that I wanted to look in on you because we're friends."

I nod that I understand.

"Tomorrow morning Mona will come see you, okay?"

"Grant?" I manage to ask.

"You'll probably see him tomorrow, too."

I nod okay, then fall asleep.

The next time I wake up, I see Mona and Evan smiling at me.

"Hey, Meredith. How're you feeling?" Mona asks in a quiet, stilted voice I don't think I've ever heard her use.

"Terrible," I say, wincing from the pain that is shooting out from every part of my body. "Where's Grant?" I ask. It suddenly seems like years since I've seen him.

"I dropped him off at school this morning," Evan says. "He asked me to tell you he loves you," he adds.

"I'll bring him in the afternoon," Mona says reassuringly. "He misses you terribly."

"I really need to see him," I say, wiping away tears with my bandaged hands.

Mona grabs a tissue out of her purse and wipes my face. "Doctor Anderson said that your hands and legs should heal pretty well," she says, "but that you'll have to be off your ankle a while."

"My friend Lei was here. She told me," I say, pausing a second before asking if they had seen Pete at the hospital.

"I don't know if Pete's heard about the fire or not, hon," Mona says gently. Do you want me to try to get a hold of him? I can call his folks."

Mona and Evan glance at each other, and I realize that I only dreamed Pete's visit.

"It seemed like he was here. He told me that he loved me, but I couldn't talk," I say sadly. "No, don't call his folks."

"Okay," Mona says, "but let me know if you change your mind."

"I don't even know how long I've been here—when did it happen?"

"Three nights ago," Mona says.

Suddenly I'm back in The Serenade, surrounded by the horrifying flames. Mona leans down over me, her cheek touching mine as she strokes my head soothingly. Evan gently touches my shoulders with his big calloused hands and suddenly I start sobbing uncontrollably.

"It's all over. You're safe now," Mona says.

"But The Serenade is gone!" I cry, mourning Uncle Duck's prize.

"The bar and restaurant are still there," Evan says. It'll just take some cleaning up from smoke damage."

"Does anyone know how the fire...?"

Nobody speaks for a long moment. "Maybe we should wait to talk about this..." Evan starts.

"Please! Tell me! What happened?" I sob. "I need to know!"

"Dave says it was arson," Evan says finally.

I know in an instant that Raymond did it. The knowledge that he actually wanted to see me dead is horrifying. No matter how much he hurt me in the past, I never thought he would have killed me. I don't want to talk anymore. I want to curl up, put the blanket over my face and fade away. Then Mona catches my eye and starts talking, fast, like she's afraid to let the room be quiet.

"Don't worry about the business," Mona says. "Sam and I talked to the employees—they all know that they'll be back at work real soon. It won't take too long to get the place cleaned up. Sam's keeping an eye on the finances—paying the bills and stuff—and I'm keeping track of everything else. Jenny's okay, too, she's just worried about you. Jenny and Jean are still in the trailer and Grant can stay with us while you're in the hospital, then when they release you, you can all stay in the trailer as long as you need to," she adds. "Jean wants to stay and help out until you're better."

"No," I shake my head. "Raymond. If he finds out she's with us, he might come over. I don't think it's Jean he's after, it's me. Because I told him he wasn't getting any part of what I inherited."

"I guess it's because she feels partly responsible for all this," Mona says, "and she wants to make up for it some-how."

"Why would she be responsible? Raymond's been mean for years, long before she even knew him," I say.

"I told her that, but no matter what, you can't really take care of everything right now," Mona says. "You're going to need help. So I'll stay with you if you don't want Jean to help. I'll hire someone to replace me at The Serenade. The doctor said it should be about six to eight weeks before you're able to get around very well."

"No, don't do that," I say, imagining The Serenade running without Mona. "I guess I better accept Jean's offer. But what about Raymond? What if he tries to take Grant? Just… to get back at me?"

"We'll keep a very close eye on Grant. The police are going to catch up to Raymond," Evan says. "There are a lot of them out there looking for him."

"Okay," I say. I'm feeling worse as the minutes tick by, and I realize that the pain medication is wearing off. "How's Grant doing, do you think?"

"He's very worried about you," Mona says, "but we've been keeping him busy. He's missing one of his 'mens', as he calls them. He's turned the house upside down looking for it. He thought he packed it with the others."

"Those mens," I say with a sigh. "That's how I broke my ankle."

"What do you mean?" Evan asks.

"I knew I had to get downstairs fast or I was going to be trapped up there in the fire, so I was running for the stairs and I slid on one of his little toys and fell down the stairs."

"Oh my God! That's awful!" Mona exclaims.

"I don't want Grant to know," I say, just as there is a short rap on the door and Lei comes in.

"Hi everyone," she says. "Nice to see you, Mona, Evan. How are you feeling today, Meredith?" she asks me.

"I really need something for the pain," I say.

"Well," Mona says abruptly, "I need to get back to The Serenade. We'll bring Grant in later today."

"They're very concerned about you," Lei says, after Mona and Evan leave.

"They're the salt of the earth," I say. Do you know them?"

"Just from the last few days. They came several times to see you when you were sleeping, and I got to talk with them for a while. I'm glad you have such good friends." she says. "Mona told me that your mom's in Florida and I already knew about Raymond, so I let them in your room as family," she explains. "I'll go get someone for your pain medication," she says.

"How long do you think I'll be here?" I ask. "I don't want to be away from Grant much longer."

"I can imagine how tough this has been for you, being away from your son," she says. "But Doctor Anderson has to make the decision of when to discharge you. He'll be in to tomorrow morning and you can talk with him about that. Now, I better get someone to take care of your medication. That will help you sleep, so you'll have more energy when Grant is here later on today," she says with a smile. "I'll check in on you a little later."

"Thanks, Lei," I say as she leaves the room. I hear the fading click of her heels as she walks down the corridor to the nurse's station.

When Doctor Anderson tells me this morning, thirteen days after the fire, that I can go home, I act like it's great news, but instead of happiness I'm overcome by a horrifying mixture of despair, failure, and fear. Grant is smart enough to realize that if he had been at home with me, he would have been in the fire too. All his life I've kept him safe, but I'm afraid this will end his trust in me. I've also lost Uncle Duck's hotel, which he trusted me to take care of. On top of all that, I know now that Raymond wants me dead, and I'm frightened of what he's going to try next.

I'm waiting for Evan to pick me up from the hospital when Dave Bunsen, who has come to see me with Roma several times since I've been here, stops by. So far he hasn't mentioned the fire to me, but today he sits in the armchair by the bed and says, "Meredith, are you up to talking now? About the fire?" I don't want to. I don't think I'll ever want to, but this is Dave, my friend, and the law. I nod an okay.

"Can you think of anything or anybody suspicious you might have seen the night of the fire?" he asks.

"I did see a person running through the parking lot that night, just after I woke up and realized there was a fire," I tell him. "There was a loud explosion, and right after that, I noticed someone running across the parking lot. Whoever it was had on a long white coat or something like that. I didn't really have much time to look because of the fire, so

I can't say much about it."

"Is there anything else you think might help with the case?

"There were several more loud explosions after that, like fireworks noise."

"It was arson—I imagine you've heard that already?"

"Evan and Mona told me," I say quietly. "They weren't going to say anything, but I needed to know what happened."

"Of course you did," Dave says. "You may have heard bottles exploding. Gasoline had been poured all over, and probably that cabinet of wine and liquor behind the staircase exploded from the intense heat. I remember that there had been a theft from that closet a few years back. You kept it locked, right?"

"Yes."

"Besides you and me, who else knew what was in that cabinet, or had keys?"

"Just Mona, Charlie and I, as far as I know. I didn't even know what was in it until I came back. Uncle Duck didn't want it to be a temptation to employees, so that's why it's out of sight, behind the staircase. I think I'm the only one who's opened it since I've been back. That wine is for romance packages or for guests who are celebrating an anniversary or something special," I say, the knowledge that there will be no more romance or celebrations in the hotel sinking in with my words.

"I'm guessing that whoever did this didn't expect that cabinet to explode like it did, and may have been injured by a blast. There was gasoline poured in other parts of the first floor, but it looks like they had to get out before they could set the other fires."

"So he had planned to destroy everything?" I ask quietly.

"The fire department and I think that whoever it was," he says, "had planned to burn the whole building down."

"It was Raymond, go ahead and say it," I say.

"I can't. I don't have proof," Dave says, but I can tell he's thinking it's a good bet. "The lady you hired to help Jenny— uh, Jean?" he asks.

"Yes?"

"What was her situation with Raymond when the fire happened? Since the day he was at The Serenade?"

"I know she's kind of scared of him, but she also talks about him like she misses him and still loves him," I say. "I guess she'll be living with us in Mona and Evan's old place until I'm back on my feet," I add, explaining what Mona had said about Jean feeling partly responsible for the fire.

Dave nods and asks, "What kind of person is she? Do you think she would take part in a crime?"

"Not unless she was forced into it," I say. "Jean is a very likable, sweet woman. That's why I hired her. Jenny and Grant get along great with her, too."

"Do you think the person you saw in the parking lot the night of the fire was Raymond's size?"

"I don't know. It was too dark to see much," I say again. "Dave, did you ever think Raymond would really try to kill me?"

"He's no good, but I didn't take him for a killer. Remember, he's innocent until proven guilty," Dave reminds me. "But he's certainly a person of interest. When we find him, he'll go to jail and he'll have his day in court."

"I'm scared just thinking that he's out there, and could show up anywhere, at any time!"

" I promise," Dave says, hugging me gently, "that we will do our best to find him."

Returning to my life, centered now in Mona and Evan's old trailer, has been a painful and exhausting mental and physical trial. The burns on my legs, which affected my knees and calves, are healing fine, the doctor says. I can walk with crutches for a little while at a time, which hurts my hands but spares my legs some of the pain, but I don't want to. I don't want to do anything.

Grant stands next to my bed for a while every day before and after school, and in the evening, his blue eyes worried, while he tells me things he did at school. It's odd—it never used to be hard to talk to Grant, but now I can't seem to think of what I'm supposed to say or do next. Not just with him, with anyone. I haven't heard from Pete. He probably heard about the fire, but I haven't gotten a card or a call to see how I am. I guess we're really through. I think about the dream I had of him in the hospital, but I don't mention it to anyone again.

I've thought a lot about MaryAnn lately, sometimes while I lie awake waiting for my next pain pill, and sometimes I dream about her—loud, exhausting dreams that many times end with her driving her car off a cliff. I wonder if the dreams are signs that I am close to driving off my own cliff.

One day Jenny knocks on my bedroom door and comes in before I say anything. I'm lying in bed, staring out the window.

"Feeling any better?" she asks in a hopeful voice.

"I've been thinking a lot about MaryAnn," I say. "It really bothers me."

"What bothers you?" Jenny asks.

"We were best friends since we were little, but she wrote in her journal that she thought I wouldn't forgive her for what she did with Raymond. Then, according to the police, she drove off a cliff on the coast highway on purpose. She killed herself instead of even giving me the chance to forgive her, and I couldn't understand it at the time. But now I'm beginning to understand."

Jenny comes to my side and clasps my hands firmly in hers. I hear desperation in her voice as she says, "You can't understand MaryAnn's choices, because you aren't living in the same circumstances. Imagine having to make a terrible decision that separates you from your child because it appears, even if it's not true, to be in their best interest at the time!"

"That's what I'm talking about," I say, before turning over and going to sleep.

I hobble through the trailer on crutches once in a while, just to look out a window, but the dirty patches of snow, brown grass and dead winter trees make me feel worse, so I just go back to bed and back to sleep. Sleep is the best way to get rid of all of it.

One day I wake up around noon to hear Mona speaking in a distressed voice on the kitchen phone.

"She's very depressed," I hear her say, "and she sleeps most of the time. Then the pain pills—I don't know if she needs them or if she's using them just so she can sleep longer! And poor Grant! Meredith's normally a very good mother, but now she barely seems to notice him."

I don't know who she's telling, and I really don't care. I close my eyes and go back to sleep.

The next afternoon I hear a little rapping at my bedroom door.

"Hmm?" I say, not even wanting to open my mouth to speak.

The door opens a little, and I see Lei.

"Hi, Meredith," she says cheerfully. "I hear you're not feeling so well?"

"I'm just tired," I say. "Why are you here?" I ask, confused. "You do house calls?"

"Mona called me. Everyone's very worried about you. May I talk to you for a little while?" she asks. She looks around for a chair, and not seeing one, sits on the edge of my bed.

"No extra chairs," I say.

"That's fine," she says, then squints a little, searching for her approach. "Meredith, I've known you for a long time. I think when I was your math tutor the year I was a senior and you were a freshman, we got to be pretty good friends. Don't you?"

"I guess so, yes," I say.

"I'm really glad that we ran into each other again at Roma's party and got reacquainted, though I'm sorry that it was such a sad thing that brought us this close together."

"Me too," I say, hoping she's not going to make me cry.

"I told you at the hospital that I'm a psychologist—that's why I'm here. From what Mona told me on the phone, it sounds like you're depressed, and maybe I can help. First of all, it's no wonder if you're depressed. I know you're still in pain, and that is no doubt part of the problem. Fighting pain for an extended period of time is wearing on a person, but you do have to know when you're using the meds, and when they start using you," she says cautiously.

"You think I'm abusing the pain pills?" I ask.

"People around you are concerned that you are," she says gently. "I hope you don't mind, but I talked to Dr. Anderson about it, and he and Jean are going to help you get a handle on that."

I nod as she continues.

"You've been through a very traumatic experience. But I suspect this was the straw that broke the camel's back. If you want to tell someone your problems, you and I are the only ones who will know what is said. I promise you."

"It's too complicated to tell," I say.

Lei nods, then sits for a little while on the edge of my bed. "I have a question for you," she finally says. "I've been wondering about it since the party at Roma's."

"Okay," I say.

"It's about MaryAnn," she says, then apologizes quickly when she sees my face.

"No, it's okay," I say quietly. "It's just that I've been thinking a lot about her lately."

"What happened?" Lei asks.

"Are we alone in the house?"

"Yes, Jenny and Jean are in town shopping, Grant's at school, and Mona and Evan are at work," she says.

"She died," I say, looking at my lap, trying not to cry.

"Oh, Meredith! I'm so sorry! When did it happen? How?" Lei asks, reaching across the bed to hold my hands in hers.

I take a deep breath and tell her everything from Raymond and MaryAnn, losing Pete, taking on Grant and Jenny, and my inheritance. Lei lowers her head a few times while I'm talking. I can see that she's close to crying herself.

"And now the fire, and physical injuries," she says when I finally finish the story.

"And now the fire," I echo her. "I miss MaryAnn so much!" I cry. "I really need her now!"

"Oh Meredith, I'm so sorry you've had to go through all of this!" Lei says softly. "I remember how close you two were. I was away at college, that's why I didn't hear about it, I guess. You and MaryAnn were true friends. Some people never have a true friend at all."

"Some friend she turned out to be! I need her now! I have too much to deal with, and I need her back!" I say, unable to hold back my sobs any longer. Lei rubs my back softly until my crying subsides.

"I'm going to help you get though this," she finally says, in a calm voice. "It is too much to deal with, you're right. If you look at everything all together. But if you take it all apart, it becomes separate little manageable pieces, which is how we can work at tackling the bigger picture." She takes a notebook out of her briefcase and draws two columns on a piece of paper.

"On one side we'll write what the problem is, and on the other side we'll write whatever you have to say about it," she says. "What would you like to start with?"

I think for a few seconds, and then, sniffling, say, "Mary-Ann."

Lei writes the name in one column. "What would you like to say about MaryAnn?"

"That I miss her every day…" I hang my head and press my fingers to my forehead to keep the tears from starting again. "And I want to tell her everything that's happened. I want her to know I've done the best I could with Grant, but that she should have stayed to raise him herself! I'm so mad at her!"

"Do you think you can ever forgive her for taking her own life?"

"I can't answer that," I say. "Sometimes I tell myself I have no right to judge, because I have no way to know what she was feeling. But other times I just get so upset, thinking that she could always have told me her problems, so I could have helped her figure them out, but instead she just checked out."

"Have you ever imagined what it would be like, to have been in her shoes? I imagine she thought it was impossible for her to tell you what she did."

"I'm sure it was terrible for her. Sometimes I can forgive her for what she did, and sometimes I can't. I'll never forgive him, though."

"Let's talk about him," Lei says, writing 'Raymond' in the left column.

"I hate him! For all the times he hurt me and Mom, and for being Grant's father, and for the fire! I don't want to talk about him!"

Lei writes quickly in the column, clears her throat, then asks, "What about Pete?"

"I've always loved Pete. I've never loved any other man. I want so badly for us to get back together, but something always goes wrong. Like that stupid photo album I told you about, that Cathy showed Pete the last time I saw him."

"You say you want to get back together with Pete, but is he worth the effort?" Lei asks.

"What do you mean? "I ask sharply.

"Well, how much work is he worth? Is he worth you getting well and finding him? Or do you just want to talk about missing him?"

"He didn't even call or come see me in the hospital! Everyone in five counties must have heard about the fire!" I almost shout

"He did visit you in the hospital!" she says. "But you were too sedated to talk to him."

"You saw him?"

"Yes. I happened to be there when he got there, and I told the nurses he could go in," she says.

"I thought I had dreamed it! Mona said a nurse told her that she and Evan were the only ones who had come in! He said he loved me! But why hasn't he called me or anything since then? I mean, he could call The Serenade and anyone could tell him where I was if he wanted to see me," I say.

"I suggest you go visit Pete's parents, let them know how you are, and that you want to talk to Pete," she adds. "They'll probably put you in touch with him."

"I can't just barge in on them like that!" I say, wondering why she would suggest such a thing.

"Please trust me on this, and go visit his parents," she says again. "Before I go, there's something else I want to tell you," she says. "I know you're a good, loving mother. But Mona told me that she thinks your depression has caused you to turn away from Grant. Roma also mentioned to me the other day—I see her quite a bit because we're neighbors—that Grant has not been himself at school since the fire, and she's concerned about him. I told her I would talk to you about it. You're the only person who is really his, Meredith, and right now he doesn't even have you."

"I hate myself, Lei. I've let him down just like my mom

let me down," I say sadly.

"Please don't hate yourself. Just try to understand yourself. Tell me, what was it like between you and your mother?" she asks.

"She wanted to be my pal, but not my mom. I always told myself that if I had kids someday, they would know they could depend on me. Now I don't know if Grant will trust me again."

"I'm pretty sure he will," she says. "Why don't you try him when he gets home this afternoon?"

"I'm going to give him a big hug," I say, "as soon as I see him. Let him know I'm feeling better."

"Are you? Feeling better?" she asks me seriously.

"Some. I feel better knowing that Pete really came to the hospital. And it does help to talk about all the problems. "

"I hope your relationship with Pete works out, but you have to put Grant before that. You have to get healthy yourself while you rebuild your connection with Grant. I'll be back next week to see how you're doing, but I can talk to you sooner if you want to."

"Thanks, Lei. I really appreciate all this," I say.

"No need for thanks, just get better," she says. "Remember, you need to help Grant get through this too."

"I will," I say.

"That's what I hoped I would hear," she says. "Just call me at home if you want to talk." She smiles warmly at me as she leaves my room.

I hear Jean and Jenny chatting in the living room as they come in from shopping.

"Hello!" I hear Jenny's voice.

"Oh, hi, I'm Dr. Jonsson. Mona called me yesterday about Meredith. I just finished visiting her."

"It's nice to meet you," I hear Jean say. "I'm Jean, and this is Jenny."

"I'm happy to meet both of you," Lei says.

"A house call?" Jean says in a surprised voice.

"I don't usually make house calls, but Meredith is a friend."

"Oh, that's good of you to help our Meredith that way," Jenny says. "Did you say your last name is Jonsson?"

"That's right," Lei says.

"Where is your family from?" Jenny asks.

"Well, originally my family was from China. My great grandfather came here first, to work on the railroads. Then his son, my grandfather, was an artist and woodworker. But if you were wondering about my married name, Jonsson—they were settlers here in Crossroads."

"Do you mind if I ask how your last name is spelled?" Jenny asks, and Lei spells it for her.

"Do you know if any of your husband's ancestors built the pink house on Sixth Street? It has a lot of gingerbread, and is across the street from the market?"

"As a matter of fact, his great-great-aunt and uncle did," she says. "One of his ancestors who lived there was named Anna."

"Anna Jonsson! She befriended me when I moved to Crossroads! Oh my goodness!"

"Small world!" Lei exclaims. "I'm sorry, I have to get back to my office, Jenny, but I know my husband and I would really enjoy talking with you more about this."

"Oh that sounds wonderful! Yes, let's arrange it some time!" Jenny says excitedly. In a moment she is in my room, smiling at me.

"Meredith! Did you hear?"

"Yes, I did!" I say. She sounds so happy that you'd think she had just run into Anna herself.

Chapter 11

Today will be the first time in the six weeks since the fire that Grant and I are going to The Serenade. My burns have healed pretty well now, and my left ankle, though still weak, has healed. Uncle Duck's old truck is too hard to drive right now, but I can drive my automatic, so at least I can get around. Lei has been a strong shoulder for me through this ordeal. I appreciate all my friends and the help they've given me, but my talks with Lei have really helped me start to feel like myself again.

"Hi honey!" I say when Grant steps down off the school bus at noon. "How was school?"

"It was fun! We traced our hands and made Thanksgiving turkeys out of colored paper! To decorate with," he explains. "I made four!"

"You can never have too many turkey decorations," I say. "I can't wait to see them."

When we get in the house Grant gets the turkeys out of his bag. I tape them to the living room windows, then we stand back admiring his handiwork for a minute.

"After you have lunch I think we'll drive over to The Serenade. I've only seen Charlie once since the fire, and I miss him and everyone else, don't you?"

"I miss them, but it won't look the same, Mom," he warns me.

"Right, because of the fire," I say.

"Yeah, and right after it happened I heard lots of kids at school say that it looked real bad," he says, obviously worried at how I will take this.

I stop and gently turn his face up toward mine. "You must have been real upset to hear that, and you didn't even tell me all this time?" I ask, taking his hand.

"I was afraid to tell you, because you were already so sad," he says, keeping himself from crying.

"I have such a tough little man. Thank you for worrying about me," I say. "I love you so much."

"I love you too, Mom," he says, hugging me.

"I think I'm getting better now. Lei has been talking to me, helping me out," I say, comforting him.

"I like Lei, too," he says. "She talked to me sometimes at the hospital when Mona and Evan brought me to see you."

"We know some pretty nice people, don't we?"

"Yep! And don't forget Jenny and Jean!"

"Right. Jenny and Jean are also nice people. So, we'll go to The Serenade after you eat. I can't start getting the place fixed if I don't even know what has to be done, okay?"

"Okay!"

I had heard reports of the initial fire damage, and Mona keeps me up to date on how the cleanup is progressing, but no amount of information could have prepared me for the shock of actually seeing The Serenade with my own eyes. When we drive into the parking lot I shudder at the sight. Draped over the hotel's skeleton of massive beams is a huge tarp as big as a circus tent, charred ends of the log framework sticking out at the ends. Large red signs on posts warn would-be trespassers to keep out. There are ugly ARSON signs posted by the authorities. I clutch my heart with my hand. I wonder where

Raymond is and what trouble he'll cause next, or if he has seen the aftermath of his handiwork.

"Dear God," I utter.

"You okay, Mom?" Grant asks in a worried voice.

I throw my shoulders back and take a deep breath. Break this mess into manageable pieces, I think, before answering him. "Yes, honey. I'm okay. I'm…I'm surprised, that's all. I know you told me it would look bad, but I'm still surprised. Now it's time for doing something about it, right?"

"Right!" he says.

We go around to the back door of the kitchen so I don't have to limp through the restaurant in front of the customers. I appreciate that they're still coming in, but I'm not ready to talk to everyone about the fire or how I'm doing.

"Meredith! Grant!" Jacob shouts when we walk in the door. He rises from the break table and runs over to help me in. The other six or seven employees in the kitchen shout a welcoming chorus.

"It's great to see you all," I say as Jacob leads me over to the seat he had just occupied. I thank him with a nod and a smile. Charlie actually comes over to me and bends over to hug me.

"How you feeling? " he asks, his voice catching.

"Much better, thanks, Charlie," I say.

"Good. That's real good. Grant? You getting to the school bus on time every morning?" he asks, getting back to his normal drill sergeant voice.

"Every morning," Grant says. "And nobody has to help me," he adds.

"I guess I got you trained, then," he says as he goes back to the grill.

"Yep," Grant says.

"Tons of work to do around here," Mona says. "We've got Thanksgiving to get ready for, ordering, cleaning, plenty of stuff to do. Ready to get to work?" she asks me with a grin.

"Mom's not ready to go back to work yet," Grant says sternly, surprising everyone.

I look up at him and smile at his determination to protect me. "Not today. Today I'm just here to see all of you, and to look at the fire damage," I say. "Is the smoky smell driving you all nuts?" I ask.

"The cleaning service I hired has gotten it to where it's pretty tolerable now, wouldn't you all say?" Everyone agrees with her, which makes me feel a little better.

"I'm going to go see what I can of the inside of the hotel," I say in a few minutes. "Just going to take a quick look and go back home." I tell Grant he can play with the toys in his corner while I go look the hotel over.

"You better let me go with you, Meredith," Jacob says. "I've been in there with the fire department, so I can show you where you can walk pretty safely."

"Okay. Thanks, Jacob," I say.

Jacob leads me part way down the corridor, then pulls back a plastic tarp where the corridor abruptly ends and a blackened forest begins. It's like walking into a nightmare— it takes my breath away. The sour post-fire stink is stronger here, and everywhere that used to be dressed in radiant polished knotty pine, including the prized staircase, is now skeletal, shrouded in black and ashen gray. The rock chimney, standing absurdly at attention, is all that remains of the once grand lobby.

"I'm so sorry, Meredith," Jacob says, looking back at me. "I can't imagine what kind of person would do this."

"Thanks," I say, knowing exactly what kind of person would do it. I blink back tears, thinking what Uncle Duck and the people who helped build this place would say if they saw it now.

"The fire department doesn't want anything touched, and your insurance company might feel that way too," Jacob says.

"Yes, I better talk to Mr. Overgaard about the insurance," I say.

"The safest thing to do is to stay in this area," Jacob says, pointing out an area about eight feet square just past what had been the end of the corridor. "The ceiling and floor are stable here. You have to do your looking from this point," he says. Under the circumstances, I'm happy to accept his direction.

"Look at that!" I exclaim. "I can see some of the top floor still intact!" I say, pointing up to where Grant and I used to live.

"The sprinkler and alarm systems I installed did save some of that, but don't let it fool you," Jacob says. It's just being held up by a few pretty badly burned support beams. It's burned right up to the flooring underneath. I saw it from the back of the building before they put the tarps up in the back." He sees the devastation in my eyes, and adds, "I'm just so, so sorry."

I swallow hard, looking around at the mess again. The antler chandeliers lie in three piles, and I make out a heap in one corner to be the burned trophy heads that had hung high on the walls. The chairs and sofas are piled in another corner, all charred through to the springs.

"Well, I'm sure glad you installed it, then," I say, remembering the discussion I had with the fire department about the new systems I should get, and the day I put the jobs on Jacob's list.

"I doubt you would have survived if I hadn't put them in," he says.

I want to tell him that I didn't even hear the alarm until I was awake and got outside my room that night, but I don't. "Thank goodness for modern technology," I say.

"Yeah," he mutters.

"Well, I've seen enough. Let's go." Jacob nods and gets in front of me. He tries to hold my hand to lead me back to the kitchen, but I shake my hand free.

"The skin on my hands is very sensitive still," I say, glad to have a reason to pull away from him. "And I know I'm limping a little, but I don't need to be led around. Thank you, anyway," I say politely.

When I get back to the kitchen, I motion to Mona that I want to talk to her privately for a minute.

"You okay?" she asks, touching my shoulder.

"Yes, I'm okay. Pretty bad mess in there, huh?" I say, trying to sound collected.

"Yes, terrible," she agrees, grimacing.

"I got the idea that Jacob thinks he saved my life because he installed the sprinkler and alarm system. It was strange, the way he was acting."

"Ah, the white knight syndrome," Mona says. "He'll get over it. Hey, do you think you can have a cup of coffee with me before you go?" I nod yes, and she gets the mugs out, then calls to JoLynn, who is heading out the double doors with a pot of coffee, "Let us have some of that, will ya?"

JoLynn turns around and comes over to us, filling our mugs. "Anything else?" she asks pleasantly.

"That's all, thanks, JoLynn," I say.

I turn to see what Grant's up to in his play corner, "would you like a snack while I have a cup of coffee?" I ask him.

"I'm busy with the blocks Evan made for me, Mom," he says, looking over the little wall at me.

"Okay, that's fine," I say. "Mona, the way Jacob talked, like he saved my life, suddenly made me think of something from the night of the fire that I hadn't remembered until now."

"What's that?" she asks.

"I don't know how I got out of that fire. It seems like after I fell down the stairs, then had to crawl on my hands and knees, it got so bad I was afraid I couldn't go on. And just then, when I guess I was passing out, it seemed that someone scooped me up and got me out of there."

"Dave Bunsen saved you," Charlie says loudly, pulling a tray of dinner rolls out of an oven close to where we are sitting. "The lobby door was locked, so he broke in and carried you outside. Yep, Dave saved your life," he says loudly again I glance at Jacob, who glares at Charlie.

"Dave Bunsen!" I exclaim, noticing that Jacob is leaving by the back door.

Mona looks after Jacob as he leaves, and raises her eyebrows at me.

"Grant!" I call over to him, "did you hear that? Officer Bunsen saved me by carrying me out of the hotel when it was on fire!"

"I always thinked he was cool," Grant says. "They should make an Officer Bunsen super hero!" he says. Everyone in the room laughs.

"That's pretty funny, Grant," I say. 'I can just imagine your little plastic Officer Bunsen, crashing through doors and walls to save people "

"That's not funny! He saved you from the fire!" Grant answers, standing up to stare at me with a hurt expression.

"I'm sorry. I just meant that if I saw you playing with a tiny Officer Bunsen it would look funny, I didn't mean that what he did was funny," I explain. "Saving someone from a fire isn't funny at all."

"Oh, okay," he says, and goes back to playing. In a few seconds he asks, "Mom? What are you going to do about the hotel? To make it look nice again."

"I think we're going to just have it torn down, as soon as the fire department and the insurance company let us," I say.

"You don't want to rebuild?" Charlie asks.

"How can I replace something as wonderful as that hotel? And how would a new building look next to the part that's left?" I ask.

"Easy. You draw what you want, get a good architect

and let them do their job. Tell them it has to look good with the rest of the place. They can make the new look old, you know," Charlie says like he's been studying the topic.

"I realize all that, Charlie, it's just that…"

"What she means is that it won't have the same ambiance, the aura, that the old hotel had," Mona explains.

"Aura, schmaura," Charlie mutters. "I'll bet Duck is rolling over right now. He's probably thinking 'make some money, girls! Build it the way you're going to profit the most! Listen to Charlie!'"

"Maybe Charlie's right," Mona says. "Maybe we're being too sentimental."

"We'll talk more about this later," I say, suddenly too weary to talk anymore. I drink the last drops of coffee in my mug. "Time to go now, Grant," I say, gathering up our coats.

"Mom," Grant asks solemnly on the way home, "do you think the bats got out of the fire okay?"

I think for a second what a gem my child is—that he would even have been thinking about the bats' safety. "I imagine that they did. I think they would have realized it was time to go as soon as it started getting hot," I say. I hope I'm right, even though we're talking about bats.

"Good," he says, looking out the window.

A few mornings after I inspect the hotel damage, I am sitting in the living room of the trailer, going through the stack of get well cards I've received since the fire. I haven't had the mental strength or energy to tackle the task until now. I'm touched that so many people, some I don't even know, cared enough to send a card to me. I note the signatures and log every name on a list so I can thank them properly later. One more for today, I think, picking up a pink envelope. The postmark was from just a few days after the fire, I notice. When I realize that it bears the McBrides' postal delivery route and box number, I nervously tear the envelope open.

'Dear Meredith,' I read in Pete's mother's beautiful script, 'We are so sorry to hear that you have been injured and have suffered such a loss. We are praying every day for your speedy recovery. Let us know if we can help in any way. Thinking of you, Evelyn, Matthew and Pete McBride. Suddenly I decide to take Lei's advice. I check the clock on the living room wall. Nine forty-five. Grant won't be home for several hours still. Plenty of time to go visit Evelyn and Matthew, I think, as I grab my coat, gloves and purse.

Only a few inches of snow remain from the last storm, but the wind is blasting against my car as I drive out the secondary road from Crossroads south toward the McBride ranch. Along the way I see small herds of cattle huddling around groves of scrub pines for shelter from the bitter wind. I remember that Pete said he visits his folks at least once a month. I wonder if his truck will be there, and if I'll actually get out of my car if it is.

I round the last bend before my destination and take a deep breath. The McBride ranch sprawls out in a huge acreage of rich land, extending over many miles of prairie and hills in the distance. I see the cluster of buildings and the old ranch house set far down a gravel lane. Something isn't right, I think, but I can't put my finger on it. Or is it just that I haven't been here for a long time? As I get closer, it hits me— there are no cattle or horses, no men working outside, no dogs, machinery, trucks or cars at all. The place is deserted. My heart skips a beat as I pull off the road at the entrance to the McBride's property, stop my car and lean heavily against the door to open it against the roaring wind. A huge padlock and chain hang down from the steel farm gate.

I remember that the return address on the card the McBride's had sent me was the address I had always known. It had been sent just a few days after the fire, so whatever happened here must have been since then. I wonder what has caused them to leave this place that they all love so much.

All the way back to Mona's place I worry about Matthew. He could have died, and I wouldn't even know it. I imagine Pete and Evelyn without Matthew, grief stricken, and tears spring to my eyes.

That evening I go over to see Mona in her new house. Sunny yellow paint greets me as I walk in the kitchen door. The odors of fresh paint, new carpet, and wallpaper glue mingle to create a slightly nauseating odor. "It's beautiful in here!" I say, trying to ignore the odor.

"Why, thank you," she says proudly. "Just here to visit?" she asks.

"Actually, I wanted to tell you something," I say. "I went to see Pete's folks today, and…"

"You went to see them? I told you a while back I thought you could call them to find out where Pete was, but wow! You go right on out to their ranch! So, what happened?" she asks.

"They're gone," I say.

"Did you leave a note or anything?"

"No, I mean they're not there at all," I explain. The place was deserted. No vehicles, no machinery, no animals, no people."

"A huge spread like that is deserted and we didn't hear about it?" Mona says in disbelief.

"I want to talk to Pete," I say. "Tomorrow morning I'm going to that market where I ran into Pete's friend Jim. He said the ranch where they were working was about five miles from there. I just want you to know where I'm going," I say.

"Well, be careful. Watch out for patches of ice on the road," she warns me.

"I will," I say. "Thanks for reminding me."

The next morning after Grant leaves for school, I pack a lunch and a thermos of coffee while my car warms up. Charlie is going to pick Grant up at school and keep an eye on him for me so I don't have to rush. I bundle up, including extra thick socks and gloves, but my ankle and hands still hurt in the bitter cold a minute after I leave the house. When I get on the road, I take it easy on the gas, vigilant about patches of ice. I'm comforted knowing that I always have emergency supplies with me, just in case I get stranded anywhere.

In a few hours I reach the store where I had run into Jim in the summer. I remember generally where he had said he was working, and I find it pretty quickly. By the time I'm driving down the gravel road to the ranch, I'm feeling awfully achy, even though the heat works fine in my car. Two large black dogs are barking at my car, so I'm afraid to get out, but I need so badly to get out and stretch. I put my head down on the wheel until the wave of pain in my ankle passes. A middle-aged man wearing a parka comes up to my car and I roll down my window.

"Atlas! Amazon! Go!" he shouts at the dogs, who lumber away. Then, turning to me he asks, "Can I help you?"

"I'm looking for Pete McBride," I say.

"Pete doesn't work here now. You a friend?" he asks, sizing me up.

"Yes," I say. "How about Jim Stewart?"

"Yeah, Jim is here. He's out working somewhere. This just a social call?" he asks, obviously not wanting me to take up Jim's time.

"No, not really. It's a private matter, though. May I see him?" I ask politely.

"Yeah, come on in the house. I'll radio him," he says. "Park over there by the barn," he adds.

I park and get slowly out of my car, then start limping over to where the man is waiting for me. He walks toward me and asks, "What're you limping for?"

"I broke my ankle. It's healed now, just gets real stiff and sore," I say.

"How'd that happen?" he asks.

"Trying to get out of a fire," I say.

"Here," he says, extending an arm for me to steady myself. "Your house catch fire?"

"No, my business. The Serenade, over in Crossroads."

"That was you? Oh geez, that was some bad deal!" he exclaims. "I'm glad to see you're okay, anyway."

"Thanks," I say, as he leads me in the ranch house and motions me to an easy chair. "Coffee?" He asks.

"That would be nice, thanks," I say, taking off my coat and gloves.

In a minute he puts a cup of strong smelling black coffee on the low table in front of me. I thank him again as he goes out the back door, pulling it shut with a loud bang. "Base to five, base to five..." I hear him calling on his radio as he walks away from the house.

Jim is alone when he comes in a few minutes later. "Meredith!" He says, his breath coming out in puffs of steam. "How are you?" He takes his parka off and sits on a chair near me. "I'm so sorry about the fire."

"Thanks, Jim. I'm doing okay now, but I was wondering there for a while," I say.

"I saw in the paper that it was arson," Jim says.

"Probably my ex-stepfather, but like Dave Bunsen says, he's innocent until proven guilty."

"Wow, that's bad," Jim says, shaking his head slowly back and forth. "Are you going to rebuild the hotel?"

"I don't really know yet. I have to wait for some insurance stuff," I say. "But anyway, I came out here looking for Pete. He used to work here with you, I know, but the man I talked to said he doesn't anymore. Do you know where he is?"

"Yeah, Pete's dad had a fall and broke a hip. He was already sick, and the fall only made it worse. He had to go to Great Falls for surgery and then he was going to be in a convalescent home for a while. Pete was setting his mom up in an apartment there, then he was going back to their ranch," he explains. "They have two hired hands, but Pete thought he should be there to oversee things," Jim says.

"How long ago? I went there yesterday and the place is deserted! There's a padlock on the gate! I didn't see any vehicles or people or anything!"

"Really? His dad's surgery was about six weeks ago. Maybe they decided they had to sell the place," Jim says.

"Do you know what might have happened to Nadia?"

"Auctioned off, most likely. Call the auction house just out of Crossroads, they might know where she ended up."

"Thanks, Jim."

"I'm sure glad you're doing okay. I have to get back out there, but I'll walk you to your car."

I stand and put on my coat and gloves, then start limping toward the door.

"That from the fire?" he asks.

"No, it's an old football injury," I laugh. "But seriously, yes, I fell down the stairs trying to get out of the fire, and broke my ankle. Burned my hands and legs, too."

"That's terrible. I'm really sorry," he says, giving me a hug. "Be safe," he says, helping me in my car. "Keep in touch."

"I will. Take care, Jim. Bye." I say, backing slowly out onto the gravel road.

"Good thing you're getting ready to come back to work," Mona says the next evening while I'm doing dishes. Since I've been home we've made sure we get together either at her new place or the trailer every day.

"Why's that? Gabe not keeping up with the dishes?" I ask with a laugh.

"As of today he's a waiter in training!" she says. "But don't worry, I hired another dishwasher."

"I'm not worried. In fact I think I'd rather be loading the dishwasher at The Serenade than piddling around here all day long. I'll be back to work soon."

"That'll be good. I really miss our chit chat—it's what keeps me going," she says. "Okay, enough small talk. So what happened yesterday? Did you find Pete?"

"No, but I found Jim," I say, and tell her what I learned from Jim about Matthew breaking his hip, and that Pete was supposed to have gone back to oversee the ranch.

"What are you going to do now?" she asks.

"Call the stables outside town, see if they have any space available," I say with a grin.

"What? Why?"

"I called this auction house that Jim suggested, to see if they knew where Pete's horse went. Well, I really hit the jackpot! After I told the woman on the phone what I was calling about, it turned out she had bought Nadia herself! I asked her if I could buy her back."

"What did you pay?" Mona asks.

"I asked her what she'd take and she said three thousand," I say. "So I said fine. She's making a profit, but that's okay. I just wanted her back for Pete. Then she asked me how much I'd give for the foal!"

"A foal!"

"Yes! She's six weeks old! I was so thrilled! I offered a thousand dollars for the foal, and she took it!"

"Are you sure you should have bought them without talking to Pete?"

"I wasn't thinking about that. I just know Pete must feel awful that he had to get rid of Nadia. He loves that horse."

"Okay, so you have horses. Now what do you know about taking care of them, town girl? And when are you going to have time, not to mention you really shouldn't be working that hard physically yet," Mona asks in a motherly tone.

"I don't know anything about them, yet." I say. "But I know the stables take care of horses and board them. And maybe I can hire someone there with a horse trailer to go get them for me."

"Gonna make a little trip to the Bridle and Bridal for your horse supplies?" Mona asks.

"I hadn't even thought that far ahead yet. Guess I'm going to have to, my ankle hurts too much to drive anywhere else. But I have a week to pick them up, so I can put that off for a few days."

"You seem to attract unusual situations, you know that?" Mona asks.

"You got that right, sister," I say, shaking my head.

Chapter 12

Mona and I just got the turkey stuffed, and Jean will put it in the oven for us in a few hours. She's still over at the trailer with Grant and Jenny, but they'll come on over here in a little while so they can watch the Thanksgiving parade on Mona's big TV. We only have a little tiny portable one here in the trailer, and parades are so much fun to watch on a bigger screen.

The restaurant and bar at The Serenade have short hours today so all the employees on the schedule can be at home with their families for the majority of the day. Mona and I are leaving for work in just a few minutes, but we plan to be back by home by three for dinner.

I walk into Mona's living room and stare for a few minutes out the picture window. I can see just the tiniest hint of dawn creeping up on the horizon, outlining the distant mountains in a purple silhouette. I'll never get tired of this beautiful place, I think.

"C'mon, let's get a move on, girl," Mona says, throwing on her coat and pulling her gloves out of her pockets.

"I want you to know that I really appreciate you letting us stay here, and all that you've done for us," I say to Mona while we're driving to The Serenade.

"You're always welcome, you know that," she says.

"I know. And you're welcome where ever I call home in the future, too," I say.

Later I'm peeling potatoes to mash for Thanksgiving dinner, which we'll start serving at eleven. I've peeled tons of potatoes since I've owned this place, and I've gotten to be pretty fast. But now my hands hurt soon after I start peeling, and I wonder how long it will be before I can do everything I used to.

"Order up!" Ralph, Charlie's assistant, shouts as he puts two plates of eggs, biscuits and gravy on the counter under the lights.

"Just a reminder, we won't have as many customers today, but make enough so that we'll have plenty of leftovers for the employees to take home," Mona says, gathering the plates up from the counter. "Including us," she adds.

"Gotcha," I say. "That'll be nice, because I don't think I'm going to have the energy to do much when we get home."

"I know I'm not going to," she says. "I'm tired already."

"Didn't you get enough sleep last night?" I ask.

She sidles up to me and whispers, "Evan was really chomping at the bit last night, if you know what I mean. There wasn't much time for sleeping!"

"Ah, something to be thankful for," I whisper back, laughing. She snickers and goes out to her customers.

I'm making salad at a back counter later in the shift, during the period when we're serving dinner. I suddenly notice that it seems very quiet out in the restaurant.

"We really are slow today," I comment to Mona when she comes in to hang a ticket.

"The customers are mostly singles today, so there isn't much talking going on," she explains. "They come so they don't have to be completely alone on Thanksgiving. Same with Christmas," she adds."

"I guess I never worked here on a holiday when I was younger," I say.

"It really gets to be noticeable when you're older," she says seriously. "You wonder if you're going to be one of those singles going out to eat alone some day."

"You just said you're getting older!" I say with a laugh, trying to steer her away from the melancholy tone she's using.

"No siree! I wasn't talking about me, it was just something I've heard other people say!" she says, grabbing a few plates on her way out of the kitchen.

At the end of the shift, Mona and I wish everyone a happy Thanksgiving as they leave. When we get back to Mona's house, we're pleased to see that her dining room table has been set with a lovely white damask cloth and her good china and silverware.

"Oh my goodness!" Mona exclaims. "Who is the darling that did all this?"

"You have the men to thank," Evan says, hugging her. "Grant helped me."

"Well, thanks, men!" she says happily, hugging Grant, who has run into the dining room at hearing his name.

"Thanks, guys," I say. "It looks wonderful!"

"Well, I knowed you wouldn't want to have to do it after work, so I helped Evan," Grant says. "I watched the parade, Mom!"

"Oh, how was it?" I ask.

"Pretty cool! There was a great big duck balloon I really liked!" Grant says excitedly. "As tall as the buildings!"

"Aren't those amazing? Did they show the people hanging onto the ropes so the balloons don't fly away?" I ask.

"Yeah," Grant says. "I think they should let go, then there would be a gigantic duck flying around," Grant says laughing. "That would be funny!" Jenny and Jean have joined us now, and they laugh with the rest of us at Grant's humor. I look around at the six of us, and I am very thankful this Thanksgiving Day.

Yesterday afternoon I called the stable from my office. I didn't really expect to catch anyone on a long holiday weekend, but I did get to talk to one of the owners for a few minutes. She told me that they do have space available, and that they can transport Nadia and her foal from the place I bought them. They explained that they could provide the stable, feeding, grooming, and exercise—although I was given a list of supplies I need to provide. There is no escaping a trip to Peterson's Bridle and Bridle now, because Nadia's saddle is the only thing on the list that I have. And I have to go today, Saturday, because they'll be transporting the horses day after tomorrow.

A buzzer rings as I walk into the Bridle side of Peterson's in the late morning. I pretend I don't see Kirsten, who is tearing plastic off a wedding dress, and she pretends she doesn't see me. I stand looking around for a minute, like I know what I want, then pull out my list. I hear Karl's voice before I see him come out of a back room.

"What can I do for you this…" he stops short when he sees me. "Oh. What can I do for you?" he asks flatly. I'm sure Kirsten has filled him in on everything.

"I'm boarding a horse at the stables just outside town," I say. "I need some supplies. I have a saddle already, so I don't need that."

"Well, that was thinking," he says.

I'd like to turn around and leave right now, but I don't want to have to drive all over the county looking for supplies.

"I have a list," I say, holding it out toward him. "Can you get this stuff together for me please? I don't want to spend a fortune, so I hope it's not too much."

"Oh no, I don't want you to spend too much here," he

says sarcastically, glancing at the list in my hand but not taking it.

I've already had enough. "Karl, if you don't want my business, I'll take it somewhere else." I push the list back in my purse.

"Just sit tight. I'll get the stuff you want," he says, walking away from me. I know that list by heart." It doesn't take long to collect a large mound of supplies. I try to conceal my shock when Karl says how much I owe him.

"Meredith!" I hear Dave Bunsen's voice behind me as I'm fishing in my purse for my wallet.

"Dave!" I say, turning around. "Wow! Great to see you!"

"How's it going?" he says. "You look good—like things are getting back to normal!" Then, as he notices the pile of supplies, he asks, "Is that yours? What are you buying tack for?"

"I got a horse and foal!" I say.

"No kidding! You keeping them at Mona's?"

"No, their barn really isn't set up for horses," I explain. "They'll be at the stable outside town," I say, not wanting to mention Pete's name in front of Karl and Kirsten, who are all ears right now.

"A foal too?" Karl butts in. "In that case, there are some more things you'll need. I'll get them for you."

"What is all this stuff?" Dave asks.

"Things the lady at the stables told me I need," I say.

Dave eyes the pile and says, "No. Uh-uh. I've had my horses there for years, and she does not want all this stuff. You have a saddle?"

"Yes, that's all I have," I say, relieved to have Dave here with me.

"Here's what you need," he says, pulling some items out of the heap. "In fact, I have all these out back in my shed," he says. "I've been collecting tack for years. Go on over to the house. I'll call Roma and ask her to get the things out that you'll need," he says.

I turn back to Karl at the register, startled by the furious look on his face. "I'm sorry for the trouble, Karl," I say. "I guess I don't need these after all."

Dave gives Karl a look of disappointment, then steers me outside. When the door shuts behind us I see Kirsten and Karl looking at us through the window, talking.

"Oh boy, more gossip," Dave says, recognizing my car and heading toward it.

"Yeah, I'm lucky you came along when you did!" I say. "And it's not the first time," I say seriously. "Thank you so much for carrying me out of the hotel the night of the fire," I say. "I'm ashamed that I haven't thanked you before this," I add.

"No, please don't feel ashamed. I'm completely aware of how things have been going for you. Besides, it's thanks enough just to have you up and about."

"Dave, I owe my life to you."

"I would do it all over again if I had to, Meredith. You can count on it."

He goes to the driver's side of my car and opens the door for me. "Now go on over to the house," he says. "Roma will be tickled to see you—you sure have had us both worried."

"I will. Thanks, Dave," I say, getting in the car.

"See you around! I'll let Roma know you're coming over!"

I wave and smile goodbye through the closed window. The world sure could use more Dave Bunsen's, I think, pulling out onto the road.

My sleep has been haunted every night recently; frightening scenes snaking their way in and out of my dreams. One weekend morning in early December I wake with the lingering feeling of a bad omen.

I imagine my uneasiness stems from obvious worries, like Raymond and the fire, but also about the McBrides. I think about how close I had grown to Matthew and Evelyn nearly as much as I think about Pete.

It seems this life of independence is not all it's cracked up to be. In fact, it's a darn lonely life. I'm lucky to have the love of a child, but I want a man to go through life with, and I still choose Pete. But if it's not meant to be, I want to know it, and get on with it.

Jenny is watching Saturday morning cartoons with Grant, and Jean left a little while ago to get her things back from Raymond's house. She told me yesterday that she doesn't think Raymond is after her anymore, and since nobody at all has seen him since that terrible day at The Serenade, she should be able to get them. I told Jean I thought she should call Dave Bunsen to let him know she was going over there, and she said she would. I'll just feel better about it if Dave's aware of it. I think he'll either tell her it isn't safe for her to go, or he'll meet her there while she picks up her things.

While Grant, Jenny and I are having breakfast, Grant asks if John can come over to play today. It sounds like a good idea to me, so after a little cleanup around the house I call Carolyn to see if we can arrange it.

In the afternoon Grant and John are outside bundled up in their colorful winter coats, playing in the front yard with a sled that belongs to Mona and Evan's grandkids. I'm in the living room on the recliner, skimming a magazine, keeping an eye on the kids through the living room window. Suddenly the police cruiser turns into the driveway, and rumbles slowly toward the trailer, frozen gravel crunching under the tires. In seconds I'm opening the door, warning the kids to stay back from the driveway.

"Hi Officer Bunsen!" the boys shout from the yard.

"Hi, kids," I hear Dave say in a tired voice. I stand in the open doorway, smiling a greeting, hoping this is a pleasure call, but when I see his ashen face I'm panic stricken.

"What's wrong?" I ask, a knot forming in my stomach.

"Let's go inside. I don't want the kids to hear," he says quietly. I'm shaking as I turn to lead him into the living room.

"I wanted you to hear it from me first," he says, grasping my shoulders, steadying me. "Raymond and Jean were killed in an accident this morning."

"Jean? Oh my God! What happened?"

"A high speed chase. He took Jean as a hostage," Dave says, hanging his head. "I saw him pulling her toward his car, but he got away from me," he says. "I'm so sorry," he says. "I know Jean was like a member of the family."

"Do we have company?" Jenny says as she comes out into the living room. "Oh! Hello, officer!" she says, then realizes there's something wrong. "What's happened?" she asks fearfully.

I turn away from Dave and lead Jenny, who's clutching tightly to my arm, to the sofa. When we're seated I look up at Dave. I want him to tell her. I don't have the heart to. He somberly repeats what he told me. "Both of them were thrown from the car when he lost control and crashed into a tree. They were killed instantly. Her next of kin in California were already notified," he adds. Jenny covers her face with her hands as she cries for Jean, and I turn to put my arms around her.

"She called you, didn't she?" I ask tearfully. "She said she'd call you to let you know she was going to Raymond's house this morning to get her things!"

"No, there was no call," Dave says. "I'm so sorry. Do you want me to go tell Mona?"

"Yes, please. She's home right now. I just can't believe it, you know? This morning Jean and I were here, talking. And now she's dead." Jenny lets out a sob and I hold her closer.

"I guess I'll go on over to Mona's then. I'll talk to you both later," he says, shaking his head sadly.

"Okay Dave," I say as he leaves. I hear him tell the boys to move up by the porch while he backs out, then their shouts of goodbye to him.

In a little while the patrol car leaves Mona's house, and I soon see her walking quickly over to my door. I stand up from my seat with Jenny just as Mona comes in. We hug each other hard, crying. Grant and John have followed Mona in and are watching us. Jenny's eyes are swollen and red from crying.

Grant asks what's wrong, and I wipe my eyes, then tell him that there was an accident that has made us sad, and I will tell him more about it a little later. I ask the boys to go in Grant's room to play, then I call Carolyn and explain what happened, and ask her to come get John.

Back in the living room I sit down with Mona and Jenny.

"If I hadn't come back here I never would have met Jean," I say, my tears starting up again. "She never would have come here and she would be alive now. Coming back here was a huge mistake!"

"You can't blame yourself for any of this," Jenny says weakly. "Don't try to figure out why these things happen. They do, that's all. It's terribly sad, and we're going to miss Jean, and other people that we don't even know will miss her, too."

"I tried to get her to stay clear of Raymond!" I cry.

"We know you tried," Mona says, holding me tightly. "You warned her about him."

"I did! I warned her! And she promised she would call the police station, and she didn't!" I burst into sobs, and Mona leads me to my bedroom and sits with me there. She leaves for a moment and comes back with a cold wet cloth and gently washes my face. Soon we hear Jenny talking quietly to Carolyn in the living room, then the kids saying goodbye to each other at Grant's bedroom door. In a few minutes Grant comes in my room and stares at me, his eyes frightened, waiting for an explanation.

"Here," Mona says to Grant, "come sit between us."

When he's snuggled in between Mona and me on the edge of the bed, Mona waits for me to speak, but I can't, so she takes over for me.

"Grant, there was a terrible car accident today. Our friend Jean was killed, and we're very sad about it," she says simply, knowing there is no reason to mention Raymond.

"Like John's dog?" Grant asks.

"Yes," I manage to say, remembering that Duke was recently killed when he was hit by a car.

"I like Jean. She's funny and nice," Grant says sadly.

"We all liked her very much, and we're going to miss her," Mona says. "Maybe Jenny will miss her the most, because she spent the most time with her."

"I don't want Jenny to be sad," Grant says, his eyes tearing up. "Like you were for so long. Let's make Jenny happy, Mom." His words make me think of what he had to go through with my depression after the fire. I sit up straight, wash my face again with the cloth Mona brought in, and clear my throat.

"You're right, Grant. We need to help Jenny." I say, standing up. "I'm going to go see how she's doing."

Suddenly I think of what Jenny's gone through in the last year or so—Uncle Duck's illness and death, living in that depressing care home, losing everything she had in the fire, and now Jean—if anyone needs uplifting, it's Jenny.

Monday I stay home with Grant. I explain to him that I'm just going to relax with Jenny today; it's not a play day. Raymond's death means I don't have to worry about fires or the constant threat he posed, but I feel sick about Jean.

Jean was Jenny's caregiver, so I'm trying to figure out what to do about that. I can't even imagine having to interview people right now, and I don't think Jenny should have to deal with a new caregiver right now anyway. Mona and I decide that we will trade off at The Serenade every other day and stay home with Jenny on alternating days. She says part time sounds good to her, so I'll talk to Mr. Overgaard about hiring another part-time waitress. It should work temporarily, anyway.

Mona is working today, so in the late morning Grant and I walk down the lane to get the Monday paper. There is a warm Chinook wind, and Grant is hop scotching his way around muddy slush puddles where the snow has quickly melted.

Grant reaches in the paper box and pulls out a skinny rolled up newspaper wrapped in plastic and fastened with a rubber band. "Here Mom," he says, handing it to me and turning to hop back up the lane. I follow him back inside the house before I open the paper. I gasp as I read the headline: "SERENADE OWNER'S FATHER, EMPLOYEE KILLED IN HIGH SPEED CHASE!"

"What's wrong?" Grant asks.

"I'm angry about something in the paper," I say, skimming the story, then throwing it on the couch. Raymond is referred to as my father at least three times in the story, and Jean is treated coldly, like she was a nobody. Grant shrugs and goes to his room to play, and I pick up the receiver of my phone and call the newspaper office.

"Mr. Teasdale," I say to the old man who puts the paper together with a few volunteers. "This is Meredith Larsson. I want to let you know that you have something wrong…"

"Oh, Meredith! Sorry about your dad! When I heard, I could have dropped my teeth if I had any!" he says.

"Mr. Teasdale, he wasn't my dad. He used to be my stepfather, and you know from the police reports you've put in the paper over the years that I wouldn't want to be associated with him. Why did you do that?" I ask him. Jenny peeks around from the hall to see who I'm talking to so angrily.

"I just print the news, I don't make it," he says.

"And also, Jean was a victim, a hostage," I snap.

"Do you have proof?" he asks.

"I heard it from the police. Look, I just want the record straight that the person who burned my hotel down and who kidnapped Jean and got both of them killed in a chase with the cops was not my father! Just print the correction, please," I say, and hang up. I'm so mad I'm shaking.

A little while later, when I've calmed down, I call Grant out from his bedroom.

"Here I am," he says.

"Grant, does it bother you that you don't have a dad around?" I ask him.

"No." he says. "Only one time when John asked me when my dad gets home from work, and I told him I just had a mom," he says.

"Well, it was the same for me. I just had a mom for many years. Then my mom married someone, and he was what is called a stepfather. Sometimes stepfathers are wonderful, and sometimes they are not friendly at all. My stepfather was not friendly at all," I explain.

"If you get married will my stepfather be wonderful?" he asks, looking up at me.

"If I ever get married I will do my best to make sure your stepfather will be wonderful to both of us," I say. "Okay?"

"Okay, Mom," he says.

"There's something else," I say, thinking of what he might hear at school after this paper is read by his classmates' parents.

"Was the man in the newspaper story your stepfather?"

"You guessed what I was leading up to. Actually, he's not my stepfather anymore, because he isn't married to my mother now," I say. "So we don't have to think about it one way or the other."

"Okay.

"That's all I wanted to talk to you about. I'm going to make hot chocolate this morning. I'll call you when it's ready, it won't be long."

I carefully climb up on a kitchen stool and begin noisily rummaging through the cupboards, looking for the can of cocoa.

"Hot chocolate?" Jenny asks behind me.

"Yes," I say, turning around. "I was going to bring you a cup when it was ready."

"Thanks," she says. "Maybe your comfort drink will be a comfort to me, too," she adds.

I find the cocoa and lean down to put it down on the counter, then get off the stool.

"I'm so very sorry about Jean," I say sadly. "I know you were getting to be very fond of her. You've had a lot to deal with these past two years."

"Yes, it has been a hard time, but thank the good Lord you and Grant came along," she says.

"Oh, Jenny, that's so sweet of you," I say. I give one of her hands a gentle squeeze. She sits down at the kitchen table and pats the chair next to her, just like she did the first time I met her. I sit down and look quizzically at her.

"Just now on the phone with Mr. Teasdale you sounded the same way as you did the day we met," she says.

"I do? What do you mean?" I ask.

"So defensive. When Duck came up behind you that day, you must have jumped three inches off the floor. He said he didn't mean to scare you, and you practically jumped down his throat. 'I seen you! You didn't scare me!' Those were the exact words you shouted at him. He spoke very pleasantly to you, and in a little while he had calmed you down and asked you to eat lunch with him. But first he took you to his office and fixed up the cut on your lip.'

"He was so gentle," I say, recalling the touch of his soft,

chubby fingers applying ointment to my face. "He made me think of Santa Claus, with that belly and handlebar mustache. His voice was jolly, like Santa, but I remember how disappointed I was when he said his real name was Steve Maddocks. It didn't sound Santa-like at all," I say, and Jenny and I laugh together.

"I was always after him about that belly," Jenny says. "But he couldn't stick to a diet. He loved good food, and plenty of it."

"You and Mona were making him eat tomato and lettuce sandwiches when I met him," I say.

Jenny doesn't speak for a minute. "I remember that Raymond had really roughed you up that day," she finally says. "I wasn't sure what had happened until Duck told me later. When he asked your name and where you lived, he contacted the police right away."

"That's right about the time Raymond stopped bothering me so much," I say.That summer, just after I turned sixteen, I started working for Uncle Duck."

"I'm glad you came into our lives, and came back the second time with Grant," she says.

"Me, too."

"Even with the struggles?"

I think of all that's happened since I came here, then imagine not having come here in the first place. "It's something to think about," I say. "You know, just being with you calms me down. Just like being around Uncle Duck used to."

"That makes me happy," she says, "Because I know how fond you were of him. I'm glad I can calm you down, because you need someone to do it! I heard what you were saying on the phone a little while ago. Try not to take it too hard if that toothless Teasdale doesn't print a correction. Nearly everyone who lives here knows about you and Raymond, and there are no tourists here right now to pick up a copy of it anyway, so don't worry about it. Jean hardly knew anybody here yet, and what the local paper says isn't going to matter in California. The whole thing is awful, but if you read the article again when your mind is settled down, you'll see he didn't say anything false about her, he just didn't say anything nice about her either."

"Okay, I'll read it again later," I say, knowing that she's going to be right. "I let things get to me when they shouldn't."

"I'll always give you my opinion when I think you need to hear it. Whether you want it or not." We both chuckle, even though we both know she's serious.

Chapter 13
⸙

Christmas came and went with an overtone of sadness. I tried to make it a happy time for Grant, but I was glad when it was over. I think Jenny felt that way too. Not only was it hard to be joyful about Christmas because of all the things that had happened lately, but the season also brought me to realize how much I miss my mother. When I was little, mom and I were always on assistance, but she was creative with whatever there was. Somehow we always had some presents to open. And we had tasty, if not traditional, holiday dinners, like thick crust pizza, which I still love, or sometimes fried chicken and mashed potatoes.

But Mom wanted to have fun, with no boundaries for either of us, because she hadn't had much herself. I love her, but it has been best for both of us to have many miles between us, the occasional call our only communication. She has the same lifestyle she had while I was being raised, and it isn't what I want for Grant. I remember her surprised voice when I told her on the phone that I had adopted a baby. I was hurt that she didn't want to know much about him, but if I had thought about it beforehand I wouldn't have expected anything else. I want to call her—it's been a long time, but I know talking to her will sap my energy, and I just don't have much to spare.

It's New Year's Eve day. My shift ended at three in the afternoon, and I spent the last hour working on supply orders. I finally start home a little after four, but I don't turn onto the road to Mona's place. I stay on the road that leads out of town, toward the McBride ranch. This time, when I turn into the drive, I see the local realtor's sign hanging on the gate. I get out of my car, and put one foot up on the lowest rung of the gate. I want to climb the gate, get over it and walk around the ranch. But I know I can't climb the gate. I'm waiting tables three full shifts a week now, and I can't risk re-injuring my ankle.

I rest my elbows over the top of the gate looking around at the buildings and house, reminding myself of the times I used to ride home with Pete in his pickup. I had met Evelyn and Matthew about a month after Pete and I started going to-gether. They treated me with respect and kindness, and made me feel completely welcome every time I was there.

I had come to love the McBride's ranch, especially the log ranch house, stands of ponderosa pine, and a beautiful rocky butte.

When Pete left for Bozeman to study animal science at the university, I used to go visit his parents sometimes be-cause it made me feel closer to him. Evelyn and I would bake together, and make Pete care packages of his favorite goodies, like fudge and snickerdoodles.

"The stars that shine down on you at night are the same ones that shine down on him. That's what my mother told me when Matthew was away in the service. It always made me feel better, somehow," she'd say when I was feeling espe-cially lonely for Pete.

In a short time Evelyn and Matthew had become like lov-ing parents to me. They were overjoyed when Pete proposed to me. Later, after DeeDee asked me to go to Oregon to help

with MaryAnn, and subsequently asked me to take Grant,
I had returned to Crossroads to tell Pete in person what I
had to do. Pete was scared to take on the responsibility, and
I couldn't blame him. He begged me to reconsider, but I
couldn't. I explained to him and his parents that on one hand,
there was a tiny baby—my best friend's baby—who needed
a mother, and on the other hand there was a full grown man
who needed me, and it was obvious to me what I had to do.
Evelyn and Matthew had taken Pete's decision to break our
engagement very hard. It was with a very heavy heart that I
had gone back to Oregon to get Grant from DeeDee, with no
Pete in my future.

Now, when I get back home from the deserted ranch, it's
dark, nearly dinner time. When I go over to Mona's house to
get Grant and Jenny, Mona's face is concerned.

"Everything okay? You're kind of late."

"I'm sorry, the time got away from me," I apologize. "I
took a drive after work. I didn't plan to, it just kind of happened. It was so chaotic today; I just needed to clear my
head."

"That's fine. I was just starting to worry, is all," she says.
"I know how crazy it can get at work, and that you have
plenty of things to think about. Just call me next time so I
don't have to worry, okay?"

"I will. I'm sorry," I say again.

"Okay," she says. "Where'd you go?" she asks a minute
later.

Hmm? Oh, I just passed your road and kept on going," I
say.

"To a certain ranch outside town, I suppose?" Mona asks,
eyeing me.

"Yes," I say. "There's a realtor sign on the place now," I
say.

"Oh yeah?" she asks. "It's too bad that they have to sell."

"It is. I feel really bad about it," I agree.

During dinner Grant tells me that he's been missing me too much, like he felt when we first moved here, and then after the fire. There have been a lot of changes in his life since we moved here, and now I've given him a little more to get used to--my new work schedule, and his spending a lot of time at Mona's while I'm gone. And while they aren't bad changes, they're changes nonetheless. I've always heard that kids are resilient, but I don't think they're as tough skinned as they're said to be.

"Would you like to help me make cookies after dinner?" I ask him. Last night I had finally made the dough for the Christmas cookies I had promised we were going to make but never got around to, and now it's chilled and ready to use.

"Yes! Like we were going to make for Christmas?" he asks excitedly.

"Yes sir!" I say.

A little later I roll out the dough on a floured board, and Grant chooses a star cookie cutter to start with. His tongue sticks out the side of his mouth as he concentrates on trimming the dough carefully around the star

"There! It's perfect!" he says, pleased. He looks at me for agreement.

"That is one of the best looking star cookies I have ever seen," I say as I put it on the baking sheet.

"I know," he says. "Wait until you see how I'm going to decorate it!"

"I can hardly wait!" I tell him. We've made cookies together before, but usually the ones Grant works so hard on don't look edible when he gets finished with them. This time, though, I think that they actually might be okay to eat. The phone rings—it's Danielle, saying that she needs someone to cover her shift in the bar because she's sick again. She's already called the two barmaids who aren't scheduled, and neither of them can take her shift. I hate to leave Grant again, but I have no choice. I call Mona and tell her what's going on.

"I'll come stay over there with Grant and Jenny," she says, "if you think you can go put in another shift."

"Of course I can." I say, adding that I hate to disturb their New Year's Eve. She's already done so many good turns for me that I know I'll never be able to repay her.

"It's okay," she says lightly. "Evan and I never stay up to watch the ball drop anymore. But I don't want you to think it's because I can't stay awake!"

"No, of course!" I laugh, not telling her that I never stay up that late either, unless I'm working. When I get off the phone I tell Jenny and Grant what's going on, and that Mona is coming over in a few minutes.

"I'm very sorry that I have to go, Grant, but we'll make more cookies as soon as possible," I tell him.

"Let's ask Mona to make popcorn, then we'll play a board game!" Jenny says to Grant, noticing his despondent look. "We'll have a little New Year's Eve party!" Grant gives a half smile, then goes into the living room and turns on the TV. "Don't worry, I'll keep him happy," she quietly assures me.

"Thanks, Jenny," I say, kissing her on the cheek.

I hurriedly clean up the cookie mess, pack my barmaid outfit, bundle up, and get out the door. I'm still a little nervous driving at night from Mona's. I'm afraid I'll hit a patch of ice, so I drive slowly. When I arrive at The Serenade, I enter through the restaurant, casting a nod and smile at Gabe, who is waiting a table. In the bar I check with the bartender to see what area Danielle was supposed to cover or if I need to know anything special before I start my shift. Suddenly Jacob comes up next to me and leans on the bar. He smells strongly of whiskey, and I make a note to myself to let the other barmaids know that Jacob doesn't need any more to drink.

"You look really hot in that!" he says, looking me up and down.

I ignore his comment. "Looks like you've been celebrating already," I say.

"Yep, I brought my new girlfriend in for the party," he slurs.

"Oh? Maybe I'll meet her later. Well, I can't talk right now." I turn back to the bartender to finish our conversation. When Jacob leaves my side, I make my way between the crowded tables to Danielle's station.

It's been a while since I filled in for a barmaid. I fleetingly think that I would really like to be at home with Grant and Jenny right now, but after I wait three or four tables I start to enjoy myself. The bar is decorated festively with New Years banners and streamers, and some of the customers are wearing party hats which are stacked on a table by the doors. The band I had hired for Serenade Nights has gone on to a string of gigs around the state, but the juke box is really getting a workout. I like the variety of songs people choose, from old time country to new rock and roll. There is a break between music selections, and Old Mr. Taubman stands up and starts singing a romantic song to his wife, Nelly. It's very sweet, I think. Suddenly Jacob stands on a chair at a table near the middle of the bar. He nearly falls off as he shouts at Mr. Taubman to stop singing. "Keep your day job!" he yells, as an uneasy ripple moves through the crowd around him.

"Shut up, fool," a man at a table near Jacob yells at him. "He's an old man, leave him be!"

"Come over here and make me!" Jacob yells back.

I'm not putting up with Jacob's behavior, and start toward him. Halfway across the bar, the woman at Jacob's table looks vaguely familiar, but from here, with the dim lighting, I can't really make out her face. Whoever she is, I think to myself, she's probably questioning her taste in men right now. I turn around and navigate back to the bar, put a cup of coffee on a tray, and head back to Jacob's table.

"Please get off the chair, Jacob," I say as Mr. Taubman

finishes his song and looks over at Jacob angrily. "I brought you a coffee…" I stop short as I realize the woman sitting at the table with him is Cathy Olson. We glare at each other for a few seconds before I say, "What are you doing here?"

"Having a drink with my boyfriend," she says, looking me straight in the eye. Jacob has noticed that he's not the star of the show anymore. He slowly climbs down off the chair and stands next to me, weaving back and forth. I turn to him and put the coffee on the table.

"Here. No more alcohol for you. You're making a scene," I say sternly.

"I remember a night you showed up here a little sloshed and I brought you the coffee," Jacob says. "But that was okay, because you own the place and I'm the employee."

"I wasn't sloshed. I had a few glasses of wine, and I was feeling bad because…" remembering details of Cathy sabotaging me at Roma's party suddenly make me very angry, and I give her a look. "Anyway, I didn't stand on a chair yelling at people," I say. "And I told you," I say to Cathy, "that you weren't welcome here anymore. Did you think I said that to hear myself talk?"

"What are you going to do, have your bouncer throw me out? I know Rick too well, if you know what I mean. He'd never throw me out."

Her comment stirs Jacob up. "What do you mean, you know Rick too well?" he shouts. "You been cheatin' on me?"

"I've only dated you twice. I had a life before you, okay?" Cathy says snidely.

"Out, both of you," I shout over the music. Jacob gives me an acid look, then grabs Cathy by the arm and tries to pull her up from the table.

"Let go of me! I already told you that I don't need you to lead me around everywhere!" she yells, jumping up and pulling herself free from his grasp. She shoves her way between the next two tables, then turns around and says loud enough that the surrounding customers will hear, "Oh, sorry about your dad," she says smugly, "I read in the paper about him and Jean being killed by the cops."

I can only stare angrily after her as she leaves the building, then I notice that Jacob is still behind me. "Aren't you going with her?" I demand.

"Yeah," he growls.

"Don't bring her in here again," I say, heading to the Taubman's table for damage control.

The Serenade is closed today for New Year's. I remember that is the one day that Uncle Duck always closed it too, so I feel okay doing it. I was tired from working late last night, though, so I slept in until ten this morning. I woke to the delicious aroma of coffee, which Jenny had made.

"Did you get enough sleep?" Jenny asks as she pours me a cup of coffee.

"Yes, I think so," I say. "Thanks for the coffee, Jenny."

"My pleasure. I was so sorry that you had to go back to work after you'd worked all day already."

"It wasn't ideal, but it had to be that way," I say. "I got home at three-thirty, so I've had plenty of sleep. I'm going to take Grant to the stables today so we can visit Nadia and the baby. Would you like to go?"

"I think I'll wait on that until the weather warms up, but thank you for the invitation," she says sweetly. "I have a good mystery I'm in the middle of, and I'm dying to find out who done it!"

"I have a mystery to figure out, too," I say, as the McBride's ranch springs into my thoughts.

"Oh? What?" she asks.

"Pete's parent's ranch is up for sale. The first time I went over there it was deserted—that was when I found the lady who had bought the horses—and then yesterday there was a realtor's sign. I'm going to go see Mr. Overgaard about buying it."

"What?" she asks, not sure she heard me right.

"Yes, I'm going to go see Mr. Overgaard, and I'm going to find out if I can sell something, like a parcel of land, so I can buy that ranch."

"That's probably a lot of land," Jenny says. "I don't like to be a pessimist, but that property is going to have a pretty high price. I doubt Sam will want you to do that."

"I really want to buy that ranch back for the McBrides," I say, worried that she's probably right again.

"I haven't seen Sam since he brought me to The Serenade the day I moved out of the care home," Jenny says, hesitating. "Would you mind if I tagged along?"

"No, not at all. Maybe we'd have time to go shopping for a little while before Grant gets home, if you'd like."

"That sounds like fun! You and I haven't done anything like that in ages! Well, if you'll excuse me, I have a mystery waiting for me," she says, going to her room.

I sit at the table alone a while longer, wondering if Jenny's right. I hear the cartoons on TV being clicked off in the living room, and Grant comes into the kitchen.

"Hi Mom!" he says. "The Serenade is closed today, right?"

"It is closed, you're right! Is your room clean?"

"Well, I throwed my clothes in the hamper and all my toys are in the box," he says.

"Okay, if you threw your clothes in the hamper, and your toys are all in the box, then it should be pretty clean. I just need to help you make your bed?"

"Yep."

"Did you have cereal with Jenny?"

"Yep."

"And then you brushed your teeth?"

"Nope."

"Let's get the bed made and the teeth brushed, and then..."

"Let's go see Nadia and the baby!" he squeals.

"Exactly!" I say, as I run to Grant's room with him.

The day is beautifully clear and cold as we drive the few miles out of town to the stables.

"There they are!" Grant shouts, pointing at Nadia and her foal as we drive past the fenced in pasture. The foal is also a golden palomino with blonde mane and tail, so she looks very similar to her mother, but she has more distinct white stockings than Nadia. I pull up at the barn and Grant races ahead of me to the fence closest to us. We've been coming here every chance we get, so they recognize us.

"Can we give them a treat, Mom?" Grant asks.

"No, they get fed plenty, and I don't think the baby is supposed to have treats yet. When she's a little older I think we can bring carrots," I say, remembering what the stable hand told me. I've lived in a little town surrounded by ranches most of my life, but I know very little about horses. I have explained to Grant that I hope Pete is going to get the horses back. I don't want Grant to think they're always going to be here for us. I told him it's like horse babysitting.

Nadia, with the foal right behind, comes up to the fence, close enough for us to put our hand through and pet her face, which she seems to like. The foal, still shy, stays back a little. I don't think Nadia will let her get any closer to us. She seems to be a very protective mama. Like me, I think.

"She sure likes us, Mom!" Grant says.

"Yes, I think she does," I agree, wondering if Nadia remembers me from the days when Pete and I used to ride her together at the McBride's ranch. "You know, I think we should give the baby a name," I say. "Even though she might go back to Pete, for the time she's with us I think she would enjoy having a special name that we choose."

Grant's eyes light up. "We get to name her?"

"Yes, in fact, why don't you name her yourself?" I say, enjoying his excitement.

"Wow!" he says, putting his mittened hands up to his mouth in thought. I can just about see the little wheels turning in his head as he looks from the foal's head down to her feet and back up again, as he searches for a name that fits. Finally he says, "Sugarfoot! Because of her white feet!"

"I love it!" I exclaim, and I do. "That's a wonderful choice!"

Grant beams proudly as he holds his hand out toward the foal. "Here Sugarfoot!" he calls softly, beckoning her over to him. Sugarfoot's ears perk up at Grant's voice. "Mom! Sugarfoot knows her name already!"

"It sure looks that way, Grant. I think she likes it," I say. We stand by the fence a little longer, talking to Nadia and trying to coax Sugarfoot up closer, but she never does venture up to the fence.

In a little while a young woman I recognize as one of the stable hands comes over to us.

"Happy New Year!" she says pleasantly.

"Happy New Year to you, too!" I say.

"I'm going to be taking these two back in the barn because it's too cold for the baby to stay out any longer," she says. "But you can come in the barn."

"Thanks," I say. We watch her lead Nadia, with Sugarfoot following closely, back to the barn. Grant and I stop by the car to get the supplies that Dave gave me before going in the barn. Before the stable hand leaves she shows me where everything goes.

"It's really something, getting to watch a mother horse with her baby, isn't it?" I ask Grant after we've been watching them a little while.

"Yeah, I hope they like watching a mother people with her baby too!" he says, which makes us both laugh.

"Well, this mother people is too cold," I say. "Aren't you, people baby?"

"I'm not really a baby!" he says indignantly.

"I know!" I laugh. "Anyway, let's go home and warm up. What should we fix for lunch?"

"Peanut butter and jelly sandwich," he says, which is just what I expected.

"I see. Aren't you ever going to get tired of peanut butter and jelly sandwiches?" I ask.

"Aren't you ever going to get tired of coffee?"

"Oh boy, you're being smart now!" I say, tickling him as he gets in the car.

"Well, Mrs. Bunsen told you at school one day that I'm smart, remember?"

"Yes, she told me, and she was right!" I say, as we head home to make Grant's pbj.

"Come in, ladies!" Mr. Overgaard welcomes us as we enter his office. "What could be better than two lovely ladies at my door the first business day of the new year!"

"It's wonderful to see you, Sam," Jenny says. "It's been a while, hasn't it? I figured it was my turn to come to see you!"

"Well, I'm glad," he says sincerely. "So Meredith," he says, turning to me. "What business do we need to discuss? More new kitchen equipment?"

"No, nothing like that. I want to buy the McBride's ranch—it just went on the market," I say. "I saw a real estate sign there the other day."

Mr. Overgaard looks surprised, and starts pushing a pencil by the eraser end around the desk, which he always seems to do when he has to think about something. Finally he asks, "Why do you want it?"

"Because it's Pete's parents' place. I'm sure they don't want to sell it, but his dad is sick and the hospital bills are mounting up, so I think they're being forced to sell."

"Do you have an idea of how you're going to purchase it? Or how much it's going for? What if they really don't want it back?"

"I don't know the price yet, but maybe I could use the

insurance money that I get from the hotel," I say. "Or sell a parcel of land?"

"First of all, it's going to take months, maybe years, before you see that settlement. I'm afraid it's going to take a long time to see any of that money. Duck had a large policy on it. I've kept up with the premiums, just as he asked me to do, from money he left that was earmarked for that purpose. Unfortunately, because arson was involved, you might have a fight getting any money at all. But if you do get it, don't you want to put that money into a new hotel?"

"I don't know about rebuilding. I need more time to figure that out. It was such a beautiful place, and of course the staircase was magnificent; how can anything compare? What about selling the property behind The Serenade, and use that money to buy the McBride's ranch?"

"I really don't think you should sell the property. That's a great piece of land to own, and some day you may need to sell it for other reasons. It's a smarter idea to hang on to it. Anyway, I doubt that Duck would have approved of spending money based on sentimentality, rather than good business sense," Mr. Overgaard says in a fatherly tone. "I know you and Pete used to be…"

"Engaged, but we might still get back together!" I say.

"So you want to buy it with the hope that you two are going to be a couple again?" he asks.

"I don't know if we'll ever get back together, but I still want to buy the ranch for the McBrides," I say, my voice unsteady. "And if they don't want it back, I guess it would go back on the market."

Mr. Overgaard stares at me for a second like he's trying to figure me out, then touches a button on his intercom and asks his secretary to get the local real estate company on the line for him. In a few seconds she calls back and tells him she has his call on the line.

"Fred? This is Sam Overgaard. Fine, fine, you? Good,

good. Say, about the McBride place, what's that going for? Oh, really? How many acres is that? Plus the house and outbuildings. I'm not sure yet if I have an interest in it, but I'll let you know. Okay, thanks Fred, goodbye," he says, and hangs up.

"It's a better deal than I thought, at least," he says, showing me and Jenny the figures he just got from the realtor. It looks like an awful lot of money to me, but I don't say anything. Jenny nods her head wisely, like she understands all of it, which knowing her, she probably does. "You're still going to have to wait until the insurance comes through, if it does, to see what your settlement will be. They may get another buyer in the meantime. But during that wait, I hope you'll think about rebuilding the hotel. I think that would be the most prudent thing to do."

Sam and I are both surprised when Jenny clears her throat and says, "Sam, sometimes it isn't prudent to be prudent. Sometimes it's best to act with one's heart instead of one's head."

"Yes, Jenny, I suppose that's true on occasion, but Meredith really shouldn't be spending money on this…"

"Well, I want to help Meredith buy the ranch," she says.

"Jenny, it's very sweet of you to offer, but I can't take your money. You might need that yourself some day."

"It's time to tell Meredith," she says, looking at Mr. Overgaard.

My heart gives a little flutter. "Tell me what?" I ask nervously.

"Are you sure?" Mr. Overgaard asks her.

"Yes," Jenny says, then turns to me. "I have quite a lot of money, dear; it was an inheritance from my father. Sam knows about it because he helps me manage it, just like he helps you with yours. You see, Steven, or Duck, as so many people knew him, was my son. I gave him the money to build The Serenade, and for all his other financial ventures. He and

I decided together that you should have The Serenade when he died."

I'm completely speechless, so she continues.

"Meredith, do you remember the story I used to tell you about a man who had gone to California during the Gold Rush, but made his fortune as a merchant instead of by mining gold?"

"Yes. And his son inherited a fortune from him," I say. "But what—that story was about your family?"

"Yes. The son who inherited the fortune was my father. I was born into a very wealthy family. Then when I was still very young I had Steven, but I wasn't married. It was very upsetting to my family. I was in love, or at least I thought so, and I would have married the man, but he abandoned me when I told him I was pregnant. My father and mother were well known and respected, and their daughter having a baby out of wedlock was not acceptable. I know they loved me very much, but they felt that my mistake would cause irreparable damage to the family name and business. They came to the conclusion that if I was going to keep the baby, I must leave home. I couldn't think of giving up a baby, so I agreed to leave, though it broke my heart. Father knew a man, Mr. Jonsson, here in Crossroads who was highly successful in the lumber business. He and his family lived in the house you were raised in: remember, I told you about that?"

I nod, and she goes on. "So I came here when I was expecting, and stayed with the Jonssons. The social structure here was a far cry from that of the San Francisco social circle. The Jonssons were very warm-hearted, and never spoke to me like I was less moral than they. And Anna, their daughter, was such a source of comfort to me! We became the best of friends. Father sent Mr. Jonsson money to pay for our expenses every month, and we lived there happily until Steven turned eighteen. Then Father gave me a terrible ultimatum: if I agreed to separate myself from Steven completely, he would pay for Steven to go to a good university, and in addition I would receive a large sum of money that he had been saving for me since I was born. My father wanted me to keep our names apart, so people wouldn't make any connection between us. I had been calling him Steven Morgan, Morgan being my maiden name, but my father wanted me to change my son's last name to Maddocks, the surname of Steven's father. He said Steven was old enough to make his own name—it wasn't going to remain Morgan."

"It was a terrible decision to have to make. If I did as my father requested, Steven could have all the advantages of a good education, and money from the sum Father would send me to do nearly anything he might want. Steven and I talked about it at length—it was as terrible for him as it was for me to imagine doing what my father asked. But we did. Steven went away to get his university education, and, since Anna had married and moved away, I moved to New York to get a fresh start. Steven and I both reaped the financial benefits, but we also took the risk of meeting a few times a year in private locations so that we couldn't possibly be found out. Steven eventually moved back to Montana and became hugely successful in mining, making his name good. He sent for me, knowing that if my parent's estate manager heard about it, he had enough of his own earnings that he wouldn't miss their money if he lost it. But I didn't want to risk my parent's estate manager hearing about it and stirring up any trouble. I'd had enough of that to last my lifetime. So at my insistence, we kept it quiet that I was Steven's mother.

Mr. Overgaard nods and says, "I tried to tell you that it wouldn't matter anymore, but you were as stubborn then as you are now."

"Their money was tied up in so many of Steven's ventures that I couldn't be sure that it wouldn't be taken away from him," Jenny says.

"Even though I'd gone over his records with a fine

toothed comb, and told you that nothing would have happened," Mr. Overgaard says.

"I had a hard time trusting anything after what I'd been through," Jenny says.

"Okay," Mr. Overgaard says, realizing he's upset Jenny. "We don't need to talk about that anymore. It's over."

"But Steven died just six months before the conditions of my parents' will would have been removed," Jenny says sadly. "For decades I looked forward to the day that we could let the world know we were mother and son," she adds.

"Oh, Jenny," I say, taking her hand.

"But Sam's right. That's all in the past," she says, shaking her head. "I find strength in making the best of the present, and doing what I can to make the future as promising as possible."

Mr. Overgaard clears his throat and looks at me. "It's a moving story, isn't it?" he asks sincerely.

"Yes, it's so sad," I say.

"Your story is also moving," Jenny says to me. "You took on your best friend's child under the worst of circumstances. Your kindness and generosity remind me of my dear friend Anna!" I look at my lap, amazed at her kind words.

"Ladies, there are many, many details that go along with a purchase of this size. It's complicated," Mr. Overgaard says. "For one thing, I'm wondering, Jenny, how do you want to help Meredith? If you give her a loan…"

"I want to pay for it outright," she says, which makes me gasp. "Let's be realistic. I'm ninety years old—what am I going to do with all the money I have? And there will be plenty left even after I buy the ranch." Then she turns to me. "Meredith, you can't be drawing enough wages from The Serenade in a month to make the kind of payments that a loan of that magnitude would cost, and that's not even considering your other living expenses. So I'll just pay for the ranch, cut and dried," she says.

Mr. Overgaard looks at Jenny. "Meredith isn't sure what she'll be doing with the property, Jenny. Do you understand that?"

"Yes. She just has a strong feeling that she can't let anyone else buy it," Jenny says, "but she needs more time to figure out what she'll do with it."

"And that's okay?" Mr. Overgaard asks her.

"Well, yes!" she says. "I've known Meredith for a long while, and I've never heard of her doing anything but good things. She took me in when I was desperate to get out of that home. She took Grant in when his mother died! I think she would be a good risk of my money," Jenny says.

I feel my face warming up from the stream of compliments. "Thank you," I say quietly to her.

"Anyway, I am a bit of a gambler—not in the conventional sense, but I gave quite a lot of money to Steven over the years to start businesses that he was never sure would pan out. Most did, a few didn't," she adds.

Mr. Overgaard runs his hand over his brow, then says, "As far as I know, everything you say about Meredith is true, Jenny, but I don't think you both realize that there are a lot of reasons you shouldn't go through with this. I can't in good conscience allow…"

"Sam," Jenny says calmly, "please just call Fred at the real estate office and tell him that Jenifer Morgan will meet the seller's asking price." Jenny stands, leaning heavily on her cane, her weary voice signaling that she's tired and wants to go. I follow her lead and also stand.

"Okay, Jenny," he says, beaten. "I'd rather take care of this than have you deal with Fred yourself." He sighs heavily and stands. "But ladies, I'm leaving town in a few days. I'll be gone a month—I just heard that my brother in Dallas is critically ill, and I want to spend some time with the family there. So someone else will be handling things for me while I'm away. I'm just telling you so you won't be surprised if you get a call from someone else on my behalf. "

Jenny and I both tell Mr. Overgaard that we're sorry to hear about his brother.

"Thank you both," he says, then clears his throat and puts his hand out to shake first Jenny's hand, then mine. "Congratulations," he says, "it looks like you two are on your way to owning the McBride ranch."

Jenny smiles at me and clasps my hand.

"I'm grateful beyond words, but shocked," I tell her.

"I'm sure you are shocked," Mr. Overgaard says. "I am too." Then he smiles and says, "Meredith, I want you to keep in mind that this transaction makes it more important than ever to keep in touch with me about finances"

"I will," I say. "Thank you, Mr. Overgaard."

"Bye now, Sam," Jenny says, clasping both his hands inside hers. "My heart tells me we've done a good thing here today."

"Okay, Jenny, so does mine," he says as he opens the door to usher us out.

Jenny and I agree that Mona and Evan are the only people we'll tell about the land purchase. Mona wants to know if we plan to move out to the ranch, but we agree that living here is the best for all of us right now because of our work schedules and sharing the care of Jenny and Grant.

"And of course the whole idea is that the McBrides can move back home, if they want to. If I ever get to talk to them about it," I explain.

We hadn't heard a thing from anyone at the bank until just last week, when Mr. Overgaard got back from Texas. He's drawing up papers for us to sign now. This morning, keys in hand, Jenny and I are going out to the McBride's place while Grant's at school. It's cold, but not so cold that we can't be outside for a while at the ranch, just looking things over.

"It's not a very long drive," I say to Jenny as I help her in my car.

'I think I remember you pointing it out to me once," she says. "I remember it's just lovely!

"Yes, it really is," I say, "especially on such a beautiful blue sky day."

At the ranch I park as close to the back door of the house as I can, and help Jenny out of the car and up the walkway to the door. It's cold inside, and dim except for the light coming in the windows. My excitement at being here suddenly turns to worry as I look around at the cold, empty rooms. The place is filled with fond memories of Matthew, Evelyn, and Pete. "Okay, let me give you a tour of the place," I say, leading Jenny into the living room.

It's strange, I think, that the last time I was in this house it was filled with warmth and love, and today it is so cold and unwelcoming. We soon go back outside into the fresh air and sunshine. I take Jenny to see the barn and other outbuildings, though we only poke around inside for a minute at each building.

"Let's walk up the lane," I say. "It's so beautiful out— and I just don't want to go back home yet!"

"That sounds like a nice idea," Jenny says. "Have you heard anything from Pete?" she asks after we've walked a little without talking, enjoying the quiet.

"No," I say.

"Try to keep your chin up," she says, leaning on my arm for support. "I know the waiting is hard, but one day you'll be able to look back and see that something good came from it."

"What was the good that came out of all your waiting? Didn't you just feel like your parents' decisions robbed you of what could have been so many good years?"

"I did feel like that for a long time, but when I was finally back with Steven, I met a lot of people in Crossroads, including you and Grant, whom I would never have met if it hadn't been for my parents' demands," she explains. "And believe it or not, I believe that part of why I ended up here, was to help you."

"Well, no matter how it all happened, I'm sure glad you're here. And you have been a tremendous help to me, beginning with the moment I met you," I say, squeezing her hand gently.

"I'm so glad you think so," she says.

"Look, we've walked clear to the highway," I say.

"Maybe a little too far. I'm afraid I'm getting awfully cold."

"The temperature dropped pretty fast. We better get back," I say, just as a car pulls into the top of the lane. I wish I had locked the gate, but I didn't figure we'd be at the ranch long enough to bother. The car looks familiar but I can't place it, and it's too far for me to see who the driver is. "Let's start walking back to the house," I say, as the car starts down the lane toward us. "Oh, crum! Who could that be?" In a few seconds the car is right behind us, and I lead Jenny into the weeds along the side of the lane to get out of the way.

"Hey! Meredith!" I recognize Cathy Olson's voice shouting over the noise of the car engine.

"What are you doing here?" I shout back.

"Why do you have Jenny out here in this cold weather? Look at her! Her lips are blue!" Cathy shouts. I look at Jenny and see that Cathy is right.

"It wasn't that cold a little while ago," I say defensively. "The temperature just started dropping."

"Seemed pretty cold to me the minute I walked out of my house," she says. "Oh, but to answer your question, I'm here because Daddy worked on the sale of the McBride ranch," she says. "He was handling all of Sam Overgaard's work while Sam was gone, and he happened to mention that you two were buying the McBride ranch," she says. "Anyway, I just wanted to see if you had moved in, and I guess you have!"

I don't tell Cathy that we haven't moved in—for some reason I think it's better if she thinks we have. Maybe she's interested in the property herself, and if she thinks I haven't moved in yet she might get us to stop the transaction. "We were just taking a walk before going to town for groceries," I lie. Would you mind giving us a ride to my car? So Jenny doesn't get any colder?" I ask.

"Yes, for Jenny," she says icily. I thank her and open the back door on the driver's side and help Jenny in, and then go around the car and slide in next to her.

I notice a dirty white blanket stuffed underneath the front seat, which I pull out and drape over Jenny's lap. Jenny looks down at the blanket, then at me. Her face goes frightfully white, and I panic, not knowing what's wrong.

"This is my blanket!" she mouths at me, pointing to a small monogram on the blanket, then at herself. 'JM', the monogram says. Jenifer Morgan! I can't imagine why Cathy has Jenny's blanket in her car, but whatever the reason, it's upsetting Jenny. I pull the blanket over to me, to get a better look at the monogram, and then I notice a big burned area on it which had been hidden in the folds.

"Please pull up as close to my car as you can," I say to Cathy, rolling the blanket up as small as I can. "I don't want Jenny to be outside any more than necessary. Thank you," I add. Cathy pulls parallel to my car, just a few feet away. "Can you help me get her to my car, please?" I ask. She sighs, and as she opens her door, I open mine on the opposite side and throw the blanket outside, close to the car. I say that I'm going to start my car to warm it up. While Cathy leans in the back seat on the driver's side of her car to help Jenny out, I pick the blanket up off the ground on the other side and quickly unlock my trunk, toss the blanket in and slam it shut. "Darn this trunk! It was open again, Jenny! I'm going to have to take it in to get it fixed!" Then, taking Jenny's free arm, I say, "Thanks for your help, Cathy. I can get her from here."

Cathy drops Jenny's arm, gives me a dirty look and moves away.

"That was my blanket!" Jenny says when we're alone in my car and Cathy has started toward the highway.

"I recognized it after you pointed the monogram out," I say. "Are you okay? Are you warming up yet?"

"I'm getting warmer. I'm okay," she says.

"You looked as white as a ghost back there!" I say.

"I was stunned to see my blanket in her car! My mother monogrammed that for me when I was very young, and I was very upset when I lost it," she says.

"I'm sure you didn't loan it to Cathy," I say.

"No. I left it out in the hotel lobby the last night I slept in my room at the hotel, before we moved over to Mona's trailer because you were going to have the bats moved out. I couldn't sleep, so I wrapped my blanket around me and went out in the lobby to read. But I fell asleep on a sofa—the one closest to the staircase. I woke up sometime during the night and went back to my room, but I forgot my blanket. I remembered it as soon as I got into my bed but I didn't want to get up again. I was going to get it the next morning, but then I forgot about it. Of course the next night was the fire, so I thought it had burned up with everything else. Why on earth would Cathy have my blanket?"

"I don't know. And what about that burned part?" Jenny and I turn and look at each other in amazement.

A little later Jenny and I are sitting on metal folding chairs in Dave Bunsen's office. Jenny hands the blanket to Dave over his desk, and asks me to explain it to Dave.

"Remember that I had told you about seeing someone running across the parking lot of The Serenade the night of the fire?" I ask Dave. He nods that he does. "And that I thought the person was wearing a long white coat?" He nods again. "Well, we may know who that person was," I say, and tell Dave about the discovery of Jenny's blanket.

"Jenny, are you certain that you had left your blanket out in the lobby?" Dave asks, eyeing the scorched area on the blanket.

"Yes," Jenny says. "I missed it right after I went back to bed in my room. But I was too tired to go back to the lobby to get it."

"Why would Cathy want to cause harm to you or your property?" Dave asks me, "if she did, that is."

"Because I fired her, I guess," I reply.

"Why?"

"Because she kept butting into my relationship with Pete. I had warned her before that if she kept it up, I would have to let her go. She had a photo album she had started carrying around, taking pictures everywhere she went. She took some in the bar, and one happened to be of me right when Jacob kissed me while we were dancing. It made her really mad. Then she showed it to Pete to blackmail me!"

"How long before the fire did you let her go?" Dave asks.

"I don't remember the exact date, but it was about a week, maybe ten days, before the fire. She knew when the building would be empty; all the employees knew that we were going to be closed to have the bats moved. But the exterminator rescheduled, and she wouldn't have known that," I explain. "She probably didn't know that I was upstairs."

"Did she take the photo album home with her the last day she was at work?" Dave asks.

"Well, hmm…" I think for a few seconds, and then remember that Cathy never had come back for her album. "No, actually, she didn't. I noticed after she left the day I fired her that the album was sticking out from under the lobby desk. I thought a few times that I should call her to come get it, but I just didn't want to talk to her. And I know she didn't want to talk to me, either. It probably burned in the fire," I say.

"That's too bad. I would have liked to have seen it," Dave says. "One more question, then I'll let you both go. Why do you suppose that Cathy wanted to know if you had moved in to the ranch? Isn't that what you told me she said this morning?"

"Yes, that's what she said," Jenny puts in. "She said her father had taken over for Sam while he was gone, and something about her father thought she'd be interested to know that we were buying the McBride's ranch."

"I wondered about that too," I say, "but I was worried about getting you warmed up, so I hadn't thought much about it."

"Well, thanks for coming in with this information. I'll be following up on everything we've just discussed," Dave says, "and I'll be getting in touch with you soon."

In the next days every time I drive up to The Serenade a dark feeling envelops me at the thought of Cathy setting the fire. It was easy to blame Raymond because I had always had problems with him, but I would never have thought the trouble I had with Cathy would trigger such a terrible thing. My fear that there would be another fire died with Raymond, but now that fear looms again. I wonder why Cathy was really at the McBride's ranch that day.

I go to work this morning exhausted, as I have each morning since Jenny and I ran into Cathy. Today will be Jacob's first day back since his vacation. I hope his little performance in the bar on New Year's Eve will be far behind him. I wonder how involved he is with Cathy, but I'll leave that questioning up to the police. I stop by the kitchen and ask Charlie if he thinks I should wait tables or if I can get some office work done.

"I'll call you if it gets busy," Charlie says. "I think JoLynn can handle it for now.

"Okay. I'll be in my office. Would you please ask Jacob to come see me in my office when he comes in?"

"Sure, I'm the cook and message man too," Charlie mutters.

"Thanks, Charlie," I say smiling. "You're a dear."

I'm at my desk, trying to get some paperwork done, but the figures are swimming around in front of my eyes. I try to keep from falling asleep, but I can't stop my head from lowering down to the desk. Suddenly my phone jars me awake.

"We're getting busy," Charlie says.

"Okay, I'll be there in a minute. Did Jacob come in? Oh, never mind, he just walked in," I say, as he appears in my office doorway. "I'll be there in a few minutes to help."

"Sure, take your time, that's why I called."

I hang up, then look at my watch. "What's up?" I ask Jacob.

"Thought I'd drop by, let you know I'm quitting," he says casually.

"Oh? Nice of you to give a notice," I say.

"I considered it, but then I thought of the crap you dish out, and I decided not to worry about it," he says.

"I'll mail your check," I say, sighing deeply, not wanting to get in a discussion with him. "I have to get out in the restaurant right now." He just stares at me for a second, then leaves and slams the door closed behind him.

In a few seconds Charlie's in my office. "What was that that just blew through the kitchen?" he asks.

"Jacob just told me he quit. It's about New Year's Eve. He was making a drunken scene in the bar, and I let him know he was out of line," I explain.

"We don't need that kind of advertising," Charlie says. "So good riddance. But we do need a maintenance man. So get right on it."

"I will. As soon as I can," I say as I go to change into my waitress uniform. I call Mona later from my office during a short break. "How would you like to write another handyman ad?" I ask.

"What? Why?" she asks, confused.

"Jacob quit this morning," I say. "He's still mad about New Year's Eve."

"Rats! He was good. And he wasn't a bad handyman, either," she says laughing.

"Mona! The things you come up with!"

"You know I'm just kidding. Okay, I'll write one now and pass it by you before I call the *Bugle*."

"No, don't bother. Just call the newspaper with it ASAP, please. I have to get back or Charlie will be calling me! Bye!"

"Okay, bye," she says and hangs up.

That evening Mona asks us all to stay for dinner. Afterward I quietly tell Jenny that I need to talk business with Mona.

"Grant," Jenny says. "I'm feeling a little tired. Will you walk me home?"

"Sure!" he says. "Is it okay, Mom?" he asks.

"Yes, it would be very nice of you to help Jenny," I agree. "And maybe, after you get your pajamas on and brush your teeth, she could tell you a story." I steal a glance at Jenny, who winks at me.

Grant looks eagerly at Jenny. "I think I'll be able to do that," she says smiling.

"Were you able to place the ad?" I ask Mona when Jenny and Grant are gone.

"I got it in for the next paper,' she says, "but then Mr. Teasdale asked me what I knew about Cathy Olson being connected in the hotel arson case!"

"What!"

"Yeah. Weird, huh?"

"It sure is. I think I'll call Dave. He's probably at home by now. Mind if I use your phone? I don't want to talk about this stuff in front of Grant."

"Of course," Mona says.

In a minute I'm telling Dave what Mona just told me. "I just thought I should let you know," I add.

"Thanks, I appreciate it," Dave says, and quickly hangs up.

"He didn't waste any time with me on that call," I say.

"Maybe he was in the middle of something with Roma, if you know what I mean," Mona says with a grin.

"Oh, Mona," I say.

"You gotta lighten up," Mona says. "All those hip swinging sessions were totally lost on you, weren't they!" she laughs. "Did you even know what to do with Pete when he came up to your room that night?"

"I know plenty," I laugh. "Mom had a string of boyfriends at our house in between dad and Raymond. Maybe I saw too much too soon."

When I get home, Grant is already asleep and Jenny is watching late night TV in the living room. I know she'd want to be kept in the information loop, so I wait for a commercial, and then tell her what Mona said about Mr. Teasdale and Cathy.

"I wonder what he'll print in the next paper," I say.

"It's probably a good thing it only comes out twice a week," Jenny says, "with Mr. Teasdale's lack of tact."

I make a pot of peppermint tea, then we sip and chat, speculating on what Mr. Teasdale had heard, and who told him.

A few days later, Mona calls me from The Serenade and asks me if I picked up the paper, since everyone is anxious to see what's in it.

"No, but I'm walking up to the road to get it now," I say.

"Well call me if there's anything interesting in it."

"You know I will." I put my coat on and hurry up the lane to the highway where the newspaper and mail boxes are. I lean down to look in the paper box, but it's empty. When I get back to the trailer I call the newspaper, but I get a recording. "This is Mr. Teasdale, editor-in-chief of the *Bugle*. If you are calling because you didn't get your paper today, please be informed that due to circumstances beyond our control, the *Bugle* production has been delayed. I apologize for any inconvenience this may cause our subscribers. Thank you and have a nice day."

Chapter 14

"I want to see that nice Dr. Jonsson and her husband," Jenny tells me at home a few days later.

"Really?" I ask, not sure where this is headed.

"Yes. I want to see her and meet her husband. Remember she said that it was her husband's relatives I lived with?"

"Yes, I remember," I say.

"She and I said we'd arrange something. I'd really like to," she says.

"Okay, I'll see what I can do, but you know she has a very busy schedule. She works part time at the hospital and sometimes sees patients in her home office, too. And she has little children to take care of," I say. Jenny says she understands, so I call Lei's home and talk to her husband, Mark, for a minute.

"I know she's terribly busy, with her work and the kids," I say after I tell him who I am and why I'm calling.

"Well, we have a lady who comes in to help with the kids," he says, his voice good natured, "because I also work at home, so I can't watch the kids sometimes."

"Oh! What work do you do? If you don't mind me asking?"

"I don't mind a bit. I love to talk about what I do. I have a woodworking shop where I make furniture, and the occasional wood sculpture."

"Oh yes, I remember Lei saying that her grandfather was a woodworker too."

"Right. I learned a lot from him," Mark says.

"I'd love to come see your work some time," I say.

"I'd be happy to show you," he says. "I'll talk to Lei and see when we can arrange a time for you and Jenny to come over. Then we'll talk about Anna and show you my wood-shop."

"Great!" I say.

"Oh, and Lei told me that you have a son in Roma's class, so he'd be about six?"

"He'll be six near the end of the month," I say.

"Bring him too. He'd be old enough that he might like to see the woodshop."

Jenny, Grant and I are on our way over to the Jonsson's now, because Lei called back this afternoon and suggested that this evening would be a good time to come over, since her schedule today had been light.

That evening, Lei greets us pleasantly at the door, waving us in.

"Thanks Lei. What a lovely home," I say.

"Well thank you, Meredith. It's simple but comfortable. No point in trying to keep a lot of fancy things around with small children, right?"

"You're right there," I agree.

Lei makes introductions all around, then Grant follows their four-year-old daughter, Maia, to the playroom. "I just put Lee in bed," she says, referring to their baby boy.

"Oh, darn," I say. "Maybe I'll get to meet him some other time."

"I'm sure you will. But here he is in a recent picture, so you can see what he looks like," Lei says, pointing to a framed photo of the family on the wall.

"That's a very nice family portrait," Jenny says to Lei. "I'm curious, how did you and Mark meet?"

"It was when Lei was a junior in high school. I was taking a community education class in wood working, and Lei's grandfather was one of the teachers," Mark says. "I had no experience in this kind of work but I seemed to have a special talent for it, and he took an interest in me."

"Grandfather invited Mark to our home to see his woodshop, and I took an interest in Mark, too!" Lei adds with a laugh.

"But I couldn't do anything about it for a few years, because I'm seven years older than she is. However, I kept at it, and finally they let me date her!"

"And while he was waiting, he learned quite a bit about woodworking," Lei adds.

"What a nice story!" Jenny says.

"But here's what you're really interested in," Mark says, bringing a big box over to Jenny. He puts it on the coffee table in front of her. "These are old family photos from my side. I haven't looked in here for ages, but I know there are some photos of Anna. Go ahead and look through them."

"Oh my goodness!" Jenny exclaims. "A treasure trove!" She begins sifting through it and immediately pulls out a large time-ravaged cabinet photo. "This is Mr. Jonsson!" Jenny exclaims. "I remember this day! He was getting ready to go on a business trip to Denver!" I've never seen Jenny as excited as she is now, holding up photo after photo, recognizing some of the people and searching her memory for the identification of others.

"You already know that the Victorian house, the pink one on Sixth Street that you asked about," Mark says, "was built by my family in Crossroad's early days. But it wasn't pink at the time," he says with a laugh. "I've been told that my family held onto that house until the nineteen-fifties, then sold it, and the new owners painted it pink. I'm sure it looked great at first, but it's looked terrible ever since I can remember. The gingerbread has chipped off and it's needed a paint job forever. I don't mind a pink house, but it needs to be kept up. It's too bad, since it was a wonderful house from the looks of these old photos." I see Lei shoot Mark a look to stop talking about the house, but he doesn't understand.

"I hate to admit it, but it was my family who bought it, I say. "My grandparents were the ones who painted it pink. I don't remember them, but I know that they left it to my mother, and that's where the downfall began."

"I'm sorry. I had no idea," Mark says.

"No, it's okay," I say. "I was just a child. I wasn't responsible for my mother's actions." I see that Lei is nodding in agreement, which gives me the courage to continue. "Mom had trouble taking care of herself, let alone a home and child. Then later, when she got divorced from my stepfather, he somehow ended up with the house, but now that he's dead, I suppose his mother will sell it."

"Oh?" Mark says. "It might be nice to get that house back in the family. I think I'll look into that. I think I'd enjoy restoring it to its original condition."

"I'll get her phone number for you if you want to call her about it," I say.

"If you buy it, I'd love to see the finished product," Jenny says, rummaging through the box of photos again. Suddenly she says, "Oh my! Here's a photo of me with Steven and Anna! Look at this, Meredith!"

I get up and move over to Jenny's side. I stare at the photo. It's a well-composed picture of a much younger Jenny, Uncle Duck at about ten years, and a woman a few years younger than Jenny, standing on the porch of the house I was raised in. It's an amazing photo, and we can barely tear our eyes away from it.

Mark takes a look, and he seems equally entranced. "It's

interesting to think — this picture is connected to everyone in this house at this moment," he says. "Please take it, Jenny. I can see how much it means to you."

"Oh, thank you! I'll cherish it forever!"

In a little while we all accompany Mark on a tour of his woodshop, a separate building behind the house. It's beautifully laid out and organized. He has some finished chairs and a few furniture pieces in progress off to one side, raw materials stored on racks, an amazing array of tools hanging neatly on a pegboard wall, and four huge tool chests on wheels with many drawers. The larger pieces of equipment are lined up against one wall.

Jenny and I compliment both his gorgeous furniture and the shop.

"The chairs are wonderful!" I say.

"Thank you," Mark says. "I hope someday I'm as skilled as Lei's grandfather was. I'm sure she's told you that her grandfather built the staircase that was in The Serenade."

"No!" I say, stunned. "Lei, why didn't you tell me? I loved that staircase! It was my favorite thing about the whole building. I've been so sad about that since the fire..." I'm afraid I'm going to burst into tears if I go on. "Why didn't he get credit for it in the brochures?"

"The Chinese weren't regarded with the same respect that a white person was, back then," Lei says. "That's probably why his name was never mentioned. When you and I met at Roma's party, nobody was discussing anything but underwear and kids, and after that, the fire brought us closer together, but I thought if I told you that the fire had destroyed an important work my grandfather had done, you would have felt even worse."

"I guess you're right," I say. "It was so beautiful. I loved it. I'm so sorry that it's gone."

"Thank you," Lei says. "I'm glad to know how much you appreciated it."

"I 'preciated it too. Mom paid me to polish it," Grant says, giving us a little comic relief. His eyes light up when he seems to realize that his comment has brightened the general mood.

"Look at all the tools, Mom!" Grant says. "I think Mark buyed all the ones at the store!"

"It looks like he bought a lot of them, anyway," I say, laughing.

"Oh, I didn't buy them all myself. I inherited a lot of them from Lei's father," Mark says.

"And father inherited them from grandfather, so some of these things are very old," Lei says. "I'm so lucky to have found Mark. It's wonderful to have grandfather's passion continue in the family."

"Why, thank you, dear," Mark says, putting an arm around Lei. Lei gives him a warm smile and tells him he's welcome.

In a little while I tell Jenny and Grant that it's getting late and we need to go. "School tomorrow, Grant. And other people have to get up for work," I say.

"Yes, I see my schedule will be more hectic tomorrow," Lei says.

"Maybe we can do this again some time?" Jenny asks, her forwardness surprising me less and less.

"Of course, Jenny. We'd love to have you come back," Lei says.

"I'll look through the basement—I know I have another box of old photos somewhere," Mark says. "I'll call you when I find them, and we'll get together."

"Thank you so much!" Jenny says. "This evening has been just wonderful!"

Lei, and Mark carrying Maia, follow us outside. "It's a lovely evening," Lei says, just as Dave and Roma come out on their porch next door.

"Hey everyone!" Roma says. "Hi Grant!"

"Hi, Mrs. Bunsen," Grant says. "Why are you at that house?"

"This is where I live," she says.

"You live in a house? I thought you lived in the school!" Grant exclaims.

"No, teachers also live in houses," Roma says. They go home a little while after the children do."

"I thought the same thing when I was little," Dave says to Grant.

"Oh, okay," Grant says.

"What brings you folks to our neighborhood tonight?" Dave asks. "Did we miss some kind of party?" he laughs.

"Lei and Mark had us over so I could look through some of his ancestral photographs. It turns out that we share a common thread, in a way," Jenny tells Roma and Dave.

"Oh?" Dave asks.

"Yes, can you believe it? The family I lived with when I moved to Crossroads as a young woman was Mark's family!"

"No kidding!" Roma says. "That's incredible!"

"I just had more fun tonight!" Jenny says. "But now I'm pretty tired. I haven't been sleeping very well."

"You haven't?" I ask, surprised.

"Well, no, what with wondering what day we're going to wake up to find who-knows-what in the paper," she says.

Dave looks concerned, and asks what she means.

I start walking with Grant to the car, since I don't know what Jenny's going to say and I might not want Grant to hear it, but it's only about fifteen yards to the house, so I hear her clearly anyway.

"Well, you know, Dave. About my burned blanket we found in Cathy's car! Then old Mr. Teasdale at the paper said something to Mona about Cathy being involved in the fire?"

After I get Grant buckled in I walk back up to the house. Lei and Mark are looking from Dave to Jenny and back.

"I'm sorry, Jenny, but I just can't say anything about

any of it," he says.

"Well, we need to go, Jenny," I say, ushering her to the car while calling out thanks and goodnight over my shoulder.

I hear Lei talking as I'm helping Jenny get in the car. "Dave, I was in Great Falls recently at a conference, and I was chatting with a doctor I met there, I can't remember which town he was from, but I have his card in my desk. He brought up something about a burn victim their hospital had earlier this winter that I really didn't think twice about at the time, but it came to mind after what Jenny just said about Cathy Olson. It might bear looking into," she adds. I've been taking my time getting Jenny situated, just so I can hear what's being said. I shudder when I hear Dave ask Lei to get the doctor's name and phone number for him.

Several weeks pass with no mention in the paper of a new arson suspect in the hotel fire. I know I can't ask Dave if he talked to the doctor Lei had mentioned because it's police business, but I sure would like to. I don't want to put Lei on the spot by asking her anything, either.

I'm glad Grant's sixth birthday is next week, so he has something exciting to look forward to. He's been worried about the bits and pieces he's been overhearing about Cathy and the fire. I've done my best to answer all his questions so that I'm not lying, but also in a way that will hopefully steer him away from thinking about it.

I am planning a surprise birthday sleepover party for Grant tonight, Friday! I had to limit the guests to six, because there just isn't much space in this trailer, even in the living room. I figure seven sleeping bags lined up in here ought to just about take up the entire living room floor. I'm going to quickly decorate with balloons and banners after the guests get here so I don't spoil the surprise.

It's six in the evening, and I'm in the kitchen heating pizzas up in the oven when Grant comes in and asks me why

I have so much pizza. "We usually only get one, Mom," he says. "Are you really hungry tonight?"

I laugh and answer, "Yes, I just feel like I could eat a bear tonight! I hope you and Jenny don't want to eat much, because I think I could eat most of this myself!"

"Really? Well, I think I want a piece, and Jenny prob'ly wants to eat some," he says, eyeing me curiously.

Right ther. there's a knock on the door. "Would you get that, please?" I ask Grant. I grab my camera from the top of the refrigerator and follow Grant quietly to the living room.

"Happy birthday!" Grant's best friend John yells as the door opens. I've moved up closer to the door so I can get a good picture of the two boys. I can't wait to see how it turns out. "Why are you here, John?" Grant asks, confused.

"For your birthday, silly!" John says, thrusting a brightly wrapped present at Grant.

John's mom, Carolyn, appears in the doorway. She wishes Grant a happy birthday, then we chat for a second and before she leaves we agree that she'll pick John up about noon tomorrow.

"Mom, can John have any of the pizza?" Grant asks. "Mom's really hungry," he says to John, "so we might have pbj's."

"I'm not that hungry any more," I say laughing. "The pizza is actually for your birthday, honey!"

"Oh," Grant says. "Can we eat now?"

"Pretty soon," I say, just as there's another knock on the door.

All the kids have arrived by six-thirty and I finally explained to Grant that they're here for a sleepover birthday party. This is his first birthday party, so he's completely over-whelmed and excited.

Jenny comes out of her room to eat with us, watch Grant open his gifts, and have cake and ice cream. She smiles, watching the boys horse around, laughing and talking. I wonder if she's thinking about Uncle Duck at Grant's age, having a great time on his birthday. I wonder if there's a photograph of him around this age in a box at Lei's house. Jenny helps me clear the table and clean the kitchen up, then tells me she'll be in her room reading.

"I think the living room is full enough without me out here too," she says with a laugh. "Let me know if you need my help with anything," she says, "otherwise, I'll see you tomorrow morning!"

"Thanks, Jenny," I say. The boys are playing make believe with Grant's little toys. They all seem to know exactly what they're expected to say and do with the little people, and everyone's happy, so I settle down on the couch, out of the way with a cup of coffee, snapping a photograph every now and then so Grant and I can look back and remember this wonderful eve of his sixth birthday.

I'm prepared to stay up late into the night, listening to seven little boys rough housing and playing, but surprisingly, the living room is quiet by ten-thirty. Of course they had all probably gotten up early and put in a day of school and homework before the party, like Grant had, so they have good reason to be all tuckered out.

Jenny and I wait until the guests leave the next day before giving Grant the gifts we got for him. I give him a robot that walks and has flashing eyes, and Jenny gives him a story she had written herself in a brightly colored notebook, about a six-year-old boy and all the things he could do. She had cut magazine photos out to serve as illustrations. Grant sits down cross legged on the sofa next to Jenny, holding the robot tightly in his arms.

"Will you read it to me, please?" he asks her.

"Once upon a time," Jenny begins, "there was a boy..."

I sit back in the easy chair, listening to Jenny read, and watching the expressions on Grant's face. My son is six today, I think. MaryAnn, wherever you are, our son is six.

Chapter 15

ᴄ᭸

"Hi, Meredith?"

"Lei? Dr. Jonsson?" I recognize her sweet accent the second I hear it on the phone one April evening while Grant and I are watching TV.

"Please! Call me Lei! How have you been? I haven't heard from you for a while, and I'm just wondering how things are going for you."

"It's so nice to hear from you! Grant and I are doing pretty well, thanks. I'm ready for spring, so any time the warmer weather wants to start, is okay with me!"

"That's how I feel about it too. Doesn't winter seem to go on forever now that we're adults? Was it always this cold in April?"

"You know, I was just thinking about that the other day. The cold didn't get to me when I was a kid, but I swear this has been the longest winter I've ever lived through."

"Of course the weather is probably harder on you this year since you had the broken ankle and things. Maybe next year it will be easier for you. I hope so."

"I think everything will be better, thanks. I'm moving on with my life. But, what about you? How are your kids and

Mark? I bet the baby's hardly a baby anymore!"

"They're both growing fast, and everyone is well, thanks. Say Meredith, I called because I wanted to tell you that I was in Great Falls a few days ago at a meeting, and I ran into Pete. But you say you're trying to move on, so maybe I shouldn't..."

My heart skips a beat before I reply. "How is he? Did he seem okay?"

"Yes, yes, he looked good. He seemed okay. I saw his parents, too."

"Oh! You did! How wonderful! "

"Yes, it was nice to see all of them. Pete said he was bringing his folks to Crossroads next Monday to meet with someone at the bank."

"Really!"

"Yes. They sold their property and someone at the bank is acting on the buyer's behalf. So they're going to take care of their business with the bank and also just stay in the area for a little vacation."

"I didn't know you even knew Pete, I mean, except for seeing him at school occasionally. He was in my class, so he was a few years behind you, too."

"I don't know him all that well, you're right. But you know how it is when you run into someone from your hometown when you're away from home. You can get a little chatty."

"That's what I've heard," I say, thinking that it just wasn't like her to spread other people's news around like she just did.

"So how's business? Have you gotten back to your regular hours yet?"

"No, Mona and I are still job sharing."

"Does that suit you both pretty well?" Lei asks, sounding more like herself now.

"It works great. We switch our schedule whenever we

want to, and we hired another part-time waitress for weekend help."

"It sounds like things are working out. How's Grant?"

"Oh, he seems fine. I know this year has been hard on him too, but I think he's going to pull through okay. He's taught me some things about being a mom, that's for sure."

"I know what you mean. You think you know what you're doing, then one little sentence from your child's mouth makes you see that you don't know what you're doing at all."

"That's it exactly."

"Well, I hate to have to hang up, but motherhood calls as we speak. I'm so glad that we could chat for a minute."

"Me too. Thanks so much for calling, and for telling me about Pete and his parents. I really appreciate it."

"I thought you'd want to know. Take care of yourself, okay? Remember I'm always here if you want to talk."

"I won't forget," I say before thanking her and hanging up.

I'm so excited that I want to call Mr. Overgaard to ask him what time the McBrides are going to meet with him this morning so I can be waiting at the door of the bank when they arrive. But I quickly realize that would make me look desperate, and I am not desperate. I put the phone down, knowing that I won't be going to the bank.

I just waved goodbye to Grant on the school bus, and I notice there aren't any footprints in the snow up to the newspaper box, so I get it out. I see Evan, who is just walking out to his truck, which is running in the driveway.

"Paper's in!" I holler to him, holding the rolled paper out so he'll see it.

"You read it first, bring it over tonight," he shouts back.

"Okay! Have a good day!" I wave as Evan jumps in his truck and backs out the drive.

I carry the paper in and pour myself some coffee. Jenny's

still sleeping. I heard her up quite a few times last night so I don't expect to see her for a few more hours. Normally when I'm home in the morning I watch the local news on TV first thing in the morning, but the walls of the trailer are thin, and I don't want to risk waking Jenny. I sit at the kitchen table, take a long drink of the delicious coffee, and open the paper.

"Oh jeez!" I say when I see a large photo of Cathy Olson, handcuffed, right on the top center of the front page. GRANDDAUGHTER OF TOWN FOUNDER ARRESTED IN ARSON CASE! I feel sick. I had known this was a possibility, but the reality of it strikes me hard. I just don't want to believe that Cathy could have done it. The article says that the police used a search warrant at the Olson home, and found evidence linking her to the fire. I don't even have the stomach to read the rest. I fold the paper up and put it away, then call Mona at work.

"I read your paper," I say when Mona picks up. "They arrested Cathy!"

"I can't believe it," Mona says. "That is too much. What happened?"

"I didn't read it all. I just read that the police searched the Olson home with a warrant and found evidence linking her to the fire. I just couldn't read any more of it alone."

"Don't read it alone. I'll read it with you tonight," she says. "Just try not to think about it, okay? I know it's very disturbing to you."

"I've got a lot not to think about today," I say.

"What do you mean?"

"I didn't even tell you, because I'm not doing anything about it, but Lei called me a few days ago and told me that Pete and his parents are going to be at the bank today to meet with someone."

"You didn't try to find out when?" Mona asks in a surprised voice.

"No, of course not."

"Oh, man. What a day. Pete and Cathy again. What is it with those two? Trying to drive you nuts?"

"It would seem so," I say. "Okay, tonight we'll read it together, but you'll probably get the whole story while you're waiting tables and won't really need to read it at all."

"I imagine that's true. And speaking of which, I have to go. Take it easy, okay?"

"Okay. I'll try. Bye."

"Bye now."

When Jenny gets up in the late morning, I fix her a scrambled egg sandwich and get out a TV tray for her. Sometimes she likes to watch a game show while she eats. It's entertaining, watching her cheer for her favorite contestants. When she's done eating and the game show is nearly over, I hear a car in the driveway. I look out the window to see who it is. The car looks familiar but I can't put a finger on it. The driver's side door opens, and Lei gets out.

"Lei! Come in!" I say, ushering her through the kitchen door. What are you doing here?" I ask happily. "Long time no hear from—since last week!"

"I was in the neighborhood, had a few free hours, and wondered if you could go to lunch with me?" she asks with a big smile.

"You saw the paper today, and want to keep me from getting depressed again," I say.

"Yes," she says. "I admit that when I saw the headline I immediately thought about you. What do you say—go to lunch with me?"

"I have to stay with Jenny, and Grant will be home pretty soon. I really can't go," I say.

"What's going on? Why are you getting depressed again, Meredith?" Jenny asks as she comes into the kitchen, then stops short when she sees Lei. "Hello, Lei, is our Meredith in trouble again?" Jenny asks, concerned.

"No, I just want her to have lunch with me, but I understand she has other obligations, so we'll make it some other time," Lei says pleasantly.

"Nonsense. Your other obligations are me, and meeting Grant. I can take care of myself for one day, and I am very capable of meeting Grant at the bus and fixing him a pbj!" she says, making Lei and I laugh.

"Well, it's not that cold out today," I say. "I guess you could wait out on the porch for him. I'll call the school so they can let the driver know you'll be waiting up here instead of at the stop, and ask them to let Grant know too."

I make the call to the school, then ask Jenny again if she's sure it's okay.

"Please, just go!" Jenny says. "I'll be fine!"

"Okay, okay. I'm gone. I'll be back in a few hours. Call Mona at work if you have an emergency, okay?"

"I will," Jenny says, closing the door behind us.

Once Lei and I are in her car, I look at her curiously. "We're not eating at The Serenade, I hope?"

"Oh, no," she says. "I wouldn't take you where you work for lunch!"

"Where else is there?" I ask. "The drive in?"

"That's a thought, but no," she says with a smile. "You'll see in a few minutes." I try to figure out where else we could be going, then finally just sit back for the ride. In a little while we pull up at the regional hospital. I guess she has to pick something up or check on a patient, so I don't make a move to get out when she parks in a reserved space.

"Aren't you coming?" Lei asks.

"Do you have to see a patient?"

"Yes. Come on," she says.

I shrug my shoulders, then follow her inside. In a few minutes we're entering the cafeteria. "This is where we're eating?" I ask. We both start laughing.

"Hey, the food isn't bad, really," Lei says as she leads me quickly between rows of tables. I'm thinking she must have a special place she likes to sit, so I trot along behind her. The place is busy and buzzing with quiet conversations.

"Here we are," she says, plopping her purse on a chair. "Sit, sit," she says, motioning me to the next chair.

"Meredith!" The familiar voice of an older woman startles me. I peer down the row of people on the same side of the table Lei and I are on and see Evelyn, Matthew and Pete eating lunch! I catch Pete's eye for a second and see that he's surprised but pleased to see me. I turn and give Lei an astonished look.

"Oh, did I forget to mention that the patient I had to see was Matthew?" Lei asks, her eyes twinkling.

I just grin at her, then get up and go to greet them. "I had no idea you'd be here! I'm so glad to see you!" I say. Pete stands up and gives me a little hug, then takes my hand and offers me a seat on the other side of him so that I'm at the opposite end of the table from Lei. I lean down and give Matthew and Evelyn hugs before I sit down, and they each squeeze my hand.

"Oh Meredith, we were so sorry about the fire," Evelyn says. "We wanted to be with you so badly, but Matthew was sick, and…"

"It was just too hard at the time," Pete says. "But it's great to be back right now."

"I've already seen two specialists here this morning," Matthew says. "And now I'm done with doctors for the rest of our visit. Oh, except for Dr. Jonsson, of course," he says, grinning at Lei.

"I'll see you in my home office tomorrow," Lei tells him. "I hope you won't mind going there?"

"Oh no, I like hearing your kids running around upstairs while we're talking. It gives it a homey touch," he says sincerely.

"It definitely is that," she says.

I turn to Pete, and he reads the confusion on my face.

"I'm not sure how…," I start, not knowing exactly what to say.

"Dr. Jonsson has been Dad's psychologist for a while," Pete explains. "We've been living in Great Falls since Dad had hip surgery, but he's been so homesick for Crossroads… well, we all are! So Dr. Jonsson said that it might do us all some good to come back to Crossroads for a little while. And here we are."

"That's right. I tell you, being sick for a long time is depressing. Dr. Jonsson has been a big help to me," Matthew says.

"I'm just glad I've been able to help," Lei tells him.

"Great Falls is a nice town, but this is home," Matthew says. "Well, it was home," he adds, a far away look in his eyes.

"Now, Matthew, we aren't going to let this trip turn melancholy," Evelyn says, hugging his arm. "We sold the property," Evelyn says to me in explanation. "The medical bills were just stacking up faster than we could take care of them."

"Well, how are you feeling, Matthew?" I ask.

Matthew says nothing for a long moment, then looks me right in the eye and says, "It's tough losing your home, isn't it? You lost your home to a fire, and I lost mine to being sick. But I tell you what, young lady. If my son was happy, I'd be happy. What do you think about that?"

I sit back quietly in my chair.

"You two better go get your food. The macaroni and cheese is very good," Evelyn says.

"Sounds yummy," Lei says, standing up.

"Lei, what's going on?" I ask when we get in the serving line.

"I didn't want to talk to you about it earlier because I was afraid you might not come," Lei says.

"Talk to me about what?"

"That Matthew was the patient I was coming to see here."

"Well, I guess I wouldn't want to butt in, you're right," I say.

"And that when I went to Great Falls to see the Mc-Bride's…"

"You said you just ran into them there," I say, cutting her off.

"Okay, I ran into them, at the apartment Pete and Evelyn are renting there," she says with a smile. "Remember I told you I had been in Great Falls and I had seen the McBrides? I had to wait for Matthew to tell you himself that I have been treating him. I couldn't just come right out and tell you about it."

I think back to the first house call Lei made at the trailer—how insistent she was that I go to the McBride's ranch to talk to Evelyn and Matthew about Pete. "So when you wanted me to go talk to Evelyn and Matthew…"

"I knew they had gone to Great Falls—but Pete was supposed to have come right back to take care of the ranch. I figured you'd run into him there. I didn't know for weeks that he stayed in Great Falls with his parents. I'm sorry for misleading you," she says sincerely.

"No, that's okay," I say, understanding that if she hadn't suggested it, I never would have known the ranch was for sale.

"When I was in Great Falls, Matthew said exactly what he just said a minute ago. If his son was happy, he'd be happy. Then he told me that Pete was still in love with you, and that he talks about you quite a bit."

"He does?"

"According to Matthew," Lei says. "Ready to sit down?"

"Yes, I can't get anything else on this plate," I say.

Pete waves me over to his end of the table again, so I excuse myself from Lei and go sit by him. "I feel like we're back in the school cafeteria," I say with a nervous laugh.

"I wouldn't mind that right about now," he says. "After school I'd take you to the ranch and we'd drive all over. Then we'd hike up the butte and watch the sunset." He gently touches my leg under the table, sending shivers up my spine. "We heard that Cathy was arrested for setting the fire," he says. "I'm very sorry. Not only about that, but also about the day I walked out when Cathy showed me that picture."

"It's okay," I say, looking at my lap.

"Can we talk privately later?"

"Yes," I say, my heart leaping.

"I can't tell you how happy I am to see you," Evelyn says to me across the table. I have really missed you, Meredith. I so enjoyed those chats we used to have."

"I did too. Remember the cookies and fudge we used to make for Pete when he was away at college?"

She laughs. "Snickerdoodles and fudge. Still his favorites."

At the other end of the table, Lei glances at her watch and clears her throat to get everyone's attention. "Excuse me, what time was it that you're supposed to meet someone at the bank?"

"It's been put off until tomorrow morning. Mr. Overgaard said his schedule was too tight," Pete says.

Lei, her lunch barely touched, suddenly scoots her chair back and says, "I'm going to have to run. Meredith, are you about finished?"

I've only eaten two bites, but I say I'm ready if she is.

"We'll give you a ride," Pete says. "If you'd like to finish your lunch."

"Sounds good," Lei says, jumping up. "Tomorrow, my office, three o'clock? Matthew? Will that work?"

"Yes, that's fine," Pete says for Matthew.

"Okay, bye!" Lei says, scurrying away from the table. She looks back at me quickly and gives me a tiny wave and a grin.

Suddenly I realize I'm not a bit hungry anymore. There's

an awkward silence, then Pete says, "We're going to take a drive out in the country, since we have this afternoon free. And we wanted to see the area anyway. I suppose you have to get back to work?"

"I'm off today," I say, to which his eyes widen in surprise. "I work every other day now. Long story. But Grant will be getting home from school soon and I don't want Jenny to have to keep up with him for very long."

"Oh, Jenny still lives with you?"

"Yes, I couldn't send her back to the old folk's home. She was so unhappy there."

"That was very sweet of you," Evelyn says. "Nobody wants to be put away in an old folk's home."

"I'm sure that's true. But Uncle Duck had to move her there because he got too sick to take care of her. I'm sure he wouldn't have if he hadn't gotten sick."

"Getting sick makes you do things you wouldn't normally do in a million years," Matthew says sadly. "Like sell your home, give up your livelihood."

"Dad, please let's not get gloomy," Pete says gently. "I was wondering if you two would mind if Meredith and her son and Jenny ride along with us?" he asks Evelyn and Matthew.

"The more the merrier," Matthew says, and Evelyn says she'd enjoy having us.

Pete turns to me and says, "We borrowed a motor home for this trip so there's plenty of room."

"A motor home?"

"Yes, I wasn't going to have my parents stay in the Greenway, and well, the reputable hotel that used to be here doesn't exist anymore," he says quietly.

"But it might, some day. I'm thinking about rebuilding," I say.

"I just can't imagine anyone deliberately burning The Serenade," Evelyn says, shaking her head. "That Cathy! She was strange even when you were all in high school. "

"What do you mean?" I ask.

"When Pete was dating you, Cathy showed up at our place on several occasions with that darn photo album. In a lot of photos taken at school activities she'd managed to squeeze in next to Pete so it looked like they were a couple. I knew what she was up to; she aimed to split you two up. She flipped through a few pages and sort of accidentally on purpose let me see where she had practiced writing Cathy McBride, Mrs. Pete McBride, Mr. and Mrs. Peter McBride— that sort of thing."

"Mom! You never told me she came out to the ranch!" Pete exclaims.

"I didn't even want to give her the satisfaction of telling you or give you the worry. She even came out once this year, to try to get your phone number. She got real chatty, acting like we were real close. It didn't work. I wouldn't give her your phone number."

"I knew she called and asked you to tell me to stop by The Serenade, but I didn't know she actually went to see you! That girl caused us some trouble," Pete sighs. "Cathy and her infamous album."

"Yes, plenty of trouble," I say. "Dave Bunsen wanted to see the album, but it was probably destroyed in the fire. I don't know if it would have been used as evidence or not."

"I don't mind telling them what was in it," Evelyn says. "If they want to know."

In the motor home, Pete asks me to sit in the chair next to the driver's seat. I tell him that we're staying in Mona and Evan's old place until I figure out where my permanent residence will be. When we get there, Matthew and Evelyn have nodded off on the couch, so just Pete and I go inside.

"Mom!" Grant shouts as he runs through the trailer to me, stopping short when he sees Pete. "You said he wouldn't be coming around anymore," he says accusingly.

"I just happened to run into Pete this morning," I say.

"Are you going to get sad when he leaves?" Grant asks me, ignoring Pete.

Just then Jenny comes into the living room. "Pete!" she exclaims, giving him a hug. "It's been ages!" I notice Grant's surprised face at Jenny's show of affection for Pete.

"It's great to see you again Jenny! Hey, we were going to go for a ride—I borrowed a motor home for a few days— there's plenty of space, so would you like to go with us? And you too, Grant," he adds.

"Three and four's a crowd, wouldn't you say?" Jenny asks, her eyes twinkling.

"My parents are with us," Pete says.

"Really? I'd love to meet them. So, I guess if you already have extras I'll go."

"Look out the window, Grant," I say. "Would you like to go for a ride in that?"

"I just want to look inside it," he says carefully.

"Sure," Pete says. "Let's go take a look."

"You two go ahead," I say to Pete and Grant. "I need to take care of a few things before I go. It'll only take a few minutes," I add, thinking a few minutes without me might be good for them. Grant looks back at me apprehensively. "It's okay," I tell him. "Go ahead. You'll love it!" He follows Pete outside.

When I'm alone with Jenny I catch her up on the day's events. She's excited that I ran into Pete and sad, like I am, to know for certain that Cathy has been arrested for starting the fire at The Serenade.

A long moment passes, then Jenny asks, "Are you sure you want me tagging along with you? I really won't turn into a pumpkin if you leave me alone a while longer," she says with a laugh.

"No, no. I want you to come along," I say, just as Grant comes bounding in the door.

"Come on!" he says insistently. "It's time to go!" He runs back outside and I help Jenny with her coat.

Evelyn and Matthew are awake and obviously enjoying Grant. I introduce them to Jenny, who sits down next to Evelyn and strikes up a conversation. I can tell they'll get along fine. I buckle Grant into a seatbelt on a cushioned bench and sit next to Pete in front. We follow the highway toward Glacier Park, reminding me of the first time Pete and I drove out this road together. Pete rolls down his window a little, letting in the fresh spring air. He looks over at me for a second and says just loud enough for me to hear, "I sure like this. Me with the woman I love, hitting the open road."

"I can't believe you remember!" I say with a laugh.

"I've thought about that weekend a thousand times," he says.

"Me too," I say. I look back and see that everyone else is contentedly chatting and looking out at the passing scenery. I hope the beautiful vistas are good medicine for Matthew. Pete and I are silent for a few minutes, which is good. I haven't had a second to think since I sat down at that cafeteria table earlier today.

Pete drives slowly, giving Evelyn and Matthew as much time as possible to enjoy the scenery. Eventually we stop for a break. The motor home is well stocked, and Evelyn and Jenny continue chatting while they get out a Thermos of coffee, some juice for Grant and some cups. Pete opens the door so we get some brisk fresh air inside.

Grant asks if he can have a pbj, and when Jenny tells Evelyn what pbj is, she's very pleased that she can oblige him. "Matthew loves peanut butter, and I always have jelly for my toast," Evelyn tells Grant. "So it's easy to make a pbj for you!"

Soon we all go outside to stretch and enjoy the beautiful scenery. We've been lucky today, as far as the weather goes. Springtime in Montana can be sunny one minute and stormy

the next, but today the sunshine prevails. In a bit we hit the
road again, stopping to enjoy several more viewpoints along
the way. Finally, Pete says it's time to go back to town.

"Do you think we could make the loop? So we don't have
to go back the same way we came?" I ask Pete.

"Well, I wasn't figuring on driving past our old place,"
Pete says quietly.

"Go ahead, son!" Matthew says from the back. "Didn't
think I heard you, did you?" he chuckles. "It's okay if we go
past the old place. I'd like to see it. I really miss it."

"I want to, too," Evelyn says.

"Okay then," Pete says, pulling out on the road. "I guess
it won't take too long." Pete and I talk about a lot of things
on the way home—what Grant is learning in school, Mona
and Evan's new truck, the weather, but we carefully avoid
our relationship and Matthew's problems. Grant falls asleep
halfway back, tired from his day of school and the excitement of riding in a motor home. We're about ten miles from
Crossroads and almost to the bend in the highway just before
the lane that leads to the McBride's old house. I look back at
Jenny, who gives me a wink.

"Pete, please stop at your old place," I say firmly.

"You actually want me to stop there?"

"Please? I just need to…"

He pulls off the road, sighing heavily. He looks back and
shrugs his shoulders at his dad, who is obviously confused.

"Are we getting out?" Evelyn asks.

"I don't think so, Mom. But you can get a good look out
the window."

"I want to walk up the butte with you," I tell Pete.

"Oh, you're talking about what I said at the hospital cafeteria at lunch? I was just taking a walk down memory lane. I
didn't mean we were actually going to do it again," Pete says.
"We sold the place," he adds. "That would be trespassing."

"I doubt the new owners are going to come out and shoot

us if we trespass. Besides, they aren't even moved in yet. There aren't any cars or anything."

"Let's do it!" Matthew says from the back.

"Dad, whatever happened to following the law? Besides, I don't know about you climbing the fence. I know Meredith can do it, but..."

"Wait a minute please," I say, "Can you all look out the windows on the other side? Nature calls. I'm going to let the motor home hide me from the highway."

"Oh, okay," Pete says as I climb out of the motor home. "I really hope they haven't moved in yet."

"Don't worry," I say, smiling at him. I walk over to the gate and look back quickly to make sure nobody is watching from the motor home. In a minute I have the gate unlocked with the key I had in my purse and am scurrying back to the motor home.

"I tried the gate, it's open!" I tell Pete.

"What?" Pete asks, then sees the open gate. "It was unlocked?"

"Yeah, I just pushed it."

"That's strange. You'd think it'd be locked. I'll tell Mr. Overgaard tomorrow so he can let the owner know. Of course he might wonder why we came here. Like I'm wondering," Pete says as he drives through the gate.

"Let's park by the barn and walk around," I suggest. "You go ahead. I'll catch up to you as soon as I get Grant up."

Pete pulls the motor home up by the barn and helps Matthew out. "Mom? Coming?" he asks Evelyn.

"I'll come with Jenny and Meredith," she says.

I get up and unfasten Grant's seatbelt and gently nudge him awake. "Grant, do you want to go out and walk around with me?"

He looks out the window. It's nearly evening, and the sun is dipping low on the horizon, leaving the house and outbuildings in shadow. "Where's this place?" he asks as he sits up and rubs his eyes.

"This is where Pete, Matthew and Evelyn used to live," I explain.

"Why are we here?" he asks.

"Just because we miss our old house and want to see it again, sweetie," Evelyn says.

"I know how that feels," Grant says. "First I left my home in Portland, then my home in The Serenade burned up."

"Yes, I guess you do know," Evelyn says, touching his hand.

"It's okay. As long as I have my mom, I can live anywhere," Grant says.

"Thanks, honey. That means a lot to me," I tell him.

"You must be a good mom," Evelyn says.

"She is!" Jenny says. "Meredith is an all around genuinely good person."

"Yep. Mom is a gennelly good person," Grant agrees.

I'm glad that Jenny and Evelyn don't laugh at Grant. "Well, thank you all," I say, walking toward the barn. Pete and Matthew are milling about between several long low outbuildings, commenting that they're surprised there isn't any machinery on the property yet.

"Pete! Let's check out the barn!" I shout. He and Matthew head my way, catching up to me at the barn door.

"Go ahead," I say. "We'll follow you."

Pete switches on the light by the door. "Hmm...they must be moving in soon, power's on," he mutters, then walks ahead of Matthew and the rest of us. He walks halfway through the huge barn. "Nadia?" I hear Pete say in an amazed voice. "What on earth?" he sticks his arm through the stable gate and reaches for Nadia. The rest of us run to see what's going on. "Look! It's Nadia!" Nadia comes right up to him and nuzzles his outstretched arm with Sugarfoot right behind.

"That's Nadia's baby, Sugarfoot!" Grant says. "But I

don't know when they comed here. They used to be at the stable. Mom?" he looks at me questioningly.

"Real recently," I say. "I think the people who are moving here are going to want them."

"So we won't get to horse babysit anymore, Mom?" Grant says, obviously upset.

"Don't worry, you'll still get to babysit," I assure him.

"Well, okay then. Here's all the stuff Off'cer Bunsen gave us," Grant says, pointing to the supplies in a large metal bin outside the stable.

"Yes, everything's here," I tell him.

"What are you talking about, Meredith?" Pete asks me. "This is great, to see her, but I don't get it. Did the new owners of the ranch buy Nadia at the auction? Do you know who it is?"

"Yes," I say.

"So that's why you knew it wouldn't matter if we trespassed."

"Yes."

"Well, when are these people moving in?" Pete asks in an edgy tone.

"I'm not sure," I say.

"Mr. Overgaard did the transaction with us, so we never met the buyer. I would never have guessed that you know her. Is she a customer at The Serenade or something? I know from the papers we signed that her name is Jenifer Morgan," Pete says.

"Jenifer sounds so formal. I prefer Jenny," Jenny pipes up.

Pete suddenly whirls around. "Jenny? You're Jenifer Morgan? You bought the ranch?"

"Yes, I did. For Meredith."

Pete looks at me, his expression incredulous. Matthew and Evelyn are speechless.

"I wanted to buy your ranch so that I could give it back to

your parents," I explain to him, before his parents have time to even ask. "It's a very long story."

"This is something Meredith really wanted to do," Jenny says to Evelyn and Matthew. "I've been fond of Meredith for years. She has a heart of gold. She never asks for anything for herself, just for the people around her. I thought her plan made perfect sense. I knew it would make her happy to get the ranch for you, and also I could enjoy the outcome while I'm alive to see it," she says.

"I don't know what to say," Matthew begins. "I'm touched beyond belief at what you've done here, but I don't have the money to put towards the ranch anymore. That's why we sold it."

"Nobody's asking you to put out any money. The place is already paid for in full. We're just asking you to move back in and enjoy your place. Or work the ranch if you want to. But I have a proposition," Jenny says with a smile.

I have no idea what this is about, so I wait eagerly with the others to hear it.

"I ask that if you sometimes come up with a little extra money, you would donate it to a children's charity. Maybe a children's hospital—there are several wonderful ones around the country. Or maybe we could even start our own charity, if we want to," she adds.

"This whole thing—you buying back our ranch, and your children's charity idea—it's the nicest thing I have ever heard of," Evelyn says, her eyes tearing up.

"Not me," Grant says suddenly.

I look at him, wondering what he's thinking. "I think when Mom bought Nadia and the baby from that lady so we could be horse babysitters until Pete came back—that's the nicest thing I ever heard of," he says.

"You bought them back yourself?" Pete asks, astonished.

"Jim told me that you probably had to put even Nadia up for auction. I just couldn't stand the thought of it. So I called the auction house and it was just luck that the lady I spoke to on the phone there was the one who had Nadia and her baby," I say.

Pete gives me a big hug and says, "You're right, Grant. Your mom did one of the nicest things I've every heard of."

"I'm worried about all this," Matthew says now. "Can you really spend all this money on total strangers, Jenny? We've never done anything for you—why should you give us all this? Of course we would happily donate whatever money we can come up with to a children's hospital, but the amount you've spent on the ranch in the first place..."

"Well, it's Meredith's now. It's up to her to decide what she's going to do with it. I understand that she wants to give it to you. And let me point out that first of all, Matthew, we aren't total strangers. Hadn't you ever heard about me from Meredith and Pete? I know I heard about you and Evelyn many times—sometimes so much that I felt like I knew you!" Jenny says.

"Sure, we heard about you, but we had never met!" Matthew says.

"Maybe not formally," Jenny says. Evelyn nods her head in agreement. "And secondly, you have done something for me. When our Meredith was in need of a stable family, the three of us took her on. I have assumed the role of grandmother, and you two were her parents. I hope you don't mind me saying that, Meredith," she says to me.

"No, you're exactly right," I say.

"And today, Jenny says, "Meredith is a pretty wonderful young woman, in part due to our investment in her."

"I agree with that," Matthew says, then turns to me. "We did feel like your parents. When you and Pete broke up, we felt almost like we had lost a child."

Nobody says anything for a minute, then Evelyn says, "If we accept Jenny and Meredith's offer, we should really have this plan drawn up legally. Don't you think so, Jenny?"

"Yes, I agree. I know Sam Overgaard will help us get that taken care of." Jenny says.

"Won't we have to pay an inheritance tax or something?" Pete asks, "even though we aren't exactly inheriting it, the ranch is still being given to us."

"Sam and I already took care of the tax matters," Jenny says. "I think we should all keep good records of everything associated with the transaction. Duck always said it was of the utmost importance to keep good records."

"Of course we will, if everyone here thinks this is all a good idea," Pete says, looking at his parents, then me.

Matthew and Evelyn look at each other. "We would both feel better living here," Matthew says, "but the fact is, son, the brunt of the work would fall on you. And we have to realize the drought could go on a lot longer. It's going to be tough getting the place going again. Realistically, we may have had to auction our cattle off at some point because of the drought, even without all the medical bills. I hate to think of taking this land from Jenny and Meredith if we won't be making money off it."

Pete is silent for a long moment, a serious look on his face, then says. "You're right, Dad, and we need to talk that over. But first, everyone, I need to talk to Meredith alone. Grant, can I borrow your mom for a minute?" he asks, but Grant doesn't answer.

"Grant, will you please tell everyone what we've learned about taking care of the horses?" I ask him. "I'll be back in a minute."

"Okay," he says, his brow knit.

Outside the barn Pete grabs me, pulls me to him and kisses me deeply. "Thank you," he says. "Thank you for what you and Jenny did. I don't know what to say, except I love you."

"I love you, too. I always have," I say, standing on my tiptoes so I can kiss him back.

He takes my hands and holds them up to his lips, kisses them, then looks at the burn scars on them, and kisses them again.

"There are plenty more like those on my legs," I say in warning.

"I'm just so sorry I couldn't stay at the hospital with you after the fire, but Dad had fallen and broken his hip, and I had to leave right away for Great Falls to be with him and Mom during the surgery. Then things went downhill with Dad after that, and I got depressed, and—well, I would have stayed if I could, that's all," he says tenderly. "I will always regret not being there for you when you needed me most." He leans down to me and kisses me softly on the mouth again.

"Lei told me that she had let you in to see me. But it was a long time until I knew it."

"You must have thought I didn't even care," he says.

"Well, yes, that's what I was afraid of," I say.

Then he lifts his head and says, "I did care. And I still do."

I can't say anything, I'm so happy there are tears escaping down my cheeks.

"We have to talk, though, Meredith. About the ranch. Dad's right, the drought is going to make it pretty difficult to get the place going again. Somehow I'll have to get a loan and I'll have to have a job somewhere too, at least for a while."

"I need a maintenance man at The Serenade," I say. "Jacob quit."

"I can't say that I'm sorry," he says smiling. "But I think I better look for a job where I won't be taking money from my wife's pockets. That wouldn't make sense."

"Your wife?" I ask, overwhelmed.

"Yes, my wife! Meredith, please marry me. I love you. I know I've let you down before, but I promise to do my best to make it all up to you. And to Grant. Please?"

I look into his eyes, marveling that this moment has arrived at last. All the months and years of missing him are over.

I know that this time it's meant to be. "Yes, yes! I'll marry you!" I say as he leans down so we can kiss again.

"We're going to have to build a second house on the property, though. It's going to be pretty cramped quarters with you, me, Grant, Jenny, Mom, Dad, and whatever other kids come along after we get married," Pete says with a laugh.

"Now I'm happy," Matthew says, startling us. "Pete and Meredith are getting married!" he shouts into the barn, bringing the others hurrying outside.

"What? You're getting married!" Evelyn gasps. "When? Where?"

"I just asked Meredith, Mom! Nothing's planned yet, just sometime soon," Pete answers.

I notice that Grant's face is worried, so I break away from Pete and kneel down by Grant. "What is it, honey?" I ask.

"I don't know if he'll be a friendly stepfather," he cries, burying his face in my jacket.

"He'll be friendly," I say softly. "I've known him for many years and I know he's a good person." I turn to the others and explain why Grant's worried.

"I think we're going to get along just fine," Pete says reassuringly.

"Okay," Grant says.

"I've known Pete a long time, too," Jenny tells Grant. "I think he'll be a wonderful stepfather for you, and I know he already loves your mom."

"Really?" Grant asks.

"Really," Jenny says.

"Matthew and I would love to be your grandma and grandpa," Evelyn tells Grant kindly.

"You'll be my grandma and grandpa?" Grant asks, his sweet face upturned to Evelyn.

"Yes! It's something we've wanted to be for a long time!" she replies. Grant is quiet. I can tell he's deciding how he feels about all this.

"I think that would be good," he says.

I'm the happiest I've been in years. I want the moment to go on forever, but it's getting dark, so I tell Pete that I have to take care of Nadia and Sugarfoot, and get home so Grant and Jenny can have dinner and go to bed pretty soon. I also can't wait to tell Mona and Evan the good news.

"I imagine your folks would like to get home too," I say.

"I'll go take care of Nadia and Sugarfoot...you ride herd on the rest of them, get them in the motor home," Pete says, chuckling. "Think about it, Meredith—pretty soon we'll be having dinner and going to bed together, right over there in that house.

"That sounds darn good, Pete McBride," I say.

"It sure does, Meredith McBride," he agrees. "That sounds darn good, too."

Chapter 16

❧

I dreamed on clouds last night, and I'm walking on them today. I relive Pete's proposal over and over. After telling Mona my news last night, Pete and I talked on the phone and picked a wedding date. Now it's four-thirty the next morning and I'm in my office at The Serenade. It's hard to stop thinking about all of it, but I have to catch up on some paperwork before I start my waitress shift. I got here very early, so I'm startled when Ralph walks in.

"Didn't mean to scare you," he says.

"What are you doing here so early?" I ask.

"I need to talk to you," he says. "I'm moving to Las Vegas. I have a friend who's a blackjack dealer there that I can live with at first. I really don't like cooking all that much, and I haven't been to Vegas, so I'm just going to go see what it's like down there."

"What kind of work do you want to do?" I ask.

"Fitness training," he says, as he turns and strikes a muscle man pose, huge biceps flexed.

"You'll be great at that," I say.

"Thanks," he says.

"I'll have to get a replacement for you—when do you want your last day here to be?"

"Today. My friend's been here at my place a few days, and he's driving back down tomorrow, so I'm gonna ride with him."

"How am I going to replace you that fast? Pete proposed to me last night and our wedding is going to be June thirteenth—that's only a month and a half away! I don't have time to fill your shift, and I can't cook that well anyway!"

"I didn't plan it this way, it just happened that he came up to visit, and the more he talks about Vegas, the more I want to go see it. I've been around here all my life and I gotta get out. You must know how that feels. Oh, congratulations, by the way."

"Thanks, Ralph," I say. I do know how it feels to want to leave a place. Or go back to one. I know I don't have any right to try to talk Ralph out of having an adventure and living his life. I hadn't left Crossroads because I was anxious to go, but I have at least had the experience of living away from here. "I'm sorry that you're leaving, but I understand. Good luck down there in Vegas."

"Thanks. Well, I might as well go do some prep work, since I'm here," he says as he leaves my office.

"Ralph." He stops at the door and turns around to look at me. "Thanks for that day you protected Jean and me from Raymond. It was really brave of you, and it meant a lot to me."

"You've already thanked me for that, but just for the record, I'd do it for you again, if I ever needed to," he says.

Some woman is going to be lucky to get him for a husband some day, I think.

When Ralph is gone I let out a huge sigh, then start composing the ad for a cook that I have to get in the paper right away. I can't call Mona to discuss this with her because it's too early, so I start making a plan. If nobody applies for Ralph's job in the next few days, I know that one of the part-time waitresses wants to be full-time, so adding her plus hiring one more part-time waitress should do it. Then I'll take Ralph's shifts myself and I won't wait tables anymore. I'm not that great at cooking, but I will be able to get us by for a little while. I stop working on the project I had out and get out the folder of employment applications. I know I still have at least ten applications for waitresses on file, and none for cooks.

Later in the morning I call the paper, place the ad, then call Mona and tell her about Ralph.

"That's really crummy. No notice! How do you like that!" Mona says indignantly.

"Well, he didn't plan it this way, it just happened. But anyway, here's my plan," I say, and tell her what I have in mind. "What do you think?"

"Yeah, hiring the waitress is a good plan to cover all the shifts, but you're still going to burn yourself out! Are you going to have time and energy to plan the wedding? I guess you can put off the date for a while," she says.

"Pete called me last night and we set a date—June thirteenth," I tell her. "I really don't want to wait longer. So I'm just going to hope there's someone around here who wants to be a cook!"

"I'm sorry, I can't volunteer," Mona says. "The three days a week is enough for me."

"No, I don't want you to volunteer," I say truthfully. "You've done so much for me this year that I don't want to ask another thing of you. This will all work itself out."

"It will eventually, anyway," she says. "I doubt you'll have to close down for lack of a cook. Bad cooking, maybe," she jokes.

I'm expecting Pete for a visit this evening, and I'm surprised to see that Evelyn is with him when he arrives.

"Evelyn!" I say when I see her. We give each other a big

hug before Pete and I exchange a quick kiss. "I'm so glad to see you! Please, have a seat. Can I get you some tea?"

"Sure! That sounds good. No sugar, please. I know you weren't expecting me, but there are some things I think we should talk about."

"Okay," I say, wondering what's on her mind.

Grant runs out from his room wearing his little black felt cowboy hat, toy six-shooter hanging off his waist in a holster.

"Hey, pardner!" I hear Pete say to Grant.

"That's what that other guy called me," Grant says.

"What other guy?" Pete asks.

"That guy that asked if we wanted to go see the ranch. That day Mom took me to the lake."

"He means Jim," I call out to the living room while I pour the tea. "It was that day last summer when we ran into him—before I opened The Serenade," I say, carrying Evelyn's tea to her on a tray. "Do you want anything to eat, Evelyn?"

"Oh no, thanks, we just had dinner," she says.

"Is it okay for me to call you pardner?" Pete asks Grant.

"I guess so," Grant says, shrugging his shoulders. "Is Jim still your friend?"

"Yes, he's my best friend," Pete says.

"I have a best friend, too. His name is John. We're both in Mrs. Bunsen's kindergarten class."

"I remember a few things about kindergarten," Pete says.

"I bet that was a really, really long time ago. Mrs. Bunsen must be pretty tired if she was your teacher, too!"

Pete stifles a laugh and says, "I lived in a different town then, so Mrs. Bunsen wasn't there."

"Oh," Grant says.

Pete and I sit down cross legged on the carpet, and Grant pushes us apart at the shoulders, squeezes in between us and sits cross legged, too. Evelyn is on the sofa.

"Jenny is already in bed, so we have to keep it down," Grant repeats exactly what I told him a little while ago, which makes us all snicker a little.

"You're right, Grant, thanks for letting everyone know, so we don't wake her up," I say. "Would you like to get out a quiet thing to do, like a puzzle you could put together right here on the floor while Pete, Evelyn and I talk?"

"No, I'll just sit right here," he says.

"Well, alright," I say.

"I told Mom about Ralph quitting," Pete says.

"Yes, it was not the kind of surprise I needed at four-thirty in the morning, and right before we start planning the wedding," I say, "but I think I have it figured out. I can cook a little, enough to get us by for a while if I can't hire anyone to take Ralph's place. And I'll be moving some waitresses' schedules around, probably hire a part-timer…we'll make it work."

"I had an idea," Evelyn says. "I've done quite a bit of cooking in my life, and I haven't had many complaints. I'd like to help out with the cooking at The Serenade, temporarily, I mean."

"I know you're a great cook—I remember eating with you many times. It's such a generous offer, but it's a lot of standing, you know. And I couldn't let you lift those heavy pots and pans, but other than that, yes! Thanks, Evelyn!"

"I know I can stand for four hours. I do that much all the time, so I can split your shift with you. When I need something heavy moved, maybe I can get some help."

I was just going to ask who was going to be helping Matthew if Evelyn worked at The Serenade, when Pete suddenly asks me if I would move out to the ranch now, before the wedding. "I already discussed it with Mom and Dad," he says, "and we think we can make it work as far as sleeping space goes. We can make the den into a room for you and Grant for now. Later on we'll just have to build more space, like we already talked about. Please say yes, Meredith, I want to see you every day. I don't want to wait another month and a half before we're living under the same roof!"

"I'd love that too, but living next to Mona has made our whole situation workable—babysitting, the way we split up our work schedules—everything."

"I think I can keep up with Grant while you're at work," Evelyn says.

"I'm sure you'd get along," I say, "but I don't want you spending all your time on us!"

"Grant is so much fun to be around that I think Matthew will start feeling better just being with him! That will make everyone happier."

"I hope you're right," I say.

"Hey, I'm part of all this too, you know," Pete says. "I can spend time with Grant, like when I'm outside working. He can help me sometimes."

I smile at Pete and thank him, and he says that Grant is our son now, so thank you's aren't needed.

"Don't worry, between Pete learning to be a dad and Matthew and I learning to be grandparents, Grant will be well taken care of," Evelyn adds with a chuckle.

Grant wriggles out from between us and runs out of the room, which leaves Pete with a concerned expression. After all, as far as Grant knows, Pete made me sad, and once played all evening at the park with him and then didn't show up again for a very long time. It's going to take some genuine effort for these two to bond.

Jenny suddenly walks into the living room, holding Grant by the hand.

"Grant! Did you wake Jenny up?" I ask sternly.

"It's okay," Jenny says. "My buddy here just needed comforting."

"Do you want to tell me what's wrong?" I ask him, although I'm pretty sure I already know.

"Evelyn says Pete is just learning to be a dad and I don't like that. And I'm worried that he won't know how to take care of you, Mom. Does he know what to do?"

"Oh, I see," I say softly. "You really have been taking good care of me, especially since the fire. I'll always need your help. But as a family, it will be up to all of us to take care of each other, okay? Pete does want to learn how to be your dad, and he's going to try very hard to be a good one."

"I'll do my very best," Pete says. "Maybe you can help me, Grant."

"Okay, I'll do my best, too," Grant says, "but everyone is talking about us moving away from here and I think if we move again I won't see Jenny anymore, or Mona and Evan."

"Come here." I take him in my arms and cuddle him. "You have an awful lot of worries on your mind! Well, let's talk it over. When we move, Mona will still work at The Serenade, and you'll see her there sometimes. And we'll visit Mona and Evan pretty often at their house. They're our good friends, and we won't be very far away from them. It only takes about twenty minutes to drive from their house to where we'll be living. That's not very long at all!"

"What about Jenny?"

"We hope Jenny will want to move with us."

"Oh, good! Jenny will you?" Grant asks her.

"If the whole family wants me to, I would love to," Jenny says.

"You're part of the family!" Grant says. "So it's all settled! Mom, can I call John?" he asks, jumping up. "I want to tell him I got a dad, and a grandma and grandpa and I get to keep Jenny too!" Jenny and I look at each other, grinning.

"I guess so. It's not very late." Pete and I exchange glances, pleased at Grant's sudden change of heart. "It is pretty important news, isn't it?" I add, thinking of all the times I've called Mona because I had something I just wanted to tell someone.

"Yeah!" Grant agrees as he runs into the kitchen, calling me over to help him dial John's number.

We want a simple wedding, but I haven't found much time in the last weeks to make plans. I did manage to have the invitations made and sent out, but that's about it so far.

Evelyn and I have been cooking up a storm at The Serenade since the three of us moved to the ranch. She is a fast, good cook, and has started making a few of her own signature dishes. Her fried chicken has become a customer favorite. When she's cooking, I'm home with Matthew, Grant, and Jenny, and Mona is at The Serenade. We're doing as much as we can, but I'm way behind on paperwork, which is very unsettling to me, so I'm relieved this afternoon when I finally find a full-time cook! When I call Evelyn to tell her, she says she had a good time, and is glad she was able to help out, but she's ready to retire again.

Our transition to the ranch has been hectic but generally positive. I think Pete and Grant's shared love for Nadia and Sugarfoot will take them a long way in the bonding process. Grant isn't scared of the horses at all, and enjoys helping Pete take care of them, which really pleases Pete. Grant s learning to ride, and it makes me happy to hear the two of them "talking horse," like some people "talk sports."

Chapter 17
❧

It's an hour before dawn, our wedding day. I could barely sleep last night and I need to get outside and walk this morning to calm down. I quietly dress in jeans and a sweater, and leave the sleeping house, carrying a flashlight.

"Meredith!" I hear Pete softly call me from behind. I turn around and give him a smile, though it's too dark for him to see my face.

"Isn't there something about the groom not seeing the bride before the ceremony?" I ask jokingly.

"That can't really apply in our situation, can it?" he asks with a laugh.

"No, I guess not."

We walk out to the meadow where we will be married. I imagine the ceremony: the guests sitting in a semicircle, the brightly colored spring wildflowers sprinkled about, and Mona and Jim standing up for us. Pete and I will exchange our vows beneath a white arch decorated with ponderosa pine boughs. He'll give me the simple gold wedding band—his maternal grandmother's—which Grant will be carrying on a silk pillow.

Around noon Mona arrives, and Evelyn tells us to use the

master bedroom to get ready, since it is the largest bedroom. Mona is carrying her dress over her arm in a clear plastic bag. When she puts it on I have to laugh. True to form, she has chosen a dress that will accentuate her attractive figure. Her dress will certainly upstage mine, which is the one DeeDee gave me long ago to sing in the high school talent show. I will wear it in honor of MaryAnn's memory.

At two o'clock I meet Matthew at the front door, and slip my arm through his for the walk to the meadow where the wedding will be. A tear springs to his eye and he says, "I'll give you away, but only because I'll be getting you back."

We walk slowly up the aisle. I smile nervously at Tressa and her husband, Carolyn with her husband, and John, Mr. Overgaard, and several of my employees. But I wouldn't be marrying Pete today if it hadn't been for Lei. When I see her with Mark and the kids, and the bright smile on her face, I'm completely happy.

When Matthew unlinks our arms and leaves me with Pete, I look up for a moment and pray that MaryAnn knows that what is said and done here today is the beginning of something beautiful for Pete, me, and our son, Grant. I think she knows. I really think she knows.

About The Author

Laurie Adair (MacFadden) Grove was raised in the northwestern USA, and spent all but one of her first seventeen birthdays in Oregon and Montana Boy Scout camps, where her father was the camp director.

The year she turned eight she wanted desperately to see what a town birthday would be like. So she had an October birthday instead of her real August one. It turned out that camp birthdays were better; the camp cook would make a special peanut butter cake for her to take to the woods or to sit at the edge of a peaceful lake to eat with her sisters and other Scouter's kids who were to become lifelong friends.

Laurie can be found writing her next book at her home in western Oregon, which she shares with her husband (George) of thirty-seven years. Together they raised a son and daughter and now thoroughly enjoy the antics of their two small granddaughters.